BLOOD OF THE WITCH

REJECTED WITCH CHRONICLES
BOOK TWO

JESSICA WAYNE

B.A.D.
PUBLISHING

B.A.D.
PUBLISHING

Blood of the Witch
Rejected Witch Chronicles, book 1
Vampire Huntress Chronicles, world book 5
by Jessica Wayne
Copyright © 2020. All rights reserved.

Edited by Dawn
Cover Design by Bewitching Covers by Rebecca Frank

CHAPTER ONE

COLE

"What the fuck was that?" I roar as soon as I'm back on two legs. Spinning to Rainey and Elijah, I search their faces for any sign that what I just saw wasn't what I think it was.

Because I'm pretty fucking sure what I saw was Delaney being ripped to who the fuck knows where.

Rainey chokes on a sob, her dark eyes wide as they fill with tears. "Where is she?" she asks. "Delaney!" She rushes toward where the portal was only seconds ago, her heart hammering so damned loud it's drowning out nearly everything else.

I whirl on Elijah. "You're old as shit. What the hell was that?"

"I've never seen anything like it," he says, his tone conveying complete bewilderment.

Every single person here is just as surprised as I am, which only makes me even more fucking terrified. My heart drums against my ribs, the repeated slamming honestly making me concerned it's going to beat right out of my chest.

Not that I would fucking care at this point. Because life without Delaney? I'll die.

I could feel her fear through our mated bond, the bone-chilling terror as she was ripped from this place, but the moment the portal closed, the bond vanished.

Which only means the distance between us is too fucking far.

Agony tears through me as my body begins to shake, the convulsions taking over my movements as the bond is severed.

A wolf without his mate is lawless, out of control. Before, when I'd been the one refusing us, I'd at least had a semblance of control.

But now? Now that she was robbed from me? The only fucking thing that matters is getting her back.

No price is too high to pay.

I stalk toward the trees, my breathing ragged. I don't fucking care how fast—how far—I have to run. I will find her.

And I will bring her home.

"Cole." It's Josiah's steady tone that has me stopping.

Slowly, I turn toward where he stands beside Willa

and a bloody Jack. "What?" I snarl the word, hoping he hears the conviction within it.

"Going in alone is not the way."

"She is my mate."

"And she's her sister," he gestures to Rainey. "She's a friend to all of us. There's not a single person here—wolf or otherwise—who would see her suffer. We will find her, but we must do it together."

"I can move faster on my own."

"Can you?"

Narrowing my eyes on his face, I let a growl emanate from my throat. *How dare he say I can't track my mate?* I take a step closer, red invading my vision as my fangs slide out, my hands extending to claws in a partial shift.

"Easy, Cole," Elijah warns.

I snap my jaws at him. "She is *mine*."

"No one is saying she's not," Josiah says quickly. "Just that we can help you. We're a family, Cole, a pack. No one here is alone."

"She is *mine*," I repeat. "Mine to protect. Mine to find."

"Well, you sure as fuck failed on that first part," Jack snaps, stepping forward with his blood-crusted blade in hand.

"What the hell are you doing?" Willa whispers loudly.

Attention focused solely on the hunter, I take a

step toward him. I will kill him, drink his blood, and then I will have the strength to find my mate.

My Delaney.

"You let her get taken, and for what? To save a vampire you don't even like?"

I drop to my knees, my body cracking as it finishes its shift. No one says a word in the few seconds it takes me to complete the change. Probably because they're all afraid of pissing me off even more.

As soon as I'm in full form, I drop my snout to the ground and inhale what's left of Delaney's scent. Then, I stalk toward Jack.

"You failed Delaney," he says, taking a step toward me. Willa grips his arm, but the young wolf won't keep me from my mark.

I will kill him.

"So, how about you let us find her."

His words fall on deaf ears as I growl and lunge for him.

Something slams into me—a body—sending me flying to the side.

Bones crack, but I'm back onto my feet as the pain fades to a dull ache, my body repairing the fractures as I face off with a white wolf. His thick fur is smeared with blood and soot, but the hazel eyes are nearly as familiar as mine.

The fact that I'm prepared to kill him would bother me if it weren't for the imminent danger my mate is in.

As of now, he's nothing but another obstacle attempting to keep me from her.

His lips draw back in a snarl, and he charges. I move to the side and clamp down on his throat, flinging my head, sending him flying.

Z grunts when he hits the dirt but is back on his feet in an instant, not wasting any time before charging back toward me as Josiah roars in response to our fight.

As pack alpha, his command should be bullet-proof, but I belong to no one but Delaney.

Such is the strength of the mate bond.

Z's teeth sink into my side as he slams into me, and pain surges up my side as his venom burns my body.

I don't let it stop me for long, though, as I twist away, feeling his teeth tearing part of my skin and fur away. *You will die,* I send his way through the bond all pack wolves share.

Not a chance in hell, dipshit. You're fucking up and wasting time.

We circle each other, every cautious step carefully planned.

You're keeping me from my mate, I remind him.

You're keeping you from Delaney. If you'd stop being such a stubborn asshole, we could find a way to figure out where the hell she is.

I can manage alone.

Can you? he asks. *Because last time I checked, you had*

absolutely zero resources. We, however, have quite a few. So how about you stop being a dickhead and let us help.

The hunter insulted me. He must pay.

If you're going to come for Jack, you'll have to go through me too, Willa's voice chimes in, and I turn my head to see her eyes glowing as she stares me down.

You would hurt another's mate? Even knowing what losing yours is doing to you? Think of Delaney, Josiah adds. *She needs you, and this is wasting time.*

I shake my head, trying to clear the voices. Trying to clear the pain. It's lesser in this form, and I know as soon as I shift back, it's going to knock me to my knees.

But I won't fucking stay there.

Shifting back to two legs, I face off with Z.

"Sorry for biting you," he apologizes.

"If she dies, I'm holding you all accountable, right along with me."

I move past Z and Josiah, stopping beside Rainey. She glares up at me, anger and grief swirling in her chocolate eyes.

"I'm sorry I failed your sister. I will find her."

"I know you will."

The pack village smolders beneath the growing light of the coming dawn. How did everything get so fucked up in a matter of hours?

Somehow, on legs that barely have the strength to carry me, I manage to make it inside. The moment I'm out of sight, I drop to my knees. The wood floor is smooth beneath my skin, but I barely notice it even when my hands hit the surface, my fingernails digging into the polished floor.

Sobs rip from my chest as my body begins to shake uncontrollably.

I can still smell her here, feel her body beneath me, beside me. Delaney's essence assaults my fucking senses as I throw my head back and roar, grief ripping through me as though I'm made of tissue paper. My head rolls forward again as I search for the bond I have with Delaney, for any sign that she's moved closer.

But I find nothing.

Not even a muted sense that she's still alive.

"What the bloody hell happened here?"

Chest heaving, I don't even have the strength to look at the fae.

"Hey, asshole, I asked you a fucking question!" he drops to his knees beside me, hands going to my shoulders and forcing me to look at him. His eyes are wide, his face flush. "Where's Del?"

"She took her," I manage.

Fearghas pales. "Who took her?"

"Lucy McClough. The original witch's daughter."

He releases me and jumps to his feet. "You have got to be fucking kidding me, wolf! One thing, I asked you to do one motherfucking thing!"

I push to my feet, still completely naked and not

the least bit fucking bothered by it. It's hard to feel a damned thing when my entire heart feels like it's been ripped from my chest. "You think I handed her over?" I growl. "The bitch attacked our village! She slaughtered families, distracting us while she went straight for what she wanted."

"Delaney."

"And Bronywyn."

"You have got to be fucking kidding me."

"There's no world in which you could say a fucking thing to make me feel any worse than I already do."

"No? Because what I will tell you is that Delaney deserved a hell of a lot better than someone who crumbles at the first obstacle."

That does it. I explode, gripping the fae by the throat and slamming him into the nearest wall. A picture falls to the ground and shatters. To my surprise, he doesn't dematerialize. Instead, he stays right where I have him, his green eyes shooting daggers at me.

"It's about fucking time you got angry."

"You have no idea what I'm going through."

"You're wrong," he spits back. "Now, put some fucking clothes on so we can find her."

CHAPTER TWO

DELANEY

S tone walls surround me, a barred door the only break in the grey. There's no furniture, no blankets, nothing we could even attempt to use as a weapon when Lucy returns.

I glance over at where Bronywyn still lies, unmoving. I'd stripped my jacket off and tucked it beneath her head, hoping to give her some kind of comfort for when she wakes. I'm pretty damn sure it will be the last bit we feel for a long time.

After threatening to shred my soul, Lucy headed out the door and up the stairs leading to what I can only guess is a house or building of some kind. Unless, of course, she has us buried somewhere in the forest.

I shiver, the thought giving me a horrible visual of slowly decaying in this place.

I've exhausted myself attempting to open the

door, to get us somewhere near freedom. The bars haven't budged. My magic is shit right now, completely unreachable. My best guess is that there's iron hidden somewhere, which is probably why she had to leave through the door.

An image of Cole's wolf lunging for me as I was thrown through the portal assaults me, and the resounding grief is suffocating. My chest aches, and my stomach churns at the thought of the other half of my soul.

How the hell is he handling this? Is he okay? Did Lucy go back to finish them off?

I push the thought away as quickly as it came. If I let myself believe there's no hope, I'm likely to just give up.

And there's no damn way I'm going to do that.

Bronywyn groans, so I leave my spot on the wall and crawl toward her, my body still aching from being flung in here like a rag doll.

"Easy, sit up slowly," I instruct as I place a hand on her back and help her up.

"Where the hell are we?" She rubs a hand over the back of her head as she scoots back against the wall.

"I have no idea. A basement somewhere?"

"An iron-lined basement." She closes her eyes and takes a deep breath. "A perfect witch cage."

"Guessing your magic is absent, too?"

"Yes."

"Fantastic."

"Lucy left through the door?"

I nod. "What is her actual name?"

"I have no clue. We didn't chat a whole lot while I was attempting to drive a dagger through her heart," she snaps, but I sense it's not in anger.

Bronywyn is terrified.

"Any idea how we're going to get out of here?"

She snorts. "We're not."

"What the hell do you mean, we're not?"

"The only way to beat a witch like Lucy is with dark magic. Since neither of us is willing to sell our souls—nor do we have the materials needed for a spell that potent—we're screwed."

"The others will find us."

"Not unless she wants them to. And then, it'll be too late." She closes her eyes, her shoulders slumped in complete defeat. Is this seriously the same woman who nearly beat the crap out of me?

"Are you really going to give up like this?"

One eye cracks open, and she stares at me. "What other options are there?"

"It's obvious, isn't it? We fight."

"All that will do is draw out our pain." She shuts her eyes for a moment, then opens them and leans forward. "You don't understand, do you?" she snaps. "When I first met Lucy, she was slaughtering an entire coven of light witches. One against thirteen.

She killed them all without remorse and without mercy."

"We took out her mother."

Bronywyn shakes her head again. "Heather was *nothing* compared to her daughter. Think about it; she was locked in a box for centuries. Centuries spent cultivating her power and tormenting innocents. You think Jane was the only one she went after?" she scoffs. "Jane was only one in an entire sea of supernaturals Lucy tortured over the years. She only survived as long as she did because Jane was Lucy's favorite chew toy."

The fact that she's completely given up just pisses me off further. I have something to live for, *someone* to live for. The last thing I want to do is lie down and die. I grind my teeth together. "I thought you didn't want her to get her hands on my magic? That I should do whatever it takes to keep it out of her hands?"

"That was before she trapped us like ferrets in a cage."

"So, your plan is to lie down and die? What about Tarnley?"

Her bottom lip quivers at the mention of the vampire. It's slight, and I barely notice it before she's stone-faced again. "I imagine he'll be a tad upset that he has no one else to annoy, but he'll move one."

"That's one hell of a selfish outlook."

She meets my eyes. "Selfish? Do you have any idea

what Lucy will do to us? She'll toy with us, playing our minds like an expert musician before finally killing us. There will be no quick death, no instant release, and there will be no afterlife for either of us. Being realistic doesn't make me a pessimist. It grounds me in reality."

I can't help but stare at her, this woman who has served as a healer to the supernatural community for decades of her long life. Sure, I've disliked her, but I never would have taken her for a quitter. Not when everything I know about her alludes to a fighter—a hunter.

"Then, I'll hold onto enough hope for the both of us."

"Good luck with that."

"Can you sense anything beyond the walls?" I ask, steadying myself against the stone as I stand and walk —slowly—to the bars.

"The entire place is lined with iron. There's no way in hell we'll be able to use magic."

"Well, luckily for the both of us, I didn't have magic for a good portion of my life and haven't come to rely solely on that to get me through."

She glares at me through thick lashes. Finally, a spark. "I assure you my strengths are not limited to my magic alone."

"You sure about that? Seems to me you're rolling over when you could be proving me wrong."

Closing her eyes again, she shakes her head. "We're near water."

"Water? How can you tell?"

"Place your ear near the stone," she instructs.

I waste no time leaning against the stone, pressing my left ear against the cool rock. Closing my eyes, I focus intently for a few moments, even holding my breath as I listen. And there it is, the muted roaring of water. "Not just any water, a fall of some kind."

"Bingo."

"Look at you, Bronywyn, you're not so helpless after all."

She flips me the bird, and I grin in return. "We know we're near water. That's something." I slide down the wall and sit back down, feeling my legs scream in protest.

"Sure. Now, if only we could get that message out."

"We'll find a way."

"A shame you're no longer a bird. Those wings could really come in handy right about now."

"You're telling me." We fall into complete silence, neither of us able to do much more than sit and wait for Lucy's return. I've already tried everything to get through the bars, and that's not happening unless she opens them. So, we'll sit, we'll wait, and then we'll take the bitch out. "What's the deal with you and Tarnley?"

"What the hell are you talking about?"

I smile at her. "Come on, Bronywyn, if your hunch is right, we're going to die anyway. What's the harm in a little chat while we pass the time?"

"I don't have idle conversations."

"Not with anyone but the vampire."

"Not with anyone," she clarifies.

"Come on, you know a lot about me, so fill in some blanks."

Bronywyn's silent a few moments, making it apparent I'm not getting anything out of her, so I close my eyes and lean my head back against the wall, willing my body to heal. What I wouldn't give to have my old hunter abilities back right about now.

"Tarnley came to me after his mate was murdered by hunters," she says softly. "Since vampires only mate once—similar to wolves—he was miserable and barely hanging on without her. I helped him by removing the mate's blood from his system, making it easier to cope with the loss."

"Wow. That's—impressive. And so sad."

"He drew the short straw when it came to mates," she says. "The woman was a psycho and ended up slaughtering hundreds of humans. She would have gotten him killed."

"But he loved her."

"He did. Still does, I imagine. It's just easier to manage now."

"Can he ever mate again?"

She shakes her head, making my heart break for the kind vampire. "They only get one shot."

The way her voice cracks at the end tells me everything I need to know. "You love him."

A tear slips down her cheek. "It doesn't do me any good to love him."

No denial though. "Doesn't make the emotion any less real," I say softly. "You can love someone even if you don't see a future with them."

"You and Cole seem to have made it work. At least if finding you naked in bed was any indication."

Heat rushes to my cheeks moments before sadness weighs heavily on my shoulders. "I have to get back to him."

"Well, if anyone is stubborn enough to will a way out of this place, it's you."

"Was that almost a compliment?"

She smiles. "Don't get used to it."

"I bet we're near the ley lines," I say as I stare out the bars at the stone stairs. "She said she needs my power, right? Why else would she need it right now if it didn't have something to do with them?"

"It's a good hypothesis, but I don't see how it helps us right now."

"If we can find a way to get a message out, Fearghas might be able to find us."

"If the fae could sense us, he would have already been here. The iron will block us from him."

"He may even still be in faerie," I say sadly.

"He went back?"

I nod. "To kill his sister."

"The fae has a sister?"

I snort. "You missed quite a bit. Short story? She killed his father in an attempt to kidnap me, which was unfortunately successful. At least until another fae came and freed us. But Fearghas killed her mate—the fae king—so she's on a rampage."

She stares at me in complete shock. "Well, shit, that's a rather impressive lineup of events."

"It was a crazy-ass two months."

"We weren't sure any of you were coming back."

"Not like it's much of an improvement," I say. "I left one prison only to be confined in another."

"But, at least, you got to have world-shifting sex before."

I snort. "That's true."

With a *pop*, a basket of bread appears in front of us, and we both jump.

"What the hell?"

Bronywyn stares at the food, then me.

"How did that get in here if the place is lined with iron?" I ask as I scoot closer to it.

"I don't—" she trails off and slowly glances around, studying the cell. "Come here and turn around."

I crawl toward her and sit, turning to face the wall

opposite of her. Fingers brush the hair from the back of my neck, and Bronywyn gasps.

"What is it?"

"Check me."

I turn, and she rotates to face the wall. Repeating her gesture, I push the hair aside to check the back of her neck. There, shimmering in silver is a Celtic knot that's been sliced down the center. "A broken knot? What does it mean?"

She turns to face me, skin pale. "It means it's not the cell that's lined with iron. She's branded us, Delaney."

"Branded us?" Fear slices through me, a knife to the gut as her words sink in. "What does that even mean?"

"It means our odds of survival just went from zero to nonexistent."

CHAPTER THREE

COLE

I grip the edge of a charred piece of wood and toss it to the side. The young girl who's spent the last hour trailing me around as we searched for her favorite stuffed animal squeals with delight and reaches down to grab the soot-covered husky.

She turns to me, beaming from ear to ear as she clutches it to her chest. "Thank you, Beta."

I force a smile and nod. "You're welcome. Go find your mother."

She does as she's told, clinging to the stuffed animal and skipping back toward the wolves gathered near Josiah's cabin. Tarnley is with them, his anger reaching me even here. He's pissed at himself for what happened to Bronywyn—just as I blame myself for Delaney.

I always knew the vampire cared for the witch, but

it seems to me his affection goes quite a bit deeper than I'd previously considered. Guess it's a good thing she'd spelled him to be able to day walk before being taken. It will make searching for them a lot easier.

Fearghas appears beside me, hands in the pockets of his slacks.

"Anything?" I ask without fully facing him. The fae and I may be speaking, but that doesn't mean I want to spend more time than I have to with the bastard.

"No. I can't sense either of them anywhere."

I whirl on him, shaking my head. "That's not possible. You said you could track her."

"Obviously, I underestimated the witch's ability to shield them."

"And overestimated yourself," I growled. "What the hell does it mean that you can't sense her?"

"It means that they aren't super close by."

"Can Delaney call for you?" I know she's done it before, during her first hunt after coming back. She'd called for him in the alley, and he'd been there.

"She can, and I should be able to hear her if she does, but if she's being shielded somehow, that's a moot point."

"Thanks for nothing," I snap.

"You're the one who lost her in the first place, wolf. Don't blame me for your complete incompetence."

I whirl on him, hands clenching into fists. "Really want to go through this again, fae?"

"Not particularly. It's a waste of my time."

"Glad we agree."

Josiah finishes speaking and waves at me a moment before he moves toward us. Exhaustion is etched into every line of his face; even his movements are strained. The only time I've ever seen him this worn down—more so even—was when his mate died during childbirth.

Our entire pack mourned for years over her death, and it had only been because of Willa that he'd had the strength to move past the loss. She'd given him a reason to get out of bed in the morning.

How the hell am I supposed to find the same strength?

"Anything?" he asks Fearghas.

"No."

"Shit."

"My sentiments exactly, Alpha."

"We need to do this the old-fashioned way. I need to go out hunting, see if I can find her."

"It's worth a try. Though, if she's shielded from my magic, I can't imagine you'll be able to find her."

"She's my mate," I snap. "If anyone can find her, it's me."

"If anyone can lose her, it's you."

"You two need to knock this shit off," Josiah scolds. "Your pointless fighting isn't going to find Delaney. You both love her. Granted, I sense it's in different ways, but that doesn't make her any more important to either of you. So instead of arguing, work together. I guarantee that's the only way we'll find her."

I know he's right, and working with the fae is probably the only way to get her back, but it's fucking difficult to imagine when the bastard keeps reminding me that her being taken was my fault, to begin with.

I never should have left with the vampire. Maybe then, she would have stood a chance at getting away. Biting down on the inside of my cheek, I fight the urge to argue with Josiah, to shift right here and take off.

"How is the rest of the pack?"

"Exhausted." He runs a hand over his face. "They hit us hard, and now most of them don't feel safe."

"Do we know how they got through the wards in the first place?"

"They broke right through them. Lauren checked this morning," he adds. "She has a friend who's coming out to help us put them back up, but I don't know how many wolves will stay here."

"It's not like the city is any safer. Hell, it's worse."

"Actually, about that." He sighs. "Rainey called. She, Jack, and Elijah are having a hell of a time sorting through what happened. It seems the war stopped pretty much overnight."

I straighten. "What?"

"They said they can't sense any supernaturals anywhere near Billings anymore."

My stomach churns as I process what he's said. Supernaturals have always saturated Billings' population. For a reason we didn't know until recently, the city was always a hot spot. So what the hell does it mean that they're all gone?

"They can't sense *any* supernaturals?" Fearghas asks, and Josiah nods.

"They went for a drive through the city. It's large, so entirely possible that they missed some, but Rainey seems to think things are dying down."

"Because Lucy has what she wants," I say, the answer hitting me right in the face.

"Delaney," Fearghas replies, and I nod.

"I'm willing to bet the war was a distraction, just as offering Rainey and Elijah those council seats was. A way to draw Delaney out or, at the very least, separate us."

"And when that didn't work, she came after the pack," Fearghas finishes.

"Motherfucker, how did we not see that?"

"She hid her intentions well, Cole." Josiah clasps a hand on my shoulder. "None of us saw it coming."

"No, but we should have. Shit, at least one of us should have pieced the damn thing together."

"How? We've all been pulled in a dozen different directions."

"Like a game of cups, and Delaney was the ping pong," Fearghas says.

I turn toward him, more than surprised about his comparison. "Seriously?"

"It's an accurate way to describe it," Josiah replies.

"What are we going to do about the pack?"

"Put the wards back up, and then see who wants to stay. I won't force anyone to stay put who feels they'd be better on their own. We lost over two dozen last night."

Bile burns my esophagus. Two dozen wolves. Men, women, and children alike. My hands clench into fists as red invades my vision, and I fight to gain control. For a wolf, their mate is a grounding rod. Before I'd accepted Delaney as mine, I'd survived. But now that she's mine? It's damn near impossible. It's like the tides trying to function without the moon.

I'm a fraction of myself.

"We will mourn them," Josiah says, "and then we'll hunt her down and make her pay for everything."

I nod in agreement, more than ready to move on to the second part of that plan. Mourning our lost ones is important to the pack, I get that, but just as mourning my brother didn't bring me peace, sitting around tonight won't. The only thing that's going to calm the storm steadily growing inside of me is tracking Lucy down, ripping out her throat, and getting my mate back.

CHAPTER FOUR

DELANEY

M y stomach growls as I stare at yet another basket of fresh-baked bread in front of me. We'd left the last one sitting there for a few hours before the next one appeared. And this one was *fresh*. As in, I can feel the heat coming off of it from where I sit.

It's torture, but there's no way in hell I'm eating something that's potentially poisoned. I have literally zero interest in making Lucy's job any easier than it needs to be. In fact, I'm going to be the biggest pain in her ass.

I'm staring at the basket, imagining eating the bread, when I notice a piece of the wicker sticking out. The piece is thin, barely even the size of a pen, but I'm taken back to when Rainey and I had been children knee-deep in an Easter egg hunt.

She'd gotten caught on the side of her basket and sliced open her leg. It can be sharp...Thought trailing off, I get to my knees and crawl toward the basket.

"Delaney, ignore it. You can't eat it."

"I'm not going to," I assure her as I come to kneel beside the bread.

The delectable aroma is torment to the max, but I swallow hard and dump the bread onto the floor before scooting back to my wall, basket in hand.

"What are you doing?"

"A piece of this wicker is damaged." I point to the piece sticking up.

"Great, you can tell our hostess that we only eat bread from pristine baskets."

I roll my eyes. "Not what I meant." Gripping the piece in hand, I tug. Nothing happens, so I twirl it around my finger and pull again. This time, it tears away from the basket, still wrapped around my finger. Careful not to make any excessive noise, I set the basket aside and twist the wicker with my fingers until it makes a solid point.

"Are you planning to shiv her with the basket?" Bronywyn asks.

I glance over at her. "Possibly. But I'm thinking more about getting this mark off my neck."

Bronywyn's eyes narrow a moment before she widens them. "You want to carve it out."

"Is it possible?"

"In theory, but since this is the first time I've ever been branded, I have no idea if it will work." She takes the makeshift shiv—great way to describe it—and touches the tip to her finger. "It's going to hurt like hell, though. The pressure will need to be intense, and if we make any noise, she'll be down here in an instant."

"I can deal with the pain." I turn and pull my hair away. "Do it."

Bronywyn hesitates. "Why don't you let me take the pain?"

"No. I can call Fearghas, he can be here in an instant for us both."

"Good point." I hear her shuffling across the stone moments before her hand comes to rest on my shoulder. "Ready?"

I take a deep breath and prepare myself. "Do it."

"Okay, here goes." She stabs the back of my neck, and I wince as pain sears my skin, frying my nerves. Fire spreads where she scrapes. Tears fill my vision, but I clamp my jaw together, terrified to even whimper and risk alerting Lucy.

"You're doing great," Bronywyn whispers in my ear. "It's working."

As warmth drips down my neck and into the back of my shirt, the familiar humming spreads along my skin once more, the magic present—but still just out of reach. So close. We're so close to getting the fuck out of here.

She scrapes again, this one on already tender skin, and I flinch. Reaching down, I ball up the bottom of my shirt and shove it into my mouth, biting down on the fabric to keep myself from making a single whimper.

What feels like hours pass as sweat beads on my forehead, my entire body shaking from the pain as I bite back cries. I focus on Rainey, Cole, Fearghas, Elijah, Jack—everyone we left behind, and who we need to get back to.

Even though they aren't here, they give me the strength I need to stay steady, to keep my mouth shut as Bronywyn does what she needs to do to remove the mark.

The magic surges again, this time, complete with green sparks coming out of my fingertips as I fall forward, hands bracing against the stone the only reason I'm not facedown.

"Try," she whispers. "Quickly."

I take a deep breath and send up prayer after prayer before opening my mouth and whispering, "Fearghas. Can you hear me?"

"Anything?" Bronywyn whispers, and I shake my head.

Come on, please work. "Fearghas?"

The metal bars slam open, and Lucy storms in, red-faced, her dark eyes narrowing on us. "What the hell is going on down here, huh?"

Magic surges through me, and I push to my feet, ignoring the blood dripping down my spine as Bronywyn stands. I move in front of her, knowing she has no active magic at the moment.

"Whatever do you mean?" I sneer. "We were just enjoying this delicious bread you sent us."

She glares back at me. "Funny, I felt quite the disruption to the mark on your neck." She shifts her focus to Bronywyn. "You know how much I hate my pets being toyed with."

"We're not your pets, you psychotic bitch," she snaps back.

Magic pulsates around me, and I throw up a hand, sending a massive blast of emerald straight at Lucy. She dodges to the side, and I grab Bronywyn's hand and yank her toward the door.

Lucy gets to her feet a hell of a lot quicker than I would have liked, but I'm already ready with another blast. She roars in anger as I slam the bars closed behind her and pull Bronywyn up the stairs.

Each one we take makes my heart beat a little faster, every step one more toward freedom. "Fearghas!" I scream, urging the fae to hear me now that I no longer have to be quiet. The pain in my neck is a dull ache compared to the panic in my gut, but I know that the moment my adrenaline wears off, it's going to hurt like hell again.

Just ahead is a door, so I grab the handle, turn it, and shove it open. We emerge in a familiar stone throne room, and all hope I had for freedom vanishes like a puff of smoke.

"Oh no," I whisper.

"What?" Bronywyn turns around slowly, seeing the inside of the castle for the first time. "Where are we?"

"Faerie," I whisper.

"Faerie? Are you fucking kidding me?"

"I really, really wish I was."

"Well, well, well, if it isn't Delaney Astor."

Fear ices my spine, and I stiffen at the new voice. One I'd sincerely hoped I'd never hear again.

"What? Nothing to say to me? Does the wolf have your tongue?" Sheelin laughs. "Of course not. That would require him to actually be here, wouldn't it?"

"Who the fuck are you?" Bronywyn demands as I turn to join her in facing Fearghas's ferociously psychotic sister.

If Lucy is crazy, Sheelin is about ten times worse. After all, how many sane people can slaughter their own father in cold blood?

Her golden eyes twinkle with absolute, twisted delight. "Your little friend here knows exactly who I am. Don't you, Delaney? After all, she and I are old friends."

Bronywyn looks to me for an answer. With a deep breath, I clench my hands into fists. "Remember Fearghas's crazy-ass sister I was telling you about?"

"Yes."

"Meet Sheelin."

She turns to face her. "Oh, shit."

"Oh, shit would be an appropriate term," I reply dryly as I refocus on Sheelin. "What are you doing working with a witch?"

Sheelin shrugs. Having traded in her pristine white uniform for an all-black ensemble, she somehow looks even more menacing now than the last time I saw her. "We have a common enemy."

"How sweet, I didn't think I'd made so many new friends."

Sheelin snorts. "My brother would be that common enemy. He's the only one who would be able to find you back in your world, no matter what safe guards were put in place. So what better place to hide you than the one place he'll never return to?"

Except that he did. "Cole will find me," I say, attempting to pull the focus off the only one who can reach us here.

"He won't. But don't you worry; he's next on my list."

I growl. "Don't even fucking think about it."

Three fae march in, each carrying a scimitar in their hands. The curved blades out and ready to defend their queen, they move toward us with purpose. "Your Majesty," they say in unison, bowing to hold a fist over their hearts.

The entire scene is disturbing.

"Head down and let our guest out of her cell. I imagine she's quite pissed by now." They leave, and Sheelin turns back to us. "See, the interior isn't lined with iron, but no magic can get out. A rather clever design if I do say so myself. I plan to use it for Fearghas while I watch him die—slowly." She bares perfectly white teeth, and magic sparks between my fingers. "Seeing him whither away, no food, no water...it's going to be the gift that just keeps on giving." She laughs. "At least until I get to burn his bones."

"Not happening." I snap my fingers and hit her with a power blast meant to knock her out. She flies backward into the wall, giving Bronywyn and me the perfect opportunity to escape. We turn on our heels and race toward the only door. If I can get outside, I can find Fearghas's mom. I know Heelean will help us if her son is no longer in Faerie.

Which, based on the fact he didn't hear me, I imagine he's not.

Our bare feet pad softly on the marble floors as we race down the hall, breathing ragged. When we follow the hall to the right, my heart comes to a stuttering stop right alongside my feet when we come face to face with an entire platoon of fae soldiers.

Blades at the ready, they're standing as a solid wall, blocking our exit. We turn on our heels but are quickly closed in. And as the crowd parts and Lucy steps through, Sheelin at her side, I know our situation has gone from fucking horrible to something far worse.

"Maybe next time, you should keep your pets on a shorter leash," Sheelin scolds Lucy.

Murder in her eyes, she nods. "Next time, I will."

CHAPTER FIVE
COLE

Arms crossed, I stare at the flaming pyre that's currently ushering the souls of those we lost into the afterlife.

Around me, those who've shifted turn their heads up to the full moon and howl, the pain in it shooting straight into my heart. Devastation curls in my belly, the link to my pack strong enough that I can feel their grief.

It mingles with my own, a dark river I could easily drown in.

Fearghas stands beside me, Tarnley on the other side. Rainey and Elijah are positioned beside him, and Josiah stands directly across with Willa and Jack.

To say the mood is somber is one hell of an understatement. There's not a single creature here who is

Some more than others, but everyone feels the loss of those we had to put to rest tonight.

"We've been knocked down," Josiah starts, his voice booming over the sound of the roaring flames. "And each time, we get back up. This will be no different. The witch hit us hard, she hit us fast, and we never saw it coming." His voice cracks. "What's worse? She slaughtered our people and took two of our own."

"Two witches," Tom, a shifter I don't know very well—and for good reason—shouts. "Her own kind who never belonged here."

I growl and lunge for him, but before I can reach him, Tarnley's there, hand around the shifters throat as he lifts him from the ground.

"Those witches fought for the lives of your people. Or are you such a coward that you'd rather ignore that?" The vampire's tone is sharp, murderous, and I'm rooting for him to snap the bastard's neck.

"Please release him, Tarnley," Josiah orders.

The vampire holds on a moment longer before dropping him. Tom barely lands on his feet, stumbling until Z steps from the shadows and steadies him with a hand on his shoulder.

"They may have been witches, but Delaney Astor and Bronywyn Walsh were as much a part of our pack as any one of us. Bronywyn has healed us, reinforced our wards for nearly a century, and I don't think I have to remind any one of you what Delaney Astor and her entire family have done for us."

I cast a glance at Rainey, not surprised at all to see her hand hovering right above the blade strapped to her thigh. I almost wish she'd unsheathe it and put Tom out of my misery. Josiah wouldn't be able to order her to stop. Rainey earned her title as a deadly hunter, and it wasn't by allowing herself to be caught up in the politics of things.

Hunt. Kill. Repeat. That's the motto that the youngest Astor has always lived by.

"Wards that were broken by one of her own kind. How do we know she didn't do it to let them in?"

"You're going to want to shut your fucking mouth before I drive a blade into it," Rainey warns.

Tom's eyes widen, and I'd be damned surprised if he didn't shit himself. Apparently, a vampire is nothing compared to a hunter, and for the first time since Delaney was taken, I grin. *Fucking mouthy coward.*

"Need I remind you that Delaney is mated to one of our own?"

Whispers break out amongst the pack, each one of them scanning for me. Dozens of eyes land on me, and my grin dissipates as I glare right back, practically fucking daring Tom to say something else. He has one more comment, and I'll kill him my damned self.

Member of the pack or not.

"She is our family, and Bronywyn has earned that title through her assistance over the years. Finding them is priority number one. While we look, we need to ensure the security of Billings. Tomorrow morning, I will be sending a group in to monitor things."

"Alpha?" Paloma Reynolds—the only human amongst us—clears her throat as her mate wraps an arm around her shoulders.

"Yes?"

"The precinct has reinstated me. Seems the supernaturals who had taken over have since disappeared."

"So it is true, then," he says with a heavy sigh. "Supernaturals have disappeared from Billings."

"It certainly seems that way," she says. "Though I'll know more once I get back to work tomorrow."

"Are you sure it's safe?" Rainey asks. As a prior detective at that same precinct, she's probably the only one here who knows the same, if not more, about the city than Paloma.

"Actually, I needed to talk to you about that, too. Seems they believe you were part of an undercover operation that went poorly. Your name has been cleared, and I'd like to formally invite you to come back."

Rainey's eyes widen, and Elijah stiffens.

I can only imagine what's going through his mind. His mate being back in the line of danger—night and day—is probably not something he was looking forward to. But I also know enough about the Astor sisters, and him, to know that he won't interfere.

Interfering with an Astor on a war path is a death wish.

"That would be fantastic," Rainey finally replies. "When?"

"Tomorrow."

"Great. That will give us good insights into crime level and what's been going on while Lucy was initiating a massive war, and we also might be able to track crime patterns, see if anything links us back to the ley lines."

"That's a great idea, Rainey." Paloma winks. "I knew we needed you back."

The youngest Astor turns to me. "It will also give me a chance to get addresses for anywhere Lucy could have hidden Delaney."

I swallow hard and nod, not trusting my voice to remain steady enough to respond. I've got plans of my own as soon as I leave here. Plans that depend on Josiah never learning about them. If he had any idea what I was going to do—well—I highly doubt he would condone it.

"What are the plans for the pack?" Bestiny questions. She and the other shifters came out to mourn with us even though they'd only been a part of the pack for a short period of time.

"There's another village just over a hundred acres

from here. It's smaller and has been vacant for some time, though everything is still in working order. We will have to build up, but it will put some distance between us and this place."

Bestiny nods but doesn't question further.

"We leave first thing tomorrow. Sleep soundly knowing we have a security team who will be out walking the village from now until tomorrow morning. You will be safe, I assure you that."

The members of the pack nod, and some begin breaking off to head to bed. Travel will be long tomorrow, and most families won't sleep tonight as they prepare their belongings for yet another move.

Which really fucking sucks since we only just got resettled. We'd been forced to retreat deep into the woods for a few years before Jack killed the Drake Beta, who'd kidnapped Willa to force her into marriage. Returning home had been one hell of a celebration, and we'd hoped to never have to leave again.

Funny how things work, isn't it? Here we are, less than a year later, and we're having to abandon the homes we all grew up in.

I turn away from the fire and start heading toward my bike. I'm nearly there when gravel crunches behind me. I don't even have to turn around to know who it is. He's been up my ass ever since returning. "What the hell do you want, fae?"

"I want to come with you."

"Not interested in you riding bitch," I snap as I climb on. I'm not even mildly surprised to see Rainey and Elijah walking towards me, Z with them.

"Where are you going?" Z crosses both arms and stares me down.

"None of your fucking business."

"If you're going to go looking for Delaney, I'm coming," Rainey snaps.

I shift my gaze from Z to the Astor. "Who said I was going to look for her?"

"You can keep acting like an asshole, but we all know how much you love her. So, stop being a fucking prick, and let me help find my sister."

If my brother were still alive, and he was the one out there somewhere, I'd insist on being a part of finding him too. So instead of continuing to deny her, I nod and then meet Z's gaze. "Fine. Meet me at Tarnley's pub."

"I'll head back and open the door for you then."

I glance over at the vampire standing just beside Elijah. "Perfect, it's a fucking party." Kicking my foot down, I start my bike and speed off before anyone else can ask me any fucking thing else.

———

The drive back to Billings is a hell of a lot longer than I'd have liked it to be, and I honestly wish I would have just asked the fae to materialize us here. Then again, the silence gives me time to process everything I'm about to do.

I don't believe for one second every supernatural who'd been in Billings is gone.

There's just no fucking way that's a legitimate explanation. My guess is they're all in hiding. Probably being shielded by witches who are either working with Lucy or hiding from her themselves.

After all, the witch did start a fucking war. There's no telling how many supernatural and human lives were lost over the course of the few months she was active in the city. It's definitely bothersome that they're laying so low, but I plan on tracking them down, one by one, if I have to, and finding out exactly what they know. She left too many loose ends, and I intend to rip each fucking one of them down.

One of those strings has to lead to Lucy.

And she will take me to Delaney.

I pull up to the curb in front of Tarnley's pub, not at all surprised to see the lights on and Fearghas leaning against the front of the bar.

"You know I could have gotten you here a lot faster," he says as I climb off and approach.

"I managed just fine." I start to move past him, but the fae grips my arm. I growl, turning my face to glare at him. "You're going to want to let me go." Fangs descend, ready to tear flesh from bone if necessary.

Thankfully, the bastard releases me.

"You and I don't like each other," he says tightly. "But we can agree that we both care for Delaney and want to see her back safe. So how about we wait to kill each other until we rescue her. Deal?" He holds out a hand, and I stare down at it before offering my own.

We shake on it, the start of a temporary truce between us. If it will lead to Delaney's safety, I'll fucking shift and let him pat me on the head.

And on that thought, I withdraw my hand and open the door. The place is host to only those in our party tonight, with Z sitting on a bar stool beside Willa and Jack, and Rainey standing in the corner with Elijah. The vampire is behind the bar, arms folded.

"Took you long enough."

"I didn't have a fae taxi," I retort.

"Care to fill us in on this master plan of yours?" Z asks, turning to face me and leaning back against the bar.

"I'm going to find the supernaturals."

"I thought they'd all left?" Willa asks.

"I'm sure they want everyone to think that," Rainey says, beating me to the punch. She meets my gaze. "But I'm pretty damn sure they're around somewhere."

"Shielded by witches would be my guess," I add with an appreciative nod.

"You want to find them because you think wher-ever they are—"

"I don't believe Lucy is stupid enough to have Delaney anywhere that will be easy to find," I inter-rupt Jack. "But I do believe someone out there knows where she is, and I plan to start at the bottom and work my way right on up the chain until someone gives me what I want."

"You're planning on going after the councils." Elijah nods in approval.

"If I have to. I'll deconstruct the entire fucking community if that's what it takes."

"And you didn't tell Josiah about this brilliant plan because you knew he wouldn't approve."

"He doesn't condone violence," Willa tells Z. "Can't say I blame you for keeping it under wraps, though after seeing what Lucy did to the pack, I don't think he still feels the same."

"It doesn't matter whether he supports it or not. I will do anything to get my mate back."

"Glad you've finally decided to stop being such a fucking asshole to my sister." At Rainey's half-hearted insult, I nod.

"Now, we need to find her so I can make it up to her."

"Where do you want to start?"

"I have no clue," I admit honestly. "They could be hiding anywhere in the city."

"Here." Tarnley reaches beneath the counter and pulls out a folded map. He unfolds it, spreading it out over the counter, and pulls the cap off a red marker before holding it out for Rainey. "Mark everywhere you've already checked."

She takes it and starts drawing x's over parts of the city, mostly the downtown area. "We drove through here twice and caught no hint of supers anywhere." After making her final mark, she hands it back to Tarnley.

"My best guess is that they could be hiding in the tunnels. That would keep them shielded from you and make it easier for the witches to ward them in. Especially if they stay near other supernatural areas. The buildings are likely already warded in those areas. All they would have to do is play off that magic and make it their own."

"You know a lot about witches," Jack comments.

"I've spent a lot of time with them," Tarnley says without looking up from the map.

"Z, Cole, and I can cover more ground as wolves," Willa offers. "You guys can take a car or have Fearghas move you around. Splitting into two teams would probably be easiest, don't you think?" She turns to me, and I nod, impressed with the strategic way her mind works.

She'd been in college, pretending to be human when the Draco's took her, so I've never really seen her as anything but a party child. It's nice to see Josiah's daughter coming into her own. Especially since eventually, she'll need to lead the pack.

"Then I say we split the city into parts," Tarnley says as he draws a grid over the map. "We start with these two and steadily work our way in."

I stare down at the massive grid. It will probably take us close to a week to thoroughly comb the entire city. There's no way in hell Lucy will keep them alive that long. Not when she instantly killed Jane every time before. "That's going to take too fucking long." I run both hands over my face.

"Then what do you expect us to do?" Z asks. "We'll move fast, Cole. We will find her, but sitting here will do us no good."

"We start with the city," I agree. "And fucking hope they aren't being held somewhere in the woods."

Everyone nods slowly, the horrible weight of our fear settling on us like stones at the bottom of a lake. If we can't find them soon—I shake my head, determined to not think of the what if's. We *will* find them alive.

Delaney has to be alive.

"Then, let's get the fuck on with it," I say as I shrug out of my jacket.

CHAPTER SIX
COLE

"This feels nice," Delaney whispers beside me.

I pull her closer, her body heat searing me.

"I never want it to end," I admit.

"It doesn't have to," she promises as she sits up, the blanket pooling around her waist. She stares down at me, bright caramel eyes so fucking beautiful I could lose myself in them. Hell, I want nothing more than to lose myself in her for the rest of my immortal life.

Even as she promises me forever, though, I feel nothing but dread.

Because even in this bliss, I know our stolen moment now is nothing but a dream.

"What are you thinking about?" Delaney asks as she reaches forward and trails a finger over one of my tattoos.

"How beautiful you are."

She grins, beaming down at me like the ray of sunshine

she is. *"You don't think we're too far gone?"* she asks as her smile fades and her eyes fill.

"What do you mean?"

"I just—I don't know how much time we have, Cole. What if—" She chokes on a sob, and I sit up, alarm bells ringing in my brain.

"What if what, mate?"

"What if this is all we can have? This moment, right here, right now?"

Leaning forward, I press my lips to hers, kissing her tenderly and cupping her face with a steady hand. I pull back and wipe a tear from her cheek. *"Then, I'll gladly spend my last moment with you."*

"I feel so robbed. We spent so many years apart to only be granted a single night."

Her words are so damned true they gut me. *"We'll make it work,"* I promise her. Even if this is just a dream, I don't want to see pain on her face.

Nothing but happiness for my mate, happiness until the day I die.

"I love you, Delaney. I hope you know that."

She grins. *"Now, I know I'm dreaming."*

I smile in return and lunge toward her, pinning her beneath my body. *"Does that make me a dream come true?"*

Her smile grows heavy, but she nods. *"You have no idea, Cole."*

"I think I do." Pressing my lips to hers again, I will her

to know everything I feel. All the passion, the hope—even the fear that I may lose her. Because in that fear lies the purest kind of love. She's my soulmate, my other half, my only love, and deep down, I know I may never get the chance to tell the real her—not the dream—how I feel.

And that kills me.

———

Hot coffee burns my throat as I drink deeply and stare out over the trees. Last night was a total and complete waste of fucking time. We ran the two planned grids and encountered nothing but a handful of teens who'd snuck off to make-out in what is evidently Horny Teenville now that the supernaturals have all gone underground.

We'd finally stopped just before dawn and returned home to help transport the rest of the pack to the new village.

I won't be leaving though. I stayed behind with a handful of other wolves. They plan to help rebuild, so eventually, we can return. I just have no intention of ever leaving the home I was born in again.

My family lived here, and it's the last place I was ever truly happy. Delaney's scent still clings to the air —fainter now—but it's there. The subtle reminder that maybe all is not lost. I'm worried that if I were to go anywhere I can't sense her, the restraints on my wolf will snap, and I'll lose my fucking mind.

I'd hardly be the first wolf it's happened to. More than one has gone mindless in their grief. The only difference is they knew their mates were gone. I have a mixture of hope and fear weighing me down like ankle weights.

The air shifts, a subtle change moments before Fearghas appears beside me. "Morning."

Apparently, I've been around the fae long enough to sense his presence before he appears. *Interesting.* Filing that information away for another time, I glance over. "Coffee?"

"That would be great, thank you."

Nodding, I head into the kitchen to pour another mug. "I don't suppose you magically found her in the few hours we've been apart?"

He shakes his head and accepts the offered mug. "If I had, you would have been the first one I told."

"I appreciate that."

"Delaney wouldn't have it any other way. Even if you don't deserve her." His half-hearted grin tells me he's fucking with me, but the words resonate.

If I'd just fucking owned up to who she was to me, maybe none of this would have happened. Maybe, just maybe, we would have had more time.

Logically, I know telling her early wouldn't have altered Lucy's actions, but they may have changed the way Delaney reacted coming face to face with her. Maybe she would have run away with me, not stayed behind.

I snort into my coffee. A day where Delaney Astor doesn't stay and fight? It would be a cold day in hell.

"We going out again tonight?"

"Today," I reply.

"You're going to run the streets of Billings as a wolf in broad daylight?"

"No. But I'm going to drive them."

"Rainey is at the precinct."

"I know that, but Elijah is available. And since Tarnley can day walk now, we have nearly a full party. I have no intention of sitting around with my thumb in my ass, waiting for nightfall. You can damn well bet Lucy isn't waiting for nighttime to do whatever it is she has planned."

"Sounds good to me. Though, I can move us around a tad faster than driving."

Nodding, I place my mug in the sink and pass the fae. "I'll be ready to go in ten."

"I'll be back." He disappears, so I head down the hall to my bedroom. Her scent is more apparent in here, so I stop and inhale deeply, letting my mind drift back to that night, to holding her, loving her.

It's in that memory I find my strength.

I dress quickly, not wanting to waste another moment on memories when I am determined to find the real thing. Grabbing my keys, my silver daggers, and my phone, I head out into the living room to wait for Fearghas.

Ten minutes on the second, he reappears in my living room. "Ready?"

"Let's do this. I'm not holding your hand," I warn him.

Fearghas grins, the first hint of humor I've seen on his face since before we escaped Faerie. "Don't flatter yourself, wolf. You aren't my type."

He clasps a hand on my shoulder, and we're gone. Less than a second later, we appear in Tarnley's pub. The vampire is just stepping out from around the bar with Elijah, both men wearing suits.

"We're going to cover as much ground as possible," I tell them as I gesture to the unchecked grids on the map.

"Rainey is going to patrol this one today," Elijah tells me. "She called me an hour ago. Seems she and her new partner were just assigned a homicide in the vicinity."

I nod in understanding and gesture to the places nestled between the ones we checked last night and the one she's going to handle today. "This is where we start. We move fast but thorough, just like last night. And when we find these cowards—" I trail off, meeting the gaze of the three men before me. "We handle them like we would any enemy."

"Not a problem," Tarnley replies, showcasing his fangs.

"Agreed," Elijah says, and Fearghas nods.

"Let's go."

I place a hand on Fearghas's shoulder while Elijah and Tarnley do the same. Seconds later, we're standing in an alley near a massive warehouse. Humans stroll the street just ahead, completely unaware of the four supernaturals who just appeared mere yards from them.

I move first, stepping out onto the street. Closing my eyes, I inhale deeply, seeking any scent that is out of the ordinary.

Anything that may belong to a supernatural. Hell, I'll take a fucking gnome at this point. Though, those are supposedly extinct now.

We start walking down the sidewalk, fanning out as we go to check buildings and alleyways. Elijah heads across the street with Tarnley while Fearghas splits off to the left to walk a street occupied with storefronts.

I'm nearly to the end of the block when something catches my attention. The hairs on the back of my neck stand on end as a trickle of awareness slips down my spine. I turn slowly, not wanting to alert whoever the hell I've discovered that I know of their presence.

Just to the left of me, I see a man disappearing into a small pawn shop. The illuminated closed sign and barred windows keep humans out, so I turn toward it, attempting to appear nonchalant when really I want to fucking run in there and demand answers.

I reach the door and turn the knob, shoving the unlocked glass-paned entryway door open and stepping inside. The place is cluttered with shit, the stale stench in the air letting me know exactly what supernaturals are hidden inside.

Fucking vampires.

"What the fuck do you think you're doing in here, pal?" The one I'd seen sneak in steps out from behind the counter and meets my gaze, his crimson eyes narrowing. "Can you not read? The sign says closed."

"Just came in to do some shopping."

"You got no business here. Leave. Now."

"Is that any way to treat a customer?" I ask, strolling through the nearly toppling piles of broken TV's, cracked tables, and other useless shit.

"You ain't no customer, and we're closed." Fearghas appears beside me, and the man jumps, his face paling as his eyes widen comically. "What the fuck are you?"

"Have you asked him anything yet?" the fae asks me, completely ignoring our new friend.

"Not just yet," I tell him. "We're getting to know each other. Isn't that right, bloodsucker?"

"I ain't got no beef with no shifters," the vampire

stammers as he steps back behind the counter. "And I ain't got no beef with whatever the fuck you are."

"We have a few questions for you." I continue toward him as he all but plasters himself to a wall, body blocking the only interior door. I don't miss the way his eyes widen as I get closer to it, nor do I miss the way his hand slips down to the knob as if to block me from reaching for it.

"What do you want to know, pal?"

"What do you know of a dark witch calling the shots?"

His eyes widen again, this time until they're nearly all white, the crimson shrinking down to nothing but a pinpoint. "I don't know nothing about her, pal. Not a damn thing."

"You're lying," I growl as I lean in, inhaling the scent of his fear. "Tell me, and I might not rip your throat out."

"He'll do it," Fearghas warns. "He's done it before. Super messy." The fae mock shivers. "Trust me, you want to avoid that at all costs. I mean, unless your buddies down there don't mind doing some repainting."

The vampire swallows hard, fangs extending down. He lunges for me, but I'm a hell of a lot faster. I close my hand around his throat and throw him into the door. It buckles, sending him toppling down a set of stairs.

I follow, Fearghas on my heels as we descend into the basement. The stairs are short, so within seconds, we're at the bottom, surrounded by vampires trying to block us from the two humans they have chained to a radiator.

The women stare at us with complete and total terror, their eyes wide, clothes streaked with blood. Rage surges through me. My hands shake, and my fangs elongate as I fight against the urge to shift.

"Anyone else want to be chattier than your buddy here?" Fearghas asks.

"You done fucked up real good coming in here, pup." A man wearing a white t-shirt and black jeans steps forward. The top of his skull is tattooed, the ink continuing down his neck and over both arms.

Fucker wants to look the part of a badass, but his fear is just as apparent as his clan mates.

"I don't think so." I step farther into the basement, reaching down to grab the first fucker by the throat and lifting him from the ground. "First off, if any of you assholes think you're going to blur out of here, I should warn you. My buddy there is a fae, and he'll rip your fucking head off before you can pass by."

One tries. He disappears from my line of sight, and I turn to see Fearghas tossing his lifeless body to the floor.

"Anyone in need of another demonstration?" the fae snarls as he cracks his knuckles.

No one else moves. Hell, they barely breathe. With a grin, I cross both arms and lean back against the wall. "Great, now that we have an understanding, how about someone tells me what they know about the dark witch—Lucy—who's been calling all the supernatural shots?"

"We ain't saying shit about no one," skull tattoo comments.

I have absolutely zero time to waste. Dropping the bloodsucker in my hand, I lunge across the space and let my fangs down. Sinking them into the vampire, I tear, ripping out his throat and spitting it to the floor like the disgusting garbage it is.

Skull tattoo falls to the ground, and I turn my attention back to the rest of them currently cowering in the corner. "In case you haven't noticed, I'm not wasting any fucking time. She has my mate, and I fully intend on killing anyone who gets in my way." I snarl, and spit more blood from my mouth.

Fearghas disappears, only to return less than a minute later, a bottle of water in his hand. He offers it to me, and I take it, cracking open the lid and rinsing out my mouth.

"Now, who wants to start talking?"

One of the vampires—one who's yet to speak—starts laughing.

"What's so funny there, Chuckles?" Fearghas demands.

"If she has your mate, you are wasting your time. Chances are she's already ripped her to shreds."

A threatening growl rips from my throat, and my vision flashes red. I shake my head, shoving the wolf back down as I cross the space and lift the vampire. "What the fuck did you just say to me?"

"I said you're wasting your time," he chokes out. "She takes no prisoners. If she *had* your mate, she's already worm food."

"You must have a death wish, bloodsucker," Fearghas growls.

"Where the hell is she?" I demand again, this time squeezing a little tighter.

"No one knows," he sneers. "She took off a few nights ago, and no one has seen her since."

"Then, why are you assholes cowering in a basement?" Fearghas demands.

"Because none of us wish to be caught in the second wave."

"What second wave?" Terror sends my heartrate skyrocketing. *Was that seriously only the beginning?*

"The witch has big plans, wolf, big fucking plans that involve a new regime. And it's going to start right here in Billings."

CHAPTER SEVEN

DELANEY

"This is a much more fitting room for you, don't you think?" Lucy asks as she steps into my new cell. Strapped to a table, I can't do much more than turn my head to glare at her.

"You afraid of me?" I ask sweetly.

Lucy snorts. "Not in the least. I'll admit I underestimated your resourcefulness, but I assure you it won't happen again." She comes to a stop at my head and reaches down, squeezing the back of my still healing neck.

I wince.

"Oh, poor thing. That little injury still bothering you?"

"Fuck. You."

"You hunters and your potty mouths. Your parents really did a poor job teaching you manners."

I don't reply, just glare up at her in hopes she can see exactly what I'm planning to do to her as soon as I'm free. I can tell you it involves my ruby blade and a hell of a lot of magic.

"I can't say I'm overly surprised though. They were a troublesome duo, weren't they?"

"Shut your fucking mouth."

"You know, I watched your dad grow up. He was a cute little hunter and a damn good looking man."

Knowing she's trying to bait me, I keep my mouth shut. I won't give her the satisfaction of knowing she got under my skin.

"It was such a shame he had to die the way he did."

"It's a hunter's honor to die for their duty," I grind out, repeating the mantra ingrained in me since birth.

Lucy snorts. "Can you believe that load of horse-shit?" she asks Bronywyn. "As though hunters *want* to die. You do realize the Astors are a dying breed, right? No other hunters actually believe that. Even your parents begged for their lives. Your father even offered himself up to the vampires in exchange for letting your mother live. Tell me, Delaney, did you know your mother was pregnant when she was killed?"

"You don't fucking know what you're talking about." Her words bring a memory to the surface. Me walking into my parent's bathroom just as my mother finished throwing up. Of her smiling at me and reassuring me that she wasn't sick.

Is it possible Lucy is telling the truth?

My stomach rolls.

"See, I couldn't let the Astor line continue. The last thing I needed was more of you little bastards running around."

She certainly has my attention now. I turn my head to her. "What the fuck are you talking about?" I growl, the words barely resonating over the sound of my pounding heart.

Lucy grins down on me. "Who do you think sent the vampires into that alley? Who do you think set the entire thing in motion? I knew your family had the box, and I knew your grandmother was protecting Jane. Of course, you made my job easier by eliminating yourself from the equation—thanks for that, by the way. But then, you just had to find a way to come back, didn't you? And not only did you come back, but you also hijacked the body of the very witch I was working so hard to build up. So, really, you did this to yourself, didn't you?"

"You killed my parents?"

"And sent the vampires after your grandmother. Though, I never actually expected her to get away. That was a bit of a surprise."

Every moment of my life spent in misery.

Every moment I was alone.

My pain.

My loneliness.

It had all been Lucy.

Power surges through my body, and I yank on my chains, trying like hell to get the iron shackles off my wrists.

Lucy's laughter echoes around me. "You sure are a spitfire, Delaney, I'll give you that."

She moves away from me, and Bronywyn spits at her from the wall to which she's chained. "You will die, very slowly," she threatens, and Lucy laughs.

"You have that backward, my dear." She claps her hands together. "Now, what do you say we get this show on the road? Since one mark was clearly not enough for you, how about we re-work it?"

"No. You already have iron on her." Bronywyn struggles against her chains.

"I apparently can't be too sure."

I bite down on the inside of my cheek, already knowing pain is coming. When she'd marked me, I'd been unconscious, but based on the way Bronywyn is struggling, I can't imagine anything pleasant is headed my way.

Lucy runs her hands over my bare arms. "Such a shame. First, how about we fix whatever the fae did to you?"

My glamour. I swallow hard, not even bothering to show any fear in the face of my tormenter. Her hands trail up over my body, hovering just over my face. Then, she snaps her fingers, and magic pulsates through my body.

It's not painful, more like the rush you get from falling.

"Much better."

I know without seeing myself that I'm back to looking like Jane.

And oddly, I'm okay with it.

"Now, onto making sure you never escape again." Her hands leave my face and hover just above my arms. "I truly am sorry for the pain you're about to experience. But yet again, you did it to yourself." An instant later, fire sears my skin, and I scream, the pain enough to have my body arching up off the table as far as the restraints allow. Every muscle in my body is aflame, my nerves burning up even as I cry out.

"Stop!" Bronywyn screams.

"Not just yet."

My entire being rejects what she's doing to me, and even as I try to fight against it, I'm useless. Never in my life have I ever felt so fucking useless.

Not even when I was bleeding to death.

The fire smolders, leaving a dull ache in its wake as I slump back to the table. I turn my head to stare at arms that are now threaded with shimmering silver lines. They cover me, climbing up my body like iron veins.

"What did you do to me?" I cry out, the pain of speaking almost too much to bear.

"I made sure you'll never try anything stupid again. At least, not unless you plan on letting Bronywyn skin you alive."

I shift my gaze to her, the sadness on her face letting me know just how fucked we are now.

Lucy crosses the room and grabs two metal buckets and carries them over to me. She unstraps one of my arms, and I try to fight against her as she wraps a leather cord around my forearm and reaches below to strap it to the table so it's situated over the side of the table—right above the bucket. *That can't be good.*

She walks around the other side, humming as if she were gardening and not torturing me, and repeats it. Just as before, I have no strength left to fight, the magic of whatever she did to me altering my very soul and draining me of everything I have.

After she has both my arms strapped out, she reaches behind her and withdraws a silver blade. "Funny thing about supernaturals and silver, our wounds won't heal. At least, not when our active magic is blocked." She heads for my left side, and I struggle against the hold, trying to keep her away from me.

"Stop!" Bronywyn roars again. "Please, take my magic instead."

Lucy grins and turns her attention to the other

witch. "I thought you might enjoy seeing Jane's body on this table."

Tears stream down her cheeks as she stares at me.

"I'm fine," I say, forcing a smile.

"Don't worry, Bronywyn. Your time is coming." Pain sears my wrist as Lucy slices me open, vertically, right over a vein. She walks around the table and does the other side, and moments later, the disturbing sound of blood drizzling into metal fills my ears.

"As I said, I will bleed you dry until there's not a drop of magic left in your body. I think you'll discover, Delaney, I'm a woman of my word."

"Fuck. You."

Throwing her head back, she laughs and stalks toward Bronywyn. "Now, now, I think it's time for us to have some fun. Don't you?"

With a snap of her fingers, Bronywyn's bindings are released. She lunges for Lucy, all fire and fury, but without her magic, she's no match for the dark witch, who, with a wave of her hand, drops Bronywyn to her knees.

"Come now, don't go ruining our fun before we have a chance to have it." Reaching down, she grips Bronywyn's hair and drags her toward the stairs.

"Leave her," I choke out. "It's me you want."

"I want you both equally as you both serve a purpose," Lucy says with a grin. "Now, don't go anywhere." She winks at me and disappears with Bronywyn, leaving me completely and utterly alone.

———

I'm not entirely sure how long it takes someone to bleed out, but what feels like hours pass before Bronywyn appears at my side. Barely awake, I can only make out her shape as she presses a cool palm to my forehead.

"Help me with the straps," she orders.

"Bron—" I trail off, my body lacking the strength to even speak.

"It's going to be okay, Delaney. We have help."

A man grunts as the straps are released from my wrists. "Hold on to me," he says, and a moment later, fresh air is blowing over my face.

"Oh, my!" A familiar voice squeals as another hand is pressed to my face. "What has that bitch done to you?" *Thick, Irish accent.*

"Heelean?" I manage, tears burning my eyes. Did Fearghas find us? Is Cole here?

"'Tis me, dear. Get her inside, and go get my son."

"We need to get her back to her mate," Bronwyn urges.

"She's barely alive," the man counters. "If Heelean doesn't get started now, she will die."

"She needs him."

"I will go look for him as soon as we get her safely inside," he promises as he begins to move again, the soft steps jostling my battered body. Bright light is replaced with something softer on my sensitive eyes.

My back rests on something soft, and I struggle to keep conscious as my eyes grow heavy. "Go get Fearghas," Heelean orders. "And be sure you bring her mate back. Their connection may be useful for keeping her alive."

"Yes ma'am."

"This is going to make you feel better," Heelean says as she opens my mouth and shoves something saturated in liquid inside. What I'm guessing are leaves are spongy in the roof of my mouth, and they taste sweet, almost soothing. *Lavender maybe?* Whatever it is, it soothes my pain, pushing the dull ache aside and relaxing me.

My eyes close, finally too heavy to stay open.

"Rest now, dear, all is well. You are safe."

"I'm here," Bronywyn whispers, and I feel someone grip my hand. "Cole is coming," she promises as I begin to drift, the world around me fading as I slip away.

CHAPTER EIGHT
COLE

"Another fucking waste of time," I snap as we appear in the living room of Fearghas's apartment. The second the words leave my mouth though, I spin, sensing another presence here with us.

"What the fuck are you doing here, Raffe?" Fearghas demands. The fae who rescued us from Sheelin's prison is leaning against the door, looking a lot grimmer than he was the last time I saw him.

"I've been waiting for you. Took you long enough."

"What's wrong? Mother—"

"She's fine. Though I did rescue two witches I feel are of value to you."

My blood runs cold. "Delaney?"

"She's one of them. We don't have much time. I need you both to come with me now."

"They were in Faerie?" Fearghas asks, his voice weaker than I've ever heard it. "This whole time?"

Raffe nods. "We need to go." He reaches out an arm and grabs my wrist. We materialize across the room, and he grabs Fearghas before we're gone again.

When we rematerialize, we're standing in the center of what looks like a war camp. Tents scattered all over the place are covered in foliage being utilized as camouflage while fae rush around us. I can feel her here, the bond finally re-emerging. Pain, fear, and exhaustion slam into me in one violent assault that nearly knocks me to my knees. I turn to the right, sensing her just ahead, and break out in a run.

"Delaney?" I call out as my boots land softly in the grass, each step bringing me closer to the tent just ahead that's shining like a fucking beacon. I know without a doubt that she's inside.

That she's alive.

I burst inside. Bronywyn turns to face me. Her face is battered and bruised, her arm bandaged, a clear tube connecting her to my mate. Crimson flows through it, and I can only guess she's giving Delaney her blood.

"She's alive," she tells me, and I all but want to fall to my knees and weep. But the look on her face, the solemnness, tells me that Delaney's not out of the woods yet.

I move closer to her, not entirely sure how my

lead-filled legs manage to carry me across the space and to Delaney's bedside. I fall to my knees and take in her sleeping form. Both wrists are bandaged, her arms shimmering with what looks like silvery veins. Her glamour is gone, giving her back chestnut hair and different features, but still, I only see her.

Her chest rises and falls slowly, and I can hear her strained heart. Taking her hand in mine, I try not to squeeze too hard, especially given how cold she is.

Fearghas appears beside me and sucks in a breath. "What the fuck happened?"

"Lucy nearly bled her out," Bronywyn tells me. "The silver is from a brand she placed on us to block out magic. We managed to cut the first one off of Delaney so she could call for you."

"I never would have heard you guys here."

"We didn't know where we were until after we carved it off the back of her neck. We were able to escape, though. And that's when we realized we were in Faerie."

"The silver is what's left of the brand?" Fearghas questions.

Bronywyn's eyes fill, and she sniffles. "No. Lucy didn't want us to be able to escape again, so she marked Delaney's arms. That way, if we wanted to try again, we'd have to all but skin her to get free."

Rage burns through me, my vision reddening as I

force the wolf back down. Shifting now will do neither of us any good. "Is Lucy still here in Faerie?"

"I can't be sure."

"She was at the castle."

Fearghas glances at me and then disappears.

The fae better just be doing recon. I want to be the one to kill the witch.

I shift my gaze back to my mate. Dark bruising circles both her eyes, and her cheeks are sunken in. Gently, I tip her head to the side and study the bandage covering the back of her neck. "Why isn't she waking up?" I choke out.

"The best I can figure is that because of the amount of blood drained from her, her body is unable to heal even as quickly as a witch would."

"What can you do about the marks?" Raffe asks, turning to Fearghas's mother.

"I am working to remove them, but to be honest with you, I'm not entirely sure I can." She sighs. "Fearghas's father could have." Her voice cracks as I look up to see her angrily wiping away tears.

"You're giving her blood?" I ask Bronywyn, and she nods.

"Only a witch can, and I was nearby."

Her stone-faced attempt to appear uncaring has always been something I've seen through. It's impossible to believe she's anything but kind, given her inclination to help those who can't help themselves.

But for some reason, keeping everyone at arm's length is easier than letting someone in. And that's something I can sure as hell relate to.

"Thank you."

With a tight smile, she nods.

"I'm going to keep trying," Heelean promises. "We also sent for another witch who may be able to help."

"There's another witch here?"

At Bronywyn's question, Heelean nods. "She came about ten years ago and has been in hiding ever since. She's a damn powerful healer, though, so if anyone can remove those marks, it's her."

"When will she be here?"

"Hopefully, within a few hours," Raffe replies. "Though it could be slightly longer depending on whether or not she's altered her wards. My people are out looking though, and we will find her."

"Thank you."

He nods. "If you'll excuse me, I have some business to tend to." With a nod, he disappears.

Something crashes to the floor behind me, so I whirl, snarling and ready for a fight. The fight vanishes when Fearghas groans from the floor beside the now shattered water basin.

"What the fuck did you do?" I cross the floor to him in two long strides and reach down to help the fae to his feet.

"Fearghas! What in the bloody hell!" Heelean

rushes in through the entrance just as her son is draping an arm over my shoulders.

I help him toward a chair in the corner as warm blood trickles from a wound in his side.

"Sheelin is what happened."

Heelean's face turns bright red. Ever see Tinkerbell when she's pissed off? Well, I have. That's what happens when you babysit three pups who are obsessed with the tiny fairy. And the red-faced Tinker-bell is exactly what the fae reminds me of right now.

"You damned fool! You went after her?"

"I went over to the castle to do some recon; not my fault the bitch was lounging in the throne room." He coughs and winces.

"I sure as hell hope you didn't lead her right to us!"

Fearghas glares at his mother. "I'm smarter than that, you know."

"Are you? Because it sure as hell doesn't seem like it!" She reaches for a fresh wash basin in the corner and dips some cloth into it before marching across to her son. I step back as he pulls his shirt up to give her access to the wound.

"Fuck, Fearghas." I cringe when I see the loose, jagged skin dangling from the softball-sized hole in his side. "What the hell did she hit you with?"

"A spear. I ripped it out in Alaska just in case it had a tracker on it."

"You could have bled to death, you fool." Heelean

sniffles, and a tear slips down her cheek as she begins wiping the blood away.

"I'm sorry, mother," Fearghas says softly. It's the kindest I've ever heard him speak, and he's damn lucky he apologized.

I'm pissed on her behalf. First, her daughter goes ape shit and kills Fearghas the First, and then her only remaining family member runs off on a suicide mission? I want to kick his ass on her behalf. And on Delany's because, as much as it pains me to admit, I think she needs the fae alive.

"You should be sorry," she snaps as she applies a bandage over his wound. He winces but doesn't make a sound. Heelean steps back and glares at Fearghas one last time before turning on her heel and marching away.

"You're a dumbass," Bronywyn declares as soon as Fearghas's mother is away. "Do you have any idea what they're capable of?"

"I don't care."

"Your sister has no moral code, which makes her completely unpredictable."

"There was a time I was more powerful than her," Fearghas replies. "I just lacked the emotional ability to kill her. Something I have now remedied."

"Regardless, you can't be going off on your own like that. It's idiotic."

The fae stands, looking more irritated than

normal. "I'm going to let the others know we found them." He disappears, and I slump down into the chair beside Delaney.

"She's brave."

I meet Bronywyn's gaze but don't respond.

"I was ready to give up, accept our deaths, but Delaney had no intention of ever doing so."

"She's tough as shit."

"She didn't make a single sound when I carved that mark out of her skin."

I wince on her behalf. The pain—it must have been excruciating. "I just wish we could have gotten to you both before she lanced Delaney open." I study her injuries. "What happened to you?"

Bronywyn shakes her head angrily. "Lucy used me as her personal punching bag. Magical and otherwise."

"We will kill her for what she did to you both," I promise.

"We'll see. How much time passed while we were gone?"

"A couple of days. How about for you?"

"I'm not entirely sure since we couldn't see the outside, but I'm going to guess it was about a day." She swallows hard. "How's Tarnley? He was unconscious when I saw him last."

"Alive and insufferable."

The ghost of a smile lifts the corners of her lips. "He is quite insufferable, isn't he?"

"When you're not around, he sure as fuck is."

Her smile fades as soon as two fae appear in the tent, a woman I haven't seen in over twenty years between them. "Candice?" I ask as I meet the gaze of the brunette witch who I met—briefly—when we rescued Lauren. She'd gone missing a few years ago after her mother was murdered. We'd always thought she'd been taken out too, but it seems she managed to escape.

And to Faerie, no less.

"Cole." Her tone is sharp, matching her rough appearance. Hair braided thickly down her back, she's wearing dirty jeans and a black sweatshirt. Her face is smeared with dirt, her eyes panicked as they dart around the room.

"What the hell happened to you?" Bronywyn demands.

The other witch glares at Bronywyn. "Let's just say my world shifted after I was almost murdered multiple times."

"You ran here?"

"Lot of good it did me." She glares at the two fae who brought her in.

Raffe appears beside her. "Candice," he greets.

"When I offered to help your kind in exchange for protection, I *only* meant your kind."

"We assumed you would be interested in helping another witch." He gestures toward Delaney.

"Yeah, well, you thought wrong. A lot of good other witches did me when my entire familial line was being wiped from the planet."

"Lauren is back," I offer. Her expression doesn't soften in the least. In fact, the announcement about her friend seems to only piss her off further.

"Good for fucking her. She ran off with her pet and managed to survive the witch sterilization of twenty-ten."

"It's not her fault."

"No, of course not."

"Will you help the witch or not?" Raffe questions, his expression betraying his irritation.

"What's in it for me?"

"Survival," I reply with a snarl.

She turns to me, her gaze unwavering. A moment passes, and she scoffs. "You have got to be fucking kidding me. Another witch mated to a shifter? What the hell is in the water?"

"This one wasn't always a witch," Raffe replies.

"No?"

"No," Fearghas snaps. "You're looking at Delaney Astor."

Candice's eyes widen. "I've met Delaney. That is *not* Delaney."

"Actually, it is." I release Delaney's hand to stand,

crossing both arms. If this witch can help her, she *will*. No matter what the fuck I have to do to make it happen. "Delaney Astor died nearly three years ago." Candice's eyes widen slightly. "Then, her soul was ripped from the afterlife by a dark witch who intended to siphon her hunter magic. When Agatha Astor discovered it, she rescued the souls of Delaney and her parents, then stuck them into three ravens. When Heather—the original witch—rose and possessed a human-turned-fae, she killed Jane—Rainey Astor's best friend. Delaney then soul-jumped into her body, and that is the one you see here."

Candice's eyes narrow on my face as though she's trying to determine whether or not I'm lying. "That's quite a story."

"It's true."

She glances from me to Bronywyn then to Fearghas and Raffe. Finally, she sighs and looks to Delaney. "I will help her because I owe her."

I'm not surprised; Delaney helped a hell of a lot of people—human and supernatural alike—when she'd been a hunter. But I don't remember her ever saying anything about the witch. Granted, I was trying like hell to avoid her and our bond. It's entirely possible I missed big chunks of her life. Hell, I know I did.

Candice cautiously moves across the tent and comes to stand directly in front of me, on the opposite side of my mate. Closing her eyes, she raises her hands and hovers them above Delaney's arm. Power pulsates from her in waves, her hands glowing gold.

Delaney's skin sizzles, steam steadily rising from where the brand is inked into her skin. Instinctively, I reach for her, but Candice's glowing eyes meet mine, and she shakes her head.

"Touch her, and you die, wolf."

Flexing my fingers, I fight the urge to rip her away from my mate, especially as Delaney's body begins to shake, convulsing up off the table with the force of Candice's power. Red streaks into my vision, tiny streams of crimson that pool as my wolf struggles to break free.

Blood.

I need to drink the blood of the one keeping me from my mate. Of the one hurting her. No matter how much I try to remind myself that Candice is here to help—someone grabs my shoulder, and a moment later, I'm standing in the center of a field.

I spin, growling as I face off with Fearghas.

"What the fuck, fae?"

"You killing Candice is hardly the best thing for Delaney. Neither is me killing her." He shrugs. "This seemed like the next best option."

I can't argue his logic. A second later, and I would have had the witch's head in my hands. So, instead of trying, I turn in a slow circle and breathe deeply. "How's your side?"

"Can't say it feels great." He grunts, and I glance over as he lowers himself onto a stump. "We're going to need to get Delaney and Bronywyn out of Faerie as soon as possible," Fearghas says. "They will be looking for them here."

"Especially now that you've drawn attention to the fact that you're here."

"Admittedly, not my best decision."

"I would have done the same."

Fearghas chuckles. "Careful, wolf, people may begin to believe we're friends."

"I've come to not want to kill you as frequently."

Fearghas throws his head back and laughs. "Just wait until Delaney sees the pair of us. She'll think she's truly died."

I can't help but chuckle. "You're probably right." We grow quiet a moment, and the only sounds are those of the breeze ruffling through the trees and the birds singing above. "How do you know Raffe?"

"He was part of my father's guard when he was attacked."

"Your father had a guard?"

"My father was the rightful king of the fae."

I whirl on him so damn fast it makes me dizzy. There's not much that surprises me these days, but Fearghas being next in line to a throne? That's a fucking whopper. "You're royalty?"

"Was." His green eyes meet mine, none of his

trademark sarcasm in them. "I want nothing to do with the throne."

"Your father?"

"He was dethroned by the bastard who brainwashed my sister, then tortured for information on me. Let's just say, I didn't take my father being ripped from his birthright so easily."

"Can't fucking blame you there."

He nods in appreciation. "Raffe was head of the guard. When he saw what happened, he offered to fight for my father, to stand beside him and help him take his throne back. But he was tired of fighting, so instead, he chose to let it be."

"And Raffe didn't want to do that?"

"Raffe's family was murdered at the request of the new king. My sister carried it out."

"Fucking-a." And I thought my pack drama was intense. This is fucking insane. "So, it's safe to say this war isn't over until your sister is dead."

"Not just her, but the elder fae who believes we're supporting his right to be king."

"The one Rainey met after you rescued her from Heather."

Fearghas nods. "He's weak, pliable, which is why he's Raffe's figurehead. But the fucker will get what's coming to him too. They all will." His eyes flash, and the air around us shifts. In an instant, he goes from the bastard I've known for the last few months to the king he should be. It's insane, the change, and gone just as quickly as it came.

"When do you think we can move them?" I ask, offering him the subject change he clearly needs.

"Candice will finish removing the brands. Then, we can speak with my mother."

Nodding, I turn away and stare out at the trees. Peace settles over me knowing that Delaney is alive and within reach. Instead of focusing on my anger that she was branded like a fucking steer, I let my mind drift to the life I hope we get to one day share.

All the light, the joy, and none of the dark.

CHAPTER NINE
COLE

Fearghas and I materialize in the dim light of the medical tent. Bronywyn's gaze meets ours, and she nods at me as I cross the floor to Delaney. With shaking fingers, I gently caress her now unmarred skin as I breathe a sigh of relief.

"She will be fine when she wakes," Candice says from the corner.

I turn to face her. "Thank you."

"You will need Lauren to remove the brand on the other one." She gestures toward Bronywyn, who pins her with a glare so icy I'm sure the lakes of hell just froze over. Without responding or even shrinking away at the threat in Bronywyn's eyes, Candice turns to the fae guard Raffe left with her. "I'm leaving now, with or without your help." He nods and touches her shoulder. The next heartbeat, they're gone.

"You have one too?" Fearghas asks Bronywyn.

After a moment, she nods and turns, lifting the hair off the back of her neck. "Lauren should be able to remove them. She has both light and dark magic residing in her, and it was dark magic that branded us."

"She does? Since when?"

"Back in the nineties when the dark coven attacked her, Lauren killed the leader and absorbed her magic. Haven't you sensed it?"

He nods. "I never understood what it meant though."

"Well, now you do." She gets to her feet. "Should we get going? I have enough equipment at my clinic we can continue the transfusion." Bronywyn sways, and Raffe appears beside her just in time to keep her from falling over.

"You're nearly at your limit, dear," Heelean says sadly. "Delaney's body will have to take over now." She removes the catheter in Bronywyn's arm and covers the wound with a bandage.

"Can I not help her?" I ask, willing to slice open a vein right now if that's what it takes to see her eyes again, to see her full lips turned up in a smirk.

"It has to be a witch," Heelean replies. "It's the only way to make sure the blood doesn't kill her."

And here I am, fucking useless to her again.

"We can take her back to my penthouse."

"No." Raffe shakes his head for good measure. "You do that, and Sheelin will find you. If I can, she can too."

Fearghas turns to me. "Then where do you suggest?"

"My clinic has a safe house beneath it." Bronywyn moves away from Raffe and stands closer to Delaney. "We can hide out there. It's warded heavily and shielded by magic a hell of a lot stronger than anything Lucy can throw our way. Until I get this mark removed, she can find us damn near anywhere else."

"Great. Let's get going, then." Fearghas reaches for Bronywyn, wrapping an arm around her waist to keep her steady, while I gently lift Delaney into my arms then turn toward the fae who rescued my mate.

"Thank you for everything you did," I tell Raffe. "You have my loyalty if ever you should require it."

"I appreciate that, Beta. And one day, I just might call you on it. Take care, all of you."

"I love you, son," Heelean says as she squeezes Fearghas's arm gently. "Take care."

"You too, mother."

She smacks him hard on the chest. "And stay the hell away from your sister until we find a way to stop her."

"Yes, mother."

The next instant, we're gone, reappearing in the clinic level of Bronywyn's place.

"We need to hurry," she says. As she proceeds to

rattle off a list of medical equipment she needs to Fearghas, I stare down at Delaney's face, studying every part of it. The slope of her nose, the shape of her mouth.

Never again will I let her out of my sight.

"We need to call Rainey," I tell them.

"I'll take care of it as soon as I know you're all safe." Fearghas appears beside Bronywyn, holding two massive bags in each hand.

"Great, this way." Using the wall to prop her up, Bronywyn leads us over to a wall that's half windows looking into the next room.

Before I can question her, she's pressing her palm to the bottom right corner of the glass. With a click, it slides backward, revealing a set of stairs. She heads down first, and we follow while lights illuminate our way as we move farther and farther into the ground.

My nerves are frayed, but I stay the course. I may hate tight spaces, but I sure as fuck hate Delaney being in danger more.

The steps end just in front of a red door, which Bronywyn opens quickly and steps through. We follow, and I find myself standing in the center of a plush living room. Windows with sun streaming in line the far wall, framed by sheer curtains on either side.

A leather couch sits before a fireplace with two throw blankets over the back of it. A pristine kitchen looks over the rest of the house, green and copper granite countertops gleaming as if the place was just cleaned.

There's one hallway to the left and another to the right, giving this place much more of a manor vibe than a tiny safe house.

"Where the hell are we?"

"Ireland," Bronywyn replies. "About four hours outside of Dublin."

Even Fearghas looks surprised. "I thought you said this was a safe house?"

"It is. The portal to it is hidden beneath my clinic, and I am the only person on the entire planet who can access it."

"How the hell did you set this up?" Fearghas questions, and if I'm not mistaken, he's in awe of the witch before us.

"I have a lot of friends who have wanted to ensure my continued safety."

"So others know of this place?"

She shakes her head. "They know of a safe house beneath my clinic. Should anyone manage to get past the panel embedded in the glass and make it down those steps, it will lead them to an empty two-room bunker. My magic is the only thing that can open this room."

"And it's warded?"

She nods. "Heavily. You can go outside if you need

to run. I assure you that the ten acres this property sits on are well-protected as well." She gestures to the counter. "Set the supplies down there, and go get Rainey and Lauren. I will leave that door open for exactly five minutes. Then, it's sealed until Delaney wakes and I find a way to get this mark off of me."

Fearghas does as he's told and disappears.

"Bring her this way." Bronywyn moves down the hall to the right and leads me into a large bedroom with a king-size bed centered on the far wall. I gently set Delaney down and move back so Bronywyn can work.

"Can you please go get me those bags Fearghas left in the kitchen?"

Without argument, I run to the kitchen, returning less than a minute later with bags in tow. Setting them down beside the bed, I move back as Bronywyn reaches down and rummages through one of them. She pulls out a blood bag and hangs it on the bed frame, which I now see is already prepped for an IV.

Whatever the hell this witch is, she's nothing if not prepared.

"Is that witch blood?"

"I keep supernatural blood on hand for cases similar to this."

"Smart."

"I like to be ready for anything." She inserts a new IV into Delaney's arm and then unblocks the line so the blood can flow freely into her. Taking her first full deep breath, Bronywyn stands back and stares down at Delaney. "I wasn't prepared for this." Reaching forward, she brushes a strand of hair from Delaney's face.

"You care for her."

"I don't like bullies," she snaps, though it lacks heat.

"You're a good person, Bronywyn. Thank you for caring for her."

She opens her mouth to respond but stops when Tarnley blurs into the room and crushes her against his body. "What the hell, vampire." I can hear her tone, though. It's the same one I use with Delaney.

She's relieved to see him even if she won't admit it.

"You can't fucking do that to me again," he orders, pulling back and cupping her face in his hands.

Feeling like I'm intruding, I walk around to the other side of the bed and take Delaney's hand in mine. Rainey rushes in next, Elijah on her heels.

"Oh my God."

"She'll survive," Bronywyn tells her.

"What the hell happened to you guys?"

Lauren walks in, Z by her side. "I'm guessing the mark on your neck and lingering dark magic is why I'm here?"

"I did just ask for Lauren and Rainey," Bronywyn

snaps at Fearghas when he appears in the room beside me.

He shrugs. "They all wanted to come."

She rolls her eyes and pushes past Tarnley. "I'll go seal the door."

"I'm not staying," Z says quickly, turning back to his mate. "Are you sure you'll be okay?"

"Yes, love, I won't do anything that will harm me or the baby."

He nods, but I can feel the tension.

I will watch after your mate, I promise him through our mental connection.

Thank you. I am happy yours has been returned.

Thank you.

"Take me home, please." Fearghas disappears with Z, then reappears a moment later.

"Door is getting sealed now," Bronywyn snaps.

"I'll come with you." Tarnley follows her out as Rainey turns to me.

"What happened?"

"Lucy marked them so they couldn't use magic. Bronywyn carved Delaney's off so she could call for Fearghas, but since they were in Faerie and he was here, he couldn't hear her." I glance up at the fae. His jaw tightens, and he looks ready to kick his own ass for what he deems as failure.

I recognize it because it's exactly how I feel too.

"That would be the lingering magic I sense on Delaney. Who removed the mark?"

"Marks," I correct. "Lucy was pissed, so she covered Del's arms in the damn things. Your old friend, Candice removed them."

Lauren's eyes widen. "Candice? I thought she was dead?" Her voice cracks, but she closes her eyes and takes a deep breath. "Later. I need to remove the last of this lingering magic from Delaney. It's what's keeping her under. Then, I'll get to work on Bronywyn."

"You can you remove them?" Rainey asks Lauren, who nods.

"Bronywyn's will only take a moment, but removing this lingering magic—" She sighs and leans down to press a hand to Delaney's forehead. "I can feel her pain." Her eyes lift to mine. "Can you?"

I nod. "I've felt it since I stepped foot in Faerie."

"I will help you, Delaney," she says softly. First, I need to remove Bronywyn's. I will be back in just a few minutes."

I want to beg her to start with Delaney, but I get the need to take care of something that will only take minutes first. Especially if Delaney's curse drains her.

"What happened to her wrists?" Rainey runs the tips of her fingers over the blood-soaked gauze.

"Lucy tried to bleed her out. I don't know much more than that."

"I'm going to fucking bleed her out." Rainey's body

begins to vibrate, so Elijah steps forward and places both hands on her shoulders. His touch calms her, and within a few seconds, she's regained control.

Bronywyn re-appears in the doorway with Lauren and Tarnley.

"Were you able to remove it?" I ask, and Lauren nods.

"I'm going to start removing the remnants of Lucy's dark magic. I may need to draw on energy in order to keep going," she warns. "So if you don't wish for that to be you, leave the room now."

Everyone stays put. In fact, Bronywyn and Tarnley both move farther into the room. I nod at them both, grateful for their willingness to sacrifice in order to save my mate.

"All right," she whispers as she brings her hands over Delaney's chest. "Let's get started."

CHAPTER TEN
DELANEY

A steady breeze rustles the tree branches while a bright sun cast in a cloudless sky shines down on me. It warms my face, my arms, and fills me with an overwhelming amount of peace.

Quiet.

Solitude.

From where I sit on a grassy knoll, I can see an expansive valley below. Soft green grass dotted with bright blooms, a shimmering pond in the center. It's stunning, this picture, and I could sit here for hours. Hell, maybe I've already been here for days.

"Funny meeting you here."

I turn, my heart stumbling in my chest as I lurch to my feet and wrap my arms around the woman I've always known as my mother. "Mom!"

She embraces me, her floral perfume filling my lungs

*and making me long for a much less complicated time.
Back before life or death, war, and pain. Back when the
only things Rainey and I worried about were who was
going to catch the biggest fish on our trip with dad.*

"Oh, Delaney, how I've missed you."

"Hey, Delly."

*I pull back enough to glance around as my father joins
us atop the hill. Tears spill from my eyes, drenching my face
as I reach for him, adding him to the embrace I'm already
sharing with mom. "Dad." We cling to each other,
unwilling to move past this moment. Somewhere in the
distance, a wolf howls. It's the pain in the sound that brings
me back to the present.*

"What are you guys doing here?"

*We pull apart, and I wipe my tears away, then stare at
the two people I never thought I'd see again.*

"Occasionally, we pop in here."

*"When we get tired of shitting on cars," dad
explains.*

I snort. "Wait, where are we? Are we in the veil?"

"Yes."

*My throat swells, the lump painful as I swallow hard.
"I guess me being here means I've run out of time." The
realization hits me like a sucker punch, and I step back,
turning to face the valley. I'd known I was somewhere, but
a part of me had hoped I'd just been dreaming.*

*Though, now I know where I am, I probably should
have figured it out sooner.*

"You're not dead, honey," dad says. I turn back toward them.

Brows drawing together, I study them. "What do you mean?"

"You're still alive. Your soul has been sent here while you are healed. Your injuries were extensive," mom tells me. "But you will survive because you are a fighter, my love."

Hope warms me, though the emotion is muted. I want to live, to return to Cole and Rainey, but once I do, how long will it be before Lucy finds me again?

"I have to figure out how to handle Lucy."

"You need to train," dad says, his tone so familiar to when he first started working with me that nostalgia makes me smile.

"I haven't had a lot of time."

"You haven't made the time," mom clarifies. "You have always been willing to run headfirst into a fight, even if you aren't fully prepared." She glances back at dad. "A character trait you get from your father."

"I like to call that bravery." He winks at me.

She chuckles. "Or stubbornness."

Their laughter fades as quickly as it came. "Lucy is powerful," dad says. "But you've faced worse."

"I'm not so sure about that."

"Really? Because I seem to remember you going head-to-head with an entire vampire clan back when you were nineteen."

He'd been so pissed that I hadn't come to get him before heading out. But I'd been convinced there were only one or two inside and hadn't wanted to pull him away from date night with mom. Sadness seeps through me.

They died two days later.

"Vampires are nothing compared to Lucy. I hit her with all of Jane's magic, and she barely flinched."

"There's your problem right there."

I turn to dad. "What do you mean?"

"You're still thinking of it as Jane's magic."

"But it is, it's her body."

"No. It's *your* body." Mom reaches out and rests a hand on my shoulder. "Your face, your voice, your blood, your magic. It may have been the shell she was born in, but you are the one living in it. Until you come to terms with that and accept yourself for who you are now instead of living in the past, you won't ever reach your full abilities."

I know her words are true, and I like to think I have come to terms with who I'd become. Then again, I'd been quick to accept a glamour from Fearghas's mother because I was so damned afraid of Cole seeing me as anyone but who I was.

"You have someone special now. Someone who sees you for who you truly are."

At mom's words, Cole's face pops into my mind. I can see him staring down at something I can't quite make out. A blurred shape, but he looks distraught, and his pain hits me hard. I wince as that pain blossoms in my chest.

"Cole is a good man."

I meet his dark gaze. "You're not mad he's a shifter?"

Dad laughs. "Why would I be mad? He can't control what he was born as, and I know Josiah's pack to be good, honorable wolves. You could do much worse. Though, no one is good enough for my daughters."

"Rainey looked happy with her vampire," mom says.

"He's a hunter now," I tell them.

"We know." Mom winks. "We also know you've got quite a friend in that fae—Fearghas."

"How do you know all of this?"

"We check in from time to time," dad tells me. "Occasionally, we leave the veil and do a fly-by."

I can't help but smile. Knowing they're still around, checking in on us, it means more to me than I can even put into words.

It means Rainey and I aren't ever truly alone.

My thoughts darken as I remember our other fallen family member and the fact that she will never know peace. "Grandmother sold her soul."

Dad's expression darkens. "We know. She did what she believed had to be done. I can tell you, she has no regrets."

"You've seen her?"

He shakes his head. "But Agatha Astor never regretted a single thing in her life. She never saw the point."

"I hate that she'll never know peace."

"We do too," mom says. "But you have much bigger problems to focus on now. Lucy is coming for you, Delaney.

And she will tear the city apart until she finds you. You must train, not just with weapons but with your magic as well. Accept it. Learn it."

"And use it to kill the bitch," Dad finishes.

"I love you guys." I wrap my arms around them both, squeezing gently.

"We love you too, baby. So much. Please, tell Rainey we love her, too, and that we're so sorry we lied to her for so long."

"She knows." I pull back.

"Now, you need to wake up. It's time to stop hiding and start fighting."

My dad's words echo through my mind as I nod. "I hope to see you around."

"We'll fly by every now and then."

Tears fill my eyes as I smile at them both. Focusing on Cole, I try to will my soul to return home. The fae said I could be trapped in the veil if not for him, but with our bond, I don't see myself ever going anywhere he's not. At least not for long.

I use that bond now, the cord connecting the both of us, to pull myself back to him. Closing my eyes, I feel air fill my lungs as pain shoots through my body.

My body is on fire.

But somewhere close by, I can feel my mate, and the pain begins to fade. "Cole?"

"I'm here." He lets out a sigh and squeezes my hand.

Vision blurry, I blink rapidly, each moment that passes clearing it a bit more until finally, I'm staring up into Cole's hazel eyes.

"Cole."

"Delaney." He lifts my hand and presses a kiss to the top of it, lips lingering. "I thought I lost you."

"I think you almost did," I say and try to sit up. Fresh burning pain shoots through me, so I still again.

"You're going to be down for a while," he tells me. "You lost a shit ton of blood, and it took Lauren two days to get all the dark magic out of you."

"Two days? I've been out for two days?"

He nods. "Longest fucking forty-eight hours of my life."

"Wait—dark magic?"

"Left behind after Candice removed your marks."

"Candice? I thought we were in Faerie?"

"It seems she discovered a way to get there herself."

"Interesting."

"You didn't know she was there?'

I shake my head. "I helped her get out of Billings and board a boat that should have taken her back to Ireland. Flying was too risky," I tell him as I recall the week I spent helping her fake her death. It had been rough, but entirely necessary, given the hunt that was going on for council witches and their families. A shiver tears through me as I recall all the dead.

"She said she owed you."

"She did. A debt that has more than been repaid now." Closing my eyes, I lean back against the pillow. "I'm sorry for everything you went through the past few days."

"Not your fault."

"Is Bronywyn okay?"

He nods. "She's in the kitchen, being annoyed by Tarnley and Elijah. Rainey is here, too, but she's showering."

"Where are we?"

"Bronywyn's Ireland safe house."

I glance up at him. "Really?"

He nods. "She gave you a bunch of her blood, but it wasn't enough, so we came here to keep you both hidden from Lucy and so she could give you another transfusion."

"She gave me her blood?"

"She did."

"Wow."

Fearghas pops into view and rushes toward me, face falling as he sinks to his knees on the other side of my bed. "You could have fucking called me in here," he snaps at Cole.

"She just woke up."

My fae friend ignores my mate. "How are you?"

I smile. "Fine." I draw my brows together as I try to remember the masculine voice who rescued us from the dungeon. "Who pulled us out of there?"

"Raffe. He found you and Bronywyn and managed to help you escape before Sheelin or Lucy could finish you both off."

Drawing my brows together, I replay what I remember of that day. The clearest picture is Lucy slicing my wrists open and letting the blood drain out. After she took Bronywyn though, everything is fuzzy.

The door opens, and Bronywyn steps in, her eyes filling when she sees me. Then, as quickly as the emotion appeared on her face, the emotion is gone, and she's strolling toward me with a fresh bag of fluids. "So glad to see you're awake." Her voice is strong, and I wish I could figure out why she's so terrified for people to realize how big her heart is.

Was it her loss? Or something else?

"Me too." Her face is still bruised, the purple turned yellow covering her left cheekbone and the right side of her jaw. "What happened to you after she took you out?"

"We had a nice little chat where her fist connected with my face quite a few times." She hangs the new bag behind the old one then steps back to talk to me.

"If Raffe hadn't shown up when he did, I imagine she would have killed me."

I clench both hands into fists, and my gaze shifts to Tarnley for a moment. The vampire's jaw is tight, his eyes hard.

"Did he kill her?"

She shakes her head. "I wish. He showed up dressed like a member of the guard, demanded she go see Sheelin for something, and offered to escort me back to my cell. As soon as she was out of view, he rushed me down to get you, and we took off."

"How much blood did she get from me?"

"A lot. You nearly bled to death."

"Shit. Will it work for what she wanted? Since I'm still alive?"

Bronywyn's expression says it all. "Whatever she needed the power boost for, she got a pretty good one from you."

"Dammit."

"We can't worry about that right now," Elijah interjects. I hadn't even seen him come in. He smiles softly at me from the doorway. "We need to focus on you getting better. Then, we can track her down."

"Do you have your magic back?" I ask Bronywyn. She demonstrates by snapping her fingers. A breeze rushes through the room.

"Me?" I glance down at my arms, noticing that the marks are gone.

"Yours will take some time. Since she took so much of your blood, your body needs to regenerate. My blood and the other witch blood I gave you will have helped that along, but don't expect to be at full power for at least a few days."

Elijah moves forward as Rainey shoves in. "Thanks a fucking lot for telling me she was awake." She elbows her fiancé, and he smiles in return as she rushes toward me. "How are you feeling?"

"Tired, mostly."

"Didn't I fucking tell you to stop dying on me?"

"I didn't die," I defend, biting down on the inside of my cheek to keep from smiling at my sister. It's just so damned good to see her again. Memories of the veil surge to the surface, and my smile falters, filled with a bit of sadness—grief.

"What's wrong?" Cole asks, and I turn to him. I hadn't realized he could sense my emotions, but the evidence is written all over his face.

"I, uh, spent some time in the veil while I was out."

"You did?"

I nod and look to Rainey. "I saw mom and dad."

Her eyes widen, and she takes a seat on the bed beside me. "How are they?"

"They're good. Said they do fly-bys to check on us."

She snorts. "I'm guessing that was dad's terminology for it."

"You'd be guessing correctly on that one. They wanted you to know they're proud of you and happy that you're happy."

Rainey tosses a glance at Elijah.

"They like him," I tell her and turn to Cole. "You too."

"What about me?" Fearghas asks, mocking shock.

"They like you all."

"Are you hungry?" Bronywyn shifts the subject, clearly uncomfortable with the personal turn things have taken.

Patting my flat stomach, I nod. "I am starved."

"I'll go make you a sandwich."

"I'll come too," Tarnley offers.

Bronywyn sighs but doesn't argue. Because of the information I'm privy to, I notice now how she relaxes around him, how unconsciously, she leans toward him.

"Where's Lauren? Bronywyn said she removed the marks?"

"She's home," Fearghas tells me. "Took her there this morning. Her mate was blowing up our phones over it."

"Z's pretty territorial," I joke.

"Not just Z," Fearghas says, with a pointed nod at Cole.

"I'm going to go clean my gun." Rainey stands. "You two care to help me?"

"Why would I want to help you clean your gun?" Fearghas asks.

"Because if you don't, I'm going to see if you can dematerialize faster than a speeding bullet."

Fearghas snorts. "I totally can."

"Great, let's go test that theory."

Accepting the challenge, Fearghas stands and heads for the door.

"Please, don't really shoot him!" I call after Rainey.

"I'll try not to! Love you!"

"Love you too!"

Soon, it's just Cole and me again. I rest back against the pillows, taking a deep breath. The air shifts, a glimmer of intense need washing over me, so I crack open my eyes. Cole's eyes are nearly black, his arms quivering as he reaches for me.

"I need to hold you."

"I need that, too."

Kicking off his boots, he shoves the comforter down and climbs into bed. Within moments, I'm tucked against his hard body, his warmth surrounding me as the steady thumping of his heart fills my ears with the sweetest melody.

His heart's song is the same as mine—his body and soul calling to my own in a way that only solidifies our bond.

Cole holds me tightly and buries his face in my hair, breathing deeply. As he does, his entire body relaxes beside me. What was it like for my wolf? To not know where I was?

"I thought I'd never see you again," I whisper as tears fill my eyes, and a lump grows painfully in my throat at the knowledge that I was so damn close for that fear to have been reality.

"Not a chance. I'd follow you into the veil if that's what it took to get back to you."

The idea of Cole dying alongside me is terrifying, even as his words make my heart swell. I love him so damn much, this man, my wolf.

"Never again, Delaney. Next time, we stand together until the end."

"Until the end," I repeat, even as I pray there will only ever be a beginning and a middle.

CHAPTER ELEVEN

DELANEY

B eing bed-ridden is getting really freaking old, really freaking fast. I've only been awake for around twelve hours, but other than to use the restroom—which, much to Cole's irritation, I refused to let him help me with—I have been forbidden from getting up.

Rainey breezes in, bag of skittles in her hand, and takes a seat on the bed beside me. Cole lays on my other side, head resting on his arm as we watch another episode of *Psych*.

"Okay, that is *not* how we actually do things," she comments dryly when Detective Lassiter begins interviewing one of the suspects Shawn's 'psychic' abilities led them to.

I laugh. "Maybe they just do things differently in Santa Barbara."

"I very much doubt they do things that differently," she comments. But less than a minute later, she's laughing her ass off as Shawn goes completely boneless on Gus.

Cole presses a kiss to my temple. "I'm going to go see what Elijah is doing." He rolls out of bed and casts one last glance at me after pulling on his boots. "Be back soon."

"Okay."

With a smile, he leaves, and I glance over at Rainey, not prepared to see her staring at me, a dopey grin on her face.

"What?"

"You guys are too adorable. I mean, it's almost nauseating. I think I threw up a little in my mouth."

"We are not." I smack her with the throw pillow in my lap, and she laughs loudly as her poor defense is met with skittles dumped all over her lap.

"Hey! That's Skittle abuse!"

"Arrest me."

"Maybe I will. Elijah! I need my handcuffs!" she calls out. Unable to keep my joy in, I laugh until my sides ache. Being back on the force has made my sister even happier than she was the last time I saw her.

And I love it. She deserves all the things, this sister of mine.

"So, how crazy is it that time moved roughly the

same here as it did in Faerie while you were gone?" she asks around a mouthful of Skittles.

"Pretty crazy. I wonder why."

"Probably because if your wolf had been separated from you any longer, he would have eaten Fearghas."

I wince. "How bad was it while I was gone?" The two have always seemed to hate each other, for who the hell knows what reason. I hadn't even considered the effect my absence had given that there was no buffer between them.

"Josiah almost kicked both their asses, but I think they came to an understanding that rescuing you was more important than comparing cock sizes."

Snorting, I shake my head. "Is that really a thing?"

She shrugs. "I'm pretty sure."

I hold out my hand for some Skittles, enjoying her side-eye when she dumps some into my palm.

"They still haven't forgiven you for making me spill them."

"I'm so sorry, Skittles." I glance back at my sister. "Better?"

"Maybe." She pops a handful into her mouth, and we both turn our attention back to the TV just in time for the episode to end and the countdown for a new one to begin.

"I can't wait to get out of this room."

"How are you feeling?"

"Normal. Well, almost normal, anyway. My magic is still absent, but physically, I'm feeling much better."

"Amazing what a few liters of blood will do for you."

"True." I shiver. "I honestly thought I was going to die in that cell."

Rainey wraps an arm around my shoulders. "Well, you didn't. Us Astor's are pretty fucking resilient."

"That's the damn truth. Loss, heartbreak, and crazy fucking witches can't even bring us down." We laugh darkly before falling silent. Her words ring true in my mind, but also make me wonder how much more the world plans to throw at us. Needing a change of subject, I clear my throat. "What's it like being back to work?"

"Great. I miss Rodriguez, though." Her mood darkens briefly. "He was a good man."

"He was."

"My new partner isn't terrible, though. He's new, on his first year as Detective."

"How's Elijah taking you working with a man?" I wiggle my eyebrows and rub my shoulder against hers.

She chuckles. "He was a tad jealous at first, but then they met, and my partner nearly pissed his pants."

"What the hell did Elijah do to make him piss his pants?"

"Nothing. His mere presence alone was apparently enough to terrify the guy." I arch a brow as I stare at her. "Fine, maybe he mildly threatened him should he let me die on the job."

"There's the ex-vampire we all know and love."

"Yeah," she says sweetly. I can all but see little hearts in her eyes. "He's pretty damn great."

"When are you two getting married?"

"Who the hell knows? Jack and Will had to postpone their mating ceremony while we figure out what's going on, so it will probably be sometime after that. I'd feel shitty if I got married first when they put it on hold to help us."

"I get that."

"What about you? You and Cole talking about making an honest woman out of you?"

"We've had sex once, so no. I'd say that's nowhere near the table at this point in time."

"Yeah, but this thing between you has been brewing for a while, hasn't it?"

I never told Rainey how I felt about Cole. It just never felt fair to put that on her when nothing could ever come of it. Then, there was the whole dying and coming back to life thing that had him running for the woods to get away from me.

By then, it was pretty damn obvious how much I loved him, though.

"I mean, it has on my side."

"I'm guessing his, too. You should have seen him when you were gone, Del. It took Z kicking his ass to get him to see reason."

My head whips around so fast my vision momentarily blurs. "What do you mean?"

"They had a fight. Cole shifted and went after Jack, and Z had to step in before Willa ripped him apart."

I gape at her. "Why the hell didn't anyone mention this before?"

"Probably because they're fine now. You know how it is. They get mad, kick the shit out of each other, get a few bites in, then all is fine and dandy again. Such is the testosterone way."

"I guess." But Z and Cole fighting? Can I even recall an argument between the two of them? I don't think I ever saw one. The closest Cole got was when Z left the pack. He'd been pretty broken up about it, but even then, he'd understood. "Why did he go after Jack?"

"Jack blamed him for you getting taken then suggested Cole was not the best one to find you."

Damn. "Jack's okay, though?"

"Yeah. There was no way Cole would have gotten through Willa. She's brutal, that one."

"She'll make a good alpha one day."

"Agreed."

"How are things in the city?"

She sits up and rotates so she's facing me. "No one has told you anything? What the hell do you and Cole talk about when you're in here if you're not having sex?"

"You've been in here for most of that time, too."

"Fair point." She swallows another few Skittles and then clears her throat. "With that mentioned, let's continue to hold off on the sex until further notice."

"If I get the chance, I'm taking it. So no promises."

She meets my gaze with a fake glare. "Noted. As far as Billings goes, the war stopped overnight, and all the supernaturals in town went underground. Tarnley's pub has been empty ever since you were taken; crime is *way* down. It's like a fucking ghost town. Supernaturally speaking."

"That's troublesome. I wonder why."

"The testosterone club cornered some bloodsuckers in the basement of a pawn shop right before we got you back. They were told that most of the supernaturals want no part in the war. Basically, they're all running scared."

"For good reason, too. Lucy is a psycho."

"Well, look at her mother. The apple didn't fall far from that tree."

"That's an understatement, I'd say that apple turned into a much larger, more twisted tree." I turn my attention to the show for a minute as Rainey settles back down beside me. "Did I miss anything else?"

"That's the gist of it. As soon as you're healed,

we'll get the band back together and get out again. With her absent, I'm not overly worried about nightshades."

"I don't know. I have a feeling she'll be back soon. If she isn't already."

"We'll be ready for her." Rainey reaches over and grabs my hand. I rest my head on her shoulder, relaxing against my sister.

Tomorrow, I will be getting out of this damned bed. Whether they let me or not. I'm tired of sitting around and playing defense. It's well past time we figure out what Lucy's next step is before she makes it.

CHAPTER TWELVE
DELANEY

S unlight pours in through the window, shining on Cole's bare chest as he sleeps. I take in the sight of him, and lust pools in my belly as I visually explore every inch of muscled, tattooed skin. A dusting of hair covers his pecs before a dark trail disappears down beneath the blanket currently covering his waist.

One arm is draped over his eyes, the other at his side. I've never wanted to lick anything more. Seriously, I would devour him like the last chocolate-covered ice cream cone in the box.

"You enjoying the view?"

I jump, not expecting his gruff voice. At my surprise, he chuckles and moves his arm so I can see amused, hazel eyes aimed at me.

"You scared the crap out of me."

"If you hadn't been eye-fucking me, you wouldn't have been scared."

That does it. The lust that was nothing but a spark explodes into an inferno at his mere mention of the word fucking. Based on the way his gaze darkens? He knows it. "You're an eye-fuckable man," I say, turning it around on him. "Can't blame me."

His body tenses as I reach out and run a finger down his chest. Cole's eyes close, and he lets out a breath. "Your touch is paradise."

Shifting in bed, I sit all the way up and lean down to press a kiss to his chest, right above his heart. It thunders beneath my lips, spurring my own to match the beat. I breathe him in, his pine scent filling my lungs.

I still can't believe he's mine.

Trailing my lips down his ribbed abdomen, I reach the waistband of his shorts. In no rush, I take my time teasing him, gently pressing kisses from one hip to the other. He groans, his body so damned stiff it might snap in two if the smallest breeze were to rustle in.

My body calls to him, and the throbbing between my legs is so fucking painful I can barely stand it, but despite the storm raging inside of me, I continue my slow movements, knowing that the waiting will only make it so much sweeter.

Slowly, I push the blankets toward the footboard and move around so I'm positioned between his powerful legs. He stares down at me, eyes nearly black as his hands fist into the covers beside him. Visual proof of his restraint.

Almost like he's worried I'm not well enough for what's to come. Which—let's just say I'm prepared to argue if he tries to pull some shit like that.

Because I've never been more ready in my life.

I slide my hands up his thighs, taking my time to knead the muscles as I go. He doesn't move. Hell, I don't think he's even breathing, and the fact that I have this much power over a predator—well—it's more than a turn on.

A soft sigh leaves his lips as I grip the fabric of his shorts and draw them down his body, moving back along with them until I can slip them down and off of his legs. "You are something else, Cole," I tell him. "So powerful." I settle back between his legs, running my hands up and down, stopping just short of the massive erection waiting for me.

Meeting his gaze, I lick my lips. A low growl emanates from him, shooting straight through me, a spark that sets off tiny bombs in my blood. My heart hammers in my chest as I lean down and press my lips to the head of his dick.

He watches me, his gaze predatory, eyes completely black, as I draw him into my mouth, tasting him. Gently, I scrape my teeth against his shaft as I take as much of him into my mouth as I can. I grip the rest of him with my hand, squeezing lightly as I fuck him with my mouth.

"Del, fuck," he growls and buries one hand in my hair, squeezing softly as I move faster and faster, trying to make him feel even a fraction of what he does for me. I want to give him the world, the galaxy, any damn thing he wants. I pull back just enough to swirl my tongue over the head again, then slide back down on top of him as he throws his head back into the pillows.

Hand still in my hair, he tugs me off of him and takes my mouth as he flips me over so I'm beneath him. He manages it so fucking fast I barely have time to react before he reaches down and shoves my over-sized t-shirt up. His hand slips beneath my underwear and finds me, his finger torturing me in the best way possible. Pleasure shoots through me as he slides his index finger over me, the friction devastating.

"You're so fucking wet, Del. Fuck, I want to be inside of you. I want to feel you on my cock." In demonstration, he thrusts against me, his hand cupping where I ache for him. A gasp leaves my lips as he slips a finger inside of me and then another.

I'm putty in his hands, and he knows it. "Then do it. What the hell are you waiting for?"

"I don't fucking know." He pulls his hand out and grips the hem of my shirt to rip it over my head and toss it to the floor. Then, he wraps both hands around the sides of my underwear and tears, tossing them to the floor. "I'll buy you knew ones," he says gruffly before taking my mouth again. His tongue slips in with mine as his hand finds my breast. He teases me, rolling my nipple between his fingers, which sends tendrils of desire straight through me, stoking the already raging flames of desire.

I bite down gently on his lip, earning a growl. "I want you, Cole. Please."

He pulls back far enough to stare down at me. "Are you sure?"

"Yes."

"I don't have a—"

I shove him off of me so he's kneeling at the end of the bed, watching me with just as much desire as I feel inside of myself. Sitting up onto my knees, I turn around, arching my back and glancing at him over my shoulder. His heated gaze is on my ass as he swallows hard then refocuses on me.

"I don't care. Please. Now." I'll beg if need be, but thankfully his argument stops there. We can consider consequences later. Right now, the only thing that matters is him and me.

He grips my hips, fingers squeezing as he positions himself behind me and fills me with a single thrust. I cry out, my body practically weeping with joy that it doesn't have to wait any longer for a release.

Magic pulsates through me, buzzing along my skin and wrapping around us as we fuck.

It's as though it had been waiting for this moment to return, or maybe Cole is my power.

Hell, at this point, I have no clue what to think.

Orgasm building, I bury my fingers in the blankets around me, keeping my back arched as he drives into me. I urge him to go faster, harder, to own me with everything he is.

Not that he has to. I'm already his. Just as he's mine. And I know, in this moment, there's not a single fucking thing in this world or the next that will keep us apart.

"Mate," he growls, voice low and deep. At his word, my body shatters, muscles quivering with the force of my orgasm.

He pulls out and falls to the side before his own completion. Wanting to be the reason he finishes, I get back to my knees and replace his hand with my own, sliding it up and down his shaft, thrilling at his hips thrusting up into my hand until his breaks free. I slow my strokes but don't stop, wanting to draw out every ounce of pleasure left in his body.

As soon as his muscles relax, I release him and roll over onto my back.

"Fuck, Del. That was—"

"Spectacular."

He grins at me. "Understatement." Reaching for

me, Cole tugs me against his side. Warm lips press against my forehead, and I smile against him.

"I love you, Delaney."

My chest tightens with those four words. I've wanted to hear them since I was nineteen, and it feels so damn surreal now. Like I'm going to wake up and discover this was all a dream.

That I'm still dead and trapped inside a raven.

"I love you too, Cole."

"I'll take on the world for you, Astor," he says softly. I sit up to look at him.

"You won't have to. Because I'll be right beside you."

He smiles up at me. "I sure as hell hope so." Then, he cups the back of my neck and pulls me down, claiming my mouth with his own.

———

Freshly showered and dressed, I take my first steps into the living room of Bronywyn's safe house. The place is impressive, more akin to a luxurious cottage than a hideaway. Everyone's gone except us with Rainey having to work today and Tarnley tending to his pub.

According to Cole, Bronywyn had to take care of things back at her clinic. Even Fearghas is gone, though to where, who the hell knows. If I had to guess,

I would say he's probably checking on Eira since she's the only one he spends more time with than me.

"Breakfast?" Cole asks as he moves into the kitchen.

"That would be great." I already know the man can cook as he made dinner for me more than once, back whenever I had a late training session with Josiah. He reaches into the refrigerator and pulls out some eggs and bacon.

"I have to say, seeing you in the kitchen, it's doing something for me."

He grins over his shoulder. "Wait until you see me pop the toast."

"I can't wait for that."

Cole chuckles, looking the most relaxed I've ever seen him. "How do you like your eggs?"

"Any way you want to make them. I'm not picky."

"You sure?"

"Positive."

"Okay, chef's choice." He pops a skillet onto the stove and flips it on.

As he preps breakfast, I move to the coffee pot and open the basket to add grounds. He reaches above me and hands me the red coffee container and then presses a kiss to my lips before going back to prepping breakfast.

It's so normal, so damn amazing, that it fills me with hope for a future I never was sure I'd have.

Then again, if Lucy has her way, I still may not.

Cole turns to me. "What's on your mind?"

"Nothing."

He arches an eyebrow. "I can sense your mood shift. What is it?"

Damn mate bond. "I'm just thinking of what's coming."

"Don't think about that shit storm right now," he says gently. "We're in the middle of bliss at the moment."

"Isn't that the best time to think about it?" I counter. "So we can be prepared?"

Cole sets down the bowl full of whisked eggs and crosses the kitchen to me. Reaching up with a hand, he cups my cheek and kisses me gently. "We're going to find a way to make this work," he promises me before turning back to the stove.

The coffee pot beeps, so I pour us both steaming mugs and take mine farther into the living room to inspect a bookcase full of novels ranging from biographies to fictional romance. *You have a broad range of interests, don't you?*

The fact that she has it so well stocked makes me wonder how long she'd planned to hide here —and why.

Is it possible she's been worried about Lucy this entire time? Or is it something else?

"Do you think Rainey and Elijah felt like this back when everything was up in the air with Heather?"

"Like what?"

"Terrified that they wouldn't see tomorrow," I reply sadly as I turn back to him.

"Possibly."

I make a mental note to ask her. Maybe we can compare notes on finding love and barely surviving.

"Do you believe the world will ever go back to normal?"

"It's hard to say." He cracks an egg. Then another. "The world goes through changes, shifts in power. Every generation brings change, sometimes small, sometimes much larger."

"So this upheaval could be our new normal?" The thought is terrifying.

"Not exactly, things always settle. Our goal is to be amongst those standing once the dust clears."

His words are heavy, but for some reason, they put my mind at ease. Every generation brings change. That much I've seen just in the time I've been around. And with as old as he is? I bet he's seen a hell of a lot of change.

Is it possible this shift is just a natural progression? That eventually, the supernatural world will find a new normal?

We've had councils for pretty damn much ever, The Accords for the same amount of time, and already both of those are damn near disbanded completely.

So what will come in the future?

"Breakfast is ready."

Thoughts interrupted, I walk toward the bar and take the plate he offers me. The scrambled eggs and buttered toast make my mouth water. And much to my horror, my stomach growls, a loud, disgusting sound that brings heat to my cheeks as I slip onto a stool.

Cole chuckles. "Don't be embarrassed. I take it as a compliment."

"I'm pretty sure I haven't had a full, warm meal since before—" The air around us shifts at the casual mention of my near-death experience. "Well, you know."

Beside me, Cole nods and starts to eat.

Fearghas appears in front of us, standing right in front of the stove. "Well, well, isn't this cozy?"

Cole turns to me. "Is it too much to hope that one of these days he materializes himself onto the hot stove and burns his ass?"

Without missing a beat, Fearghas replies, "Not everyone shares your penchant for eating ass, wolf."

I spit out my coffee, spraying the counter before me while Fearghas merely watches, his grin spreading. "What the fuck, Fearghas?"

He grins at me. "Your boy toy started it."

Rolling my eyes, I can't keep my own smile from appearing. The two couldn't possibly be more opposite. And not just because Fearghas is a fae and Cole a shifter. While Cole has light, sandy hair and hazel eyes, Fearghas's hair is nearly black, his eyes a mossy green.

"Is there a purpose to your visit?" Cole growls, interrupting my comparison. "Or are you just here to piss me off?"

"Maybe a little of both." He tosses me a towel. "I'm actually here to check on my favorite hunter witch. How are you feeling?"

"Almost back to normal." In demonstration, I snap my fingers, and the light turns off. When I snap them again, light floods the kitchen, and I beam at Fearghas.

"Good."

"Any news from Faerie?"

Fearghas shakes his head at Cole's question. "According to Raffe, the witch has taken off while Sheelin is still busy attacking his camps."

"I thought he said it was heavily warded."

"That one is. But his others are not."

"Why?"

"To draw her attention," Cole answers. "If she's always finding a location, she won't be searching out the one he doesn't want her to find."

"Right on the money, wolfie." Fearghas grabs an apple from the bowl and bites into it.

"Interesting strategy. Except for the ones caught in the crossfire."

Fearghas crunches down on the apple again, chewing and swallowing quickly. "War always has casualties, H.W., the idea is to keep them to a minimum. Raffe's main base is home to thousands of refugee fae. If Sheelin were to discover them, it would be a blood bath."

"So, if she's distracted by all the small things, she'll miss out on the larger one."

"Exactly."

I consider his words, swapping out Lucy for Sheelin. What if it were possible to pull the same kind of wool over her eyes? What if we took Raffe's method, just swapped out the targets?

A smile spreads across my face, and I glance up to see both men watching me carefully. "What?"

"You were smiling like you're getting ready to stab someone."

I roll my eyes at Fearghas and set down my fork. "I think I know of a way to handle Lucy," I tell them. "And get rid of her for good."

CHAPTER THIRTEEN
DELANEY

T arnley's pub is eerily quiet tonight as Cole and I make our way through the foyer and past the second set of doors meant to shield any vampires inside from the rays of the sun. The meeting couldn't be held at the safe house, mainly because Bronywyn didn't want "everyone and their fucking mother" knowing where her house is.

Her words, not mine.

Rainey and Elijah stand near the bar, chatting up Jack and Willa. They all glance our way and smile as we enter but continue whatever conversation they're having. Which, I'm sure, Cole has heard every word of.

Damn, how I miss my hunter hearing.

Josiah makes his way toward us, Z by his side, along with a female shifter I've never seen before. She stares at Cole, her eyes widening, and I can all but feel her fucking hormones from here.

Casually, I drape an arm around his waist, enjoying the way he chuckles because he knows exactly what it is I'm doing. He slings his arm around me and shakes the pack leader's hand with his free one.

"Josiah, Z, Bestiny, this is my mate, Delaney."

The female shifter turns her dark gaze to mine, jealousy etched in damn near every line of her face. *That's right, bitch, he's taken.* "Nice to meet you." I offer my hand, and after a moment, she takes it.

Fearghas pops into a booth toward the back and raises a hand in greeting before taking a seat. I turn my attention back to Bestiny, who's still holding my hand.

"You're the witch who used to be a hunter."

"That would be me."

"Huh."

I want to ask her what in the hell she means by that, but before I can, Tarnley steps in from the back room, Bronywyn beside him. Based on the set of his jaw, whatever conversation they were having wasn't pleasant.

Why is she so damned afraid of telling him how she feels? I pocket the thought for later as Paloma and her husband walk in, our party finally complete. Nerves dance in my belly as I realize I'll soon be addressing everyone here.

Something that doesn't feel right coming from me. I'm no leader. I'm a loner—a hunter turned witch, who never worked well with others. So why in the world would they choose me to deliver such an important plan? Even if it was mine, to begin with. I even tried to get out of it by letting Cole in on everything, but I'm guessing he'd realized what I was doing because he shut me down, saying that he wanted to wait until we were all together.

The door opens again.

I turn just in time to see Eira and four body guards walk in. The tension in the room grows immensely with the appearance of the siren. And for good reason. Not many here know that she's peaceful, and her kind has long been feared.

After all, she can drown you with a glass of water before you even have the chance to defend yourself.

"Am I late?" she asks, her feminine tone filling the room as she comes to stop beside me. I glance over to where Fearghas was, but he's gone.

"Not at all, love, you know the party doesn't start until you arrive," Fearghas says from behind me.

I turn, not even a little surprised to see the handsome fae leaning against the door and eyeing the siren like she's the last slice of pizza on a buffet for starving men.

Dressed in black leather pants, a cropped blue

shirt that showcases the pale skin of her abdomen, and a black jacket, she's every bit femme fatale.

"Good." She grins and walks past us, taking a seat at the back booth, her bodyguards taking their places, standing beside it.

"All you, H.W.," Fearghas whispers in my ear before materializing in the seat across from her. Her guards didn't even flinch at his arrival. Removing my arm from Cole's waist, I clasp my hands together in front of me.

Why is it that running headfirst into a vampire den is a hell of a lot easier than addressing a room full of allies? My gaze briefly flits across the room to Bestiny. *Well, mostly allies, anyway.*

Clearing my throat, I force a half-smile. "Hi, everyone. I'm pretty sure you all know me, but just in case —I'm looking at you four back there." I gesture to Eira's guards. "I'm Delaney Astor. Since I don't see the point in beating around the bush, the introduction ends there." No one makes a sound as I glance around the space. Rainey smiles softly at me while Elijah offers a curt nod. I continue, "Recently, I had the displeasure of being captured by the original witch's daughter—a witch we all know as Lucy McClough."

Eira's eyes widen at that, and she looks to Fearghas for confirmation.

"She also grabbed Bronywyn, her intentions to drain us of our magic."

"Why?" Bestiny asks. "Was there a purpose to it, or is this chick just a massive bitch?"

I snort. Despite her Cole attraction, I'm pretty sure I could like her. "She is a massive bitch," I confirm. "But as some of you know, she cursed the soul that was in this body before me." I take a deep breath, and Cole's hand presses against my lower back.

Okay, maybe this mate bond isn't such a bad thing. The contact gives me strength, so I straighten and take one last deep breath before speaking again. "She tracked and killed Jane over and over again for centuries. We believed she was doing it because Jane —or Zeira, as she was known back then—was the first one to kill the original witch."

"You say you thought that; what do you mean?" Eira calls out.

"She was cultivating the magic," Bronywyn answers. "Letting it build in Jane's soul over time so that, one day, when she needed it, she could harvest centuries worth of magic."

Bestiny's eyes widen and Paloma gasps.

"Why did the magic not leave with Jane's soul?" Eira questions. "I always believed witch magic to be directly related to the power connected to the immortal soul."

"My grandmother put a block on Jane's magic when she was still alive. She was attempting to shield her from Lucy's reach. Because of that block, the magic stayed behind in her body, even after her soul departed."

"Fuck." Bestiny shakes her head. "Rough fucking blow for you. Being that your number one on her hit list now."

"Lucy won't win this," Rainey says, as she comes to stand beside me. Cole on one side, my sister on the other, my two rocks. With them, I can take on the world. Which, all things considered, is a pretty fucking good thing.

"How the hell do you plan on stopping a powerful witch like Lucy? If what you're saying is true, she's a dark witch. The only way to beat one—"

"Is to join one," Bronywyn interrupts Bestiny and crosses her arms.

"Then, that leaves us the fuck out," Bestiny retorts. "Unless either you or Astor here are willing to sell your souls."

"No one is going to sell their souls." My tone is sharp, but just as I thought I could like this chick before, she's starting to get on my damned nerves. "I think I have another way." While all eyes follow me, I walk over to Tarnley where he stands behind the bar. "Do you have any foam cups?"

Nodding, he reaches down and pulls out a stack of them.

"I need three, please."

He sets them out on the counter.

Reaching into my pocket, I pull out a crumbled-up piece of paper I brought with me for this exact reason. I set it on the counter, lining the cups upside down, and place the paper ball under the center one.

"Watch carefully," I order as I begin to lift each cup one by one, passing the ball around. I move fast, just like I practiced for hours at the house earlier.

Thankfully, making an ass out of myself doesn't seem to be on the docket for this evening.

"Pretend the ball is what Lucy truly wants—the ley lines. The cups represent all the supernaturals moving about, going through the motions of their day-to-day life." *Outside left, middle, outside left again, middle, right.* I stop moving and look up at the room. I hadn't realized Eira moved, but she stands just beside Fearghas and Rainey, watching me with fascination glittering in her violet eyes.

"In continuing to live normally, we will give her too many moving pieces to control." I stop moving the cups and glance up at the shifter who I'm trying really freaking hard not to throat punch. "Where is the ball?" I ask sweetly.

Bestiny snorts. "I hardly think we're going to beat her with a magic trick invented for children's parties."

Yup. Definitely can't stand her.

"Where is it, then?" Cole questions.

"Obviously in the middle cup."

I lift it.

"Right one then."

I lift it again and it's not there. Fighting the urge to smile at Bestiny's frustration is a real struggle, especially when she crosses her arms and shakes her head.

"To be fair," I lift the last cup, and the ball still isn't there.

"You cheated!"

"Exactly. Tarnley?"

Wordlessly, he kneels behind the bar and retrieves the ball I sent over the edge.

"Brilliant," Rainey whispers. "So what she wants is never actually on the table."

"Exactly, we just make her think it is."

"Do we know what she wants? What the ball represents?" Eira asks.

"The ley lines," Fearghas replies. "If I were a betting fae, I would say she's looking to use Delaney's power to open them."

"In which case, she would have limitless magic at her disposal to do whatever the hell she wants. She could practically annihilate everything in her path with nothing but the snap of her fingers." I demonstrate, and the room falls to complete silence as everyone processes what I said.

I can't blame them; it's a hell of a lot to consider.

"We've been one step behind her since she started this war. We need to get as many supernaturals to our side as possible."

"I very much doubt you're going to convince them to work with you," Bestiny says. "You and your sister have killed hundreds over the last few years.

"Try thousands," Rainey replies sweetly.

"Fine. Thousands. What makes you think they'll want to work with you?"

"We don't need them to work with us. We just need to make the game board messy so we can hide the piece that matters."

CHAPTER FOURTEEN

COLE

"You're saying that you expect the entire supernatural community based in Billings to play along and be your pawns?"

I groan as Bestiny asks for yet another clarification. Through our bond, I can sense Delaney's frustration. I get that everyone needs to be on the same page, but fuck, she's already clarified what she meant.

"I need them to go about life like normal. We need Lucy to think she's won—at least temporarily."

"Why the hell do we need that? Don't we want her to think there's nothing to find here?"

"The ley lines she's looking for give off an energy signature," Fearghas says, sounding almost bored. "With fewer supernaturals around, they will stick out like the center of a magical bullseye should she get

"More supernaturals equals a more jumbled radar for her," Rainey snaps at the shifter. The youngest Astor has always had a short chain on her temper, and fuck me if I don't want to witness her kicking Bestiny's ass.

I know the bartender has helped me out in the past, but the fact that she's been leader of her degenerate pack for a time now is apparently going to her fucking head.

The last damn thing we have time for is a pissing contest between her and Delaney. Not that it will be much of a match. My mate could kick her ass with both hands tied behind her back and no access to her magic.

"So, we keep the board messy." Eira crosses both arms. "How does one defeat her when the time comes?"

"We're going to find the ley lines first," she says. "And open them."

The room erupts in chatter as I tense. She'd failed to mention that particular part of her plan when we'd spoken earlier, and I get it now. Because I would have told her there was absolutely no fucking way she was going anywhere near those damned lines.

"Are you out of your damn mind?" Fearghas snaps. "Opening them will kill you!"

"I don't think it will."

"Oh, well if you don't think so." He rolls his eyes

and moves to the back of the bar to pace. I want to be right there alongside him, would be if I didn't need to stand so close to Delaney to keep my fear-induced rage at bay.

"Hear me out. And we'll of course do research and testing before we get to that phase." She glances over at me. "I have no intention of risking my life unless I know the odds of survival are stacked in my favor."

I bite down on the inside of my cheek and clench both hands into fists at my sides. The battle against throwing her over my shoulder and living out the rest of our days in Bronywyn's warded Ireland property is intense.

"Lucy was intent on needing *my* magic."

"Yeah, because, apparently, you have a fuck ton of it," Bestiny says.

Willa growls. "How about you shut your damned mouth and let her finish speaking."

Bestiny looks back at her. "How about you make me."

Josiah places a hand on his daughter's arm to keep her steady. Jack, however, makes no move, his tense body telling me that he'd rather be the one removing the newcomer's head.

Why she's here is anyone's best guess.

Josiah narrows his gaze on her face. "Bestiny, please be respectful. I allowed your pack to remain on my lands, to be with my people. The least you can do is show our friends respect."

"Yes, Alpha." She dips her head and turns back to face Delaney. "I apologize. The most I've ever had to worry about was what drink to serve. This war is new for me."

To my surprise, Delaney relaxes at her apology. "I understand."

She doesn't say *me too*, and I know it's because to Delaney and Rainey—hell, to a good number of us in this room—we've been fighting this battle for years.

"I've been thinking on it for a few hours and remembered something I read in one of Bronywyn's books after I first came back." Delaney glances back at the other witch. "It said that a witch's magical resistance can grow as her magic does. That as it expands, so does her ability to contain it."

"That's true," the other witch confirms, though based on her tone, she's nearly as nervous as I am in regards to this plan.

"Then, I believe she wanted to use me to open the lines, that she was bleeding me out, not to kill me but to force my body to work harder to produce more magic."

"So you would have a higher tolerance for taking in more power," Bronywyn finishes. "She was going to bleed you nearly to death and then use you as a supernatural sponge to absorb the power."

"Exactly."

The thought is chilling and makes my skin fucking crawl like a thousand nightshades are approaching and I'm without a weapon.

"Let me get this straight." Rainey clears her throat. "You want us to find the ley lines, bleed you nearly dry, then let you open them so that maybe—hopefully—you'll be able to hold all the power that is released?"

"Not all of it," Delaney replies. "From what I understand, the initial power boost is what I'll need to hold. After that, I would stay tapped into it. Kind of like an invisible cord connecting me to a power outlet."

"This is really fucking risky," I say, unwilling to stay silent anymore.

"It's about damn time you spoke up," Fearghas snaps at me. "One of the only people in this room who has any hope of talking her out of this suicide mission, and you're standing there, keeping your gob shut."

I glare at him, sending all kinds of threats through my mind and willing him to hear them. "It's risky," I repeat, turning to her. "You can't come back from the dead again, Delaney. This is your life you're playing with."

"And not just your life," Fearghas interjects. "Do you realize that if this goes wrong, you will be unleashing enough supernatural energy onto the world that it might as well be a fucking nuclear bomb?

If there is no tether to hold it, it will reach out in all directions, seeking the next host, killing anyone unable to hold it. You could kill thousands with this ill-advised plan, Delaney. And that's just within the first day."

Her senses shift, her concern growing, and it pisses me the fuck off that she's not worried about her own life as much as she's worried about everyone else's.

Why the hell are they any more important than her?

Why is any of this worth her life?

My mate sighs. "That being said, I think it's worth looking into. Wouldn't you agree?" She turns to Rainey. "We were taught that, as hunters, it's our duty to shield humans from crimes committed by supernaturals—at any cost. This is no different. In fact, this could be the war we've been training for our entire lives."

Rainey's jaw tightens, her eyes narrowing. Elijah's hand goes to her lower back, much like how I comforted Delaney earlier. I know without her answering that she will agree with her sister.

That's the problem with hunters—it's always been their fucking problem—and why a good portion of the lines are extinct. If the odds of survival are zero in a billion, but there's a chance to save a single human life, they will take the gamble.

Live to fight another day? Not in their playbook. It's risk all, give all. End of story.

But I'll be damned if my mate is going to be a lamb to slaughter.

"The only way we do this is if we are absolutely fucking sure you're going to survive."

She turns to me. "I will do everything I can to look into it before I take the leap."

"No. That's not good enough. Promise me, Delaney. Swear to me that you will let us all figure this out before just making a jump."

She lets her gaze travel around the room before it lands back on me. "I promise."

Letting out a breath, I nod and step back.

"Now that that's settled," Josiah says, his attempt to lighten the mood not at all appreciated by me. "How do we go about finding the supernaturals who are hiding?"

"I can help with that," Eira says cheerfully. "I'll re-open the club."

"My pub's been open this entire time, and they've refused to come out."

Eira's violet eyes shift to the vampire. "No disrespect, Tarnely, but my club is nothing like your pub. It's warded from the council, and everyone within the walls is protected by me and mine."

"That went really well when Heather sent those

succubae hearts in and fed them to your patrons," Tarnely retorts.

Fearghas appears behind the vampire, nostrils flaring.

"Easy, Fearghas, he's not wrong," she says sadly. "That was a tragedy and one I've taken painstaking care to ensure never happens again."

Fearghas appears back beside her.

"I can re-open my doors, and while I can't force them to return..." She trails off and locks eyes with Tarnley. "I can reassure them that I've taken the necessary precautions to keep them safe while they're within my walls. The people want normalcy; they want routine, safety, and if we can give them that, well, I imagine a lot of them will stand with you, Delaney."

Elijah clears his throat. "This is all of our war. Lucy will destroy Billings if we don't stop her. It's not even a matter of just standing with Delaney. They will be standing up for their homes, their families. We need to make sure they understand the danger they're in should they remain complacent. She's out for blood, and if we don't get rid of her, she'll get every last drop."

"Then, we stand and we fight," Z says.

"Agreed." Bestiny crosses her arms. Behind her, Willa rolls her eyes and groans.

"So, first step, Eira re-opens her club. What's next?"

Delaney glances at Rainey. "We prepare for war."

———

With almost everyone having left, Delaney, Elijah, Rainey, Fearghas, Bronywyn, Tarnley, Jack, Willa, and myself are all that remain behind in the vampire's bar.

"So that Bestiny," Rainey says as she lifts her whiskey to her lips and drinks deeply. "She's quite a bitch."

Beside me, Delaney snorts. "That's an understatement." She turns to me. "How do you know her again?"

Fuck. "We used to be friends."

"Meaning you two used to be more than." Rainey shakes her head. "We can read between the lines, shifter."

I glare at Delaney's sister, thankful that I can feel Delaney's amusement—albeit laced with jealousy—beside me. "It was a long time ago," I clarify. *Back when I didn't think I could have what I wanted most in the world.*

"We all have pasts," Delaney assures me with a smile.

I try not to let it bother me that hers is standing in this very bar.

"Why was she here?" Elijah asks. "She's not a full member of the pack is she?"

Jack shakes his head. "She insisted on coming as the alpha for her pack."

I snort. "If you can call them that."

"Agreed. They've been more trouble than they're worth, so far." He runs a hand through his short hair. "We've had to break up a few fights over the last couple of months."

"Let them get their asses kicked," I advise him. "Josiah won't like it, but I can promise you it will put them in their places."

The hunter shrugs. "You're probably right."

"I am right."

"Cole's had his ass kicked by Z a few times." Willa's smile has one of my own popping up.

"I let him win."

"Sure you did." She laughs and leans into her mate.

"Just so we're clear," Fearghas starts. "I won't be taking you anywhere near those ley lines until I know for sure you're ready. Hell, I'm not even going looking for them until we know you are."

"Wait, look for them? I thought you've been there."

"I have been, but they shift over time."

"So you don't even know where they are?"

He shakes his head. "I have a general idea, though, and can get us close enough to sense them. When the time is right, that is."

"And who gets to decide that?" Delaney questions.

"Me."

She shakes her head, irritation rolling off of her. I, however, have never liked the fae more.

"When was the last time you were there?" Rainey asks.

"A couple of decades ago."

"Maybe you should go look for them now so we're ready to go when Delaney gives us the go-ahead."

"Not a damned chance, vampire," he tells Tarnley. "I won't be going anywhere near those lines while Sheelin and Lucy are looking for them."

"You think they're still working together?"

He shifts his attention to Delaney. "My sister is stubborn and vengeful. She won't quit until my head is on a silver platter."

Delaney stiffens, the scent of her fear filling my lungs. "That won't happen."

"Here's hoping. I'll be sticking close to Eira until Sheelin is dealt with," he adds. "There's nothing stopping her from going after her in an ill-advised attempt at revenge for my killing her mate."

"Do what you have to do," Delaney tells him before glancing back at me. "Feel like training with me?"

I nod, not feeling overly chatty at the moment. Not when she's still fucking determined to move forward with the plan.

The rest of the meeting only solidified it.

Her hand goes to my thigh, and she squeezes gently. I reach under the table and thread my fingers through hers, but it still isn't close enough.

My body is all but vibrating with the need to do *something*, anything to prove to my mate that her enemies are my own.

The very DNA in my body is urging me to hunt Lucy to the ends of the earth even as, logically, I know I need to wait for the plan to fall into place.

It's a good one, Delaney's suicide mission aside. And should it come to that, and she still won't back down, I guess we'll see if a shifter is affected by ley line magic.

Because there's no way in hell she's going in alone.

CHAPTER FIFTEEN
DELANEY

Delicious coffee aside, being out in the real world has me on edge. I watch everyone sitting at the tables scattered around the café as though each and every one of them is Lucy in disguise. Who the hell knows? They absolutely could be.

You know, since she apparently has the ability to alter her appearance whenever the fuck she wants to.

A woman glances over at me. She's young, maybe early twenties, and with the blonde hair piled high on top of her head and pink fingernails wrapped around a coffee cup, she's the exact opposite of Lucy.

Still, I find myself staring at her until she blushes and looks away. Obviously, I can't be too careful these days.

"There's my girl," Fearghas walks out from the

hallway leading to the bathrooms and takes a seat beside me in the booth.

I glance up at him, completely surprised to see him here. "Where did you come from?"

"Your fantasies?"

I snort and lean against my friend briefly, a half-hug to let him know how much I appreciate him.

"How does it feel being out in the world without your pet?" he asks as he leans back and drapes an arm over the back of the seat.

Pretty-in-pink glances back at me, her hungry brown eyes perusing Fearghas like he's the last low-cal muffin in the case. I raise an eyebrow, just so she knows I see her, then turn my attention back to my company.

"Cole is not my pet, Fearghas."

The fae shrugs. "Might as well be."

I shake my head and take a sip of my caramel macchiato. "Hey, how was Lucy able to alter her appearance? I don't remember ever seeing that in any of the books I've read on witch magic. Is it just rare?"

Fearghas plucks my coffee from my hand and takes a sip. "This is disgusting."

"Good. Then I don't have to worry about you stealing it anymore." I snatch it back.

"Definitely not." He eyes my coffee with complete disgust before faking a shiver. "As far as queen witch bitch is concerned, I'm guessing she somehow managed to get her hands on a fae."

"Your sister?"

He shakes his head. "The fae would need to be dead in order for her to steal the abilities. But her ability to glamour, in combination with the portal Cole says she conjured to take you and Bronywyn on a one-way trip to hell, I'd say she's fae-adjacent at this point."

My pulse quickens. Fae-adjacent? Heather had possessed a half-fae, and we'd nearly all died. "What does that mean?"

"That she probably didn't get her hands on a very powerful fae. A young one maybe, few decades old."

"A child?"

"Not exactly. We age roughly the same as all of you do but slow down in our twenties."

"What other abilities could she have stolen?"

"Other than glamour and portaling? Probably not much. The ability to grow shit?"

I snort. "I can't see how that can be dangerous for us."

"That's because you've never spent time in the forests of Faerie. Some of the plants there will eat a grown man alive in a single gulp."

"Remind me to never vacation there."

"Consider yourself reminded."

I take another drink, letting myself relax for the

first time since I walked into this coffee bar just over an hour ago. My intentions had been to appear casual, to move about my life as I would if I weren't being hunted by some crazy bitch.

That being said, you won't catch me in any alleyways alone anytime soon. That's for damn sure.

"You know, if ever you wanted to just get the hell away from all of this, Paris is only a blink away."

I glance up at him, surprised that he's not looking down at me, but rather awkwardly at the coffee menu in the center of the table. He's fidgeting, completely and totally uncomfortable with what he'd just said.

Which tells me that he's actually serious.

"We can't just leave."

"Why not?" Now, he glances over at me, green eyes hard. "Why do you insist on risking your life for lesser beings?"

"Lesser beings?" Taken completely aback, I turn to face him, propping a knee up in the space between us. "They aren't lesser beings. They are innocents who are being unfairly targeted."

"They are supernaturals who have probably more than earned their sentence."

"A death sentence. Because that's what will happen if Lucy manages to get the ley lines open. And what about Rainey? Cole?"

"Fuck Cole. And we can take Rainey. Elijah as well."

"Fuck Cole?" His casual dismissal pisses me off. "Fearghas, he's my mate."

"No. You're his. Witches don't mate."

"I'm a hunter."

"They don't either."

I glare at him, angry at the fae for the first time since we met. "I love him."

"You really don't think you could be happy without him?"

"Could you be happy without Eira?"

He swallows hard, jaw tightening.

"Did something happen between you two?"

"Nothing that's any of your business."

As I glance around us, I'm grateful to see no one is paying us any attention. Well, no one but pretty-in-pink, who keeps casting sideways glances at my companion. "Bull-fucking-shit. You coming in here insulting people I care about because you're pissy about something else is what makes it my business."

With a sigh, he leans back in the booth and runs both hands over his face. "I'm sorry. It's been a day."

All of my anger vanishes at his tone. I've never heard him so broken down before. Exhausted? Sure. Pissed off? Absolutely. But broken? Not in however many years he's been alive would I have imagined the smartass tone being shoved out by something so sad. And why am I surprised? He just lost his father.

"What happened, Fearghas?"

"It's just been a long few days. Hell, a year even."
He smiles at me, but it doesn't reach his eyes.

"Tell me what happened with Eira."

"Nothing."

Pursing my lips, I wait for him to retract the lie. I
can see it from here, the broken heart he's so desperately trying to hide.

"I'm serious, Delaney, everything's fine."

"Then why do you look like someone just stole
your favorite toy?"

"Because you're insisting on being out and about,
won't bring your pet along for protection, the world is
falling apart at the seams, and Eira refuses to leave
Billings."

I arch an eyebrow. "So you gave her the whole
Paris speech, too, then?"

"Why the hell wouldn't I? You people don't seem
to realize the danger you're in by taunting Lucy. She
and Sheelin will tear this world apart should they see
fit. Shit, she didn't even hesitate when she killed our
father."

Eyes glittering with angry tears, he turns away
from me to stare at the wall across from us.

Reaching over, I rest a hand over his. It's a casual
touch, simple, but through it, I try to convey all the
sorrow, the pain, I'm carrying for him. Maybe then he
won't feel so alone. "I'm so sorry about your dad,
Fearghas. Lucy and Sheelin working together is exactly

why we need to pretend everything is fine so that, when they do come, we're not scrambling for a plan."

"Seems to me everyone is so fucking spread apart you'll all be scrambling anyway."

"Which is exactly what we want her to believe," I whisper. "Now. How about you let me buy you a coffee."

He's silent for a few minutes, and I mentally prepare myself for another argument. Fearghas is nothing if not stubborn. Finally, he sighs and nods. "I guess. As long as it's not one of those." He scrunches his nose. "I'd rather drink toilet water."

———

Sunset bathes the mountainside in orange, yellow, and red, a gorgeous canvas with bright paints that brings a smile to my face as I sit on the back porch of Cole's cabin.

While the rest of the pack is settled in the new village, Cole and I, Rainey, Elijah, Jack, Willa, and even Fearghas, have all taken up residence in the old cabins just in case she does come looking for us again.

The rest of our little army is only a Fearghas blink away and have been prepped to be ready to go at a moment's notice should Lucy and Sheelin show up before we're fully ready.

Tomorrow, I'll start retraining, getting this body

ready for the fight that we're facing. And hopefully, we'll have enough time to locate the ley lines and figure out just how in the hell we're going to open them.

As much as it pains me to say, keeping Billings safe is now our second priority. Logically, I recognize that if Lucy gets her way, the city is damned. Though I do feel like shit for asking the supernaturals to return to the streets.

Unfortunately, we need them, though. Something shiny for Lucy to follow while we sneak around.

"I'm going to bleed you dry." Her words ring out in my ears, and I clench my hands into fists as the image of her hovering over me, blade in hand, comes to mind. For a brief moment, I can feel the chill of the stone beneath me, the dank, damp, dark of the cell.

My pulse quickens, my heart hammering in my chest with panic. One deep breath after another, I work to calm myself down. *She will never get me again.*

I will never give that bitch another chance to take me out. I'm not going down, not this time. Everything she throws at me, I'll give back tenfold.

No fucking matter what. I lift my knees and tuck my blanket more tightly around my waist. I'm safe now, I know that. But I can't help this feeling of total vulnerability that keeps sneaking up on me.

At least not until Lucy McClough is nothing more

than a steaming pile of ash. The wicked witch of Billings, Montana is going the fuck down.

"Hey."

I jump, glancing up as Cole steps all the way out onto the porch. Clad in dark jeans and a white t-shirt, he's mouthwatering. Heartrate speeding up for a completely different reason now, I smile. "Hey, yourself."

He takes a seat in the chair beside me, hands in his lap as he stares out at the fading sunlight. "How was coffee?"

"Not bad. At least not until Fearghas showed up and tried to rain on my parade."

Cole glances over at me, hazel eyes narrowed. "What did the fae do?"

"Nothing terrible. He was just in a pissy mood. How was your day?" *No way in hell I'm telling him that the fae wanted to leave him behind and head to Paris. Can't imagine that would go over well.*

"Some pack business to deal with, just things I had to get caught up on since I was MIA for a while."

"Everything is okay, though?"

The set of his jaw, the slump in his shoulders— they tell the story of an incredibly stressful day. Leaving me to wonder what, exactly, happened?

"It'll all be okay."

"Cole."

He sighs and leans forward, resting his face in both

hands. "The pack is being difficult about certain things."

"Like?"

He glances at me, and I know without him saying that they're pissed off I'm still here. I would be too if I were them. My presence brought them grief and pain. Having someone who's currently rocking a massive target staying near you—that's a hard pill to swallow.

"I can leave," I offer. "I don't have to stay here."

His eyes darken, turning nearly obsidian. "You're not going anywhere. They're going to have to get the fuck over themselves."

I reach for his hand. "Cole, they lost people recently. Because of me."

"Because of Lucy."

"Sure. But I had a hand in that, too. My presence here is what drew her to pack lands in the first place."

He shakes his head. "No, not your fault."

Pushing my blanket aside, I pull my nightshirt back down over my thighs and shove out of my chair to kneel in front of him. "I'm okay. We can go somewhere else."

"Nowhere else is as safe as we are here," he growls back. Watching his fangs elongating, eyes flashing, I can see he's fighting against his wolf.

"Cole." I press my palm to his racing heart. "I'm here. It's okay." He's torn between his pack and me. I see that now, and I hate it for him. I've been so damn preoccupied with everything I'm dealing with that I hadn't stopped to consider him and what he's going through.

His hand snakes up my arm and around, gripping the back of my neck and pulling me into his lap. Cole's mouth finds mine. My lip stings when his fang nips it. But I don't pull away because the pain is completely obliterated by lust when he growls, low and deep, gripping my hips and grinding me against his erection.

Fuck, this is hot. I grind my hips against him, gripping his hair in both hands and pulling just enough for a slight pain. Which—if his growl is any indication— he is thoroughly enjoying.

He releases my hips and slides his palms up, fingers turning my skin to ash as he grips the bottom of my shirt and rips it up over my head. We separate for a split second before I'm against him again, mouth on his.

Dropping my hands down, I run them beneath the fabric of his shirt, over his ribbed abdomen, and up his chest. Heart hammering beneath my palm, the steady drum matches my own. The same beat because we were made for each other.

Born to meet.

To fuck.

To love.

I pull back just enough to rip his shirt over his head. My mouth finds his again, desperate now, the passionate kiss lighting my blood aflame. Match to gasoline, he grips my hips, thrusting up against where I desperately ache for him.

I reach between us, undoing the button of his jeans and pushing up on my knees so I can free him. My hand wraps around his length, and I squeeze gently as he thrusts up into my palm.

"Fuck, Del."

"Getting there." I grin against his mouth and guide him toward my entrance. He pushes the crotch of my underwear to the side, and I slide down on top of him. He fills me completely, and I moan, head falling back.

Cole lifts me and spins, slamming me against the side of the house. I wrap my legs around his waist as he drives into me, the furious pace shoving my building orgasm over. White lights explode in my vision as I cry out and dig my fingers into his shoulders, desperate to hold on so this moment never ends.

His body begins to shake, and he pulls back, letting me slide to the ground as he covers himself with his hand.

I shove him back against the wall and drop to my knees. Pulling his hand away, I replace it with my mouth. His hands go to my hair, his head dropping back against the wall as I take as much of him as I can, letting my hand take care of the rest.

"Del," he chokes out and tries to pull me away as

his body begins to shake. I refuse to let him remove me, though, wanting to finish what I started.

So, I hold on, moving at a faster pace, his pleasure spurring my own as I finish him.

As I own him.

Looking up through my lashes, I meet his gaze, holding it without breaking. And in this moment, there is no denying it. I may be the one on my knees, but make no mistake.

Cole Miller belongs to me.

CHAPTER SIXTEEN

COLE

I shove my cell back into my pocket for what must be the tenth time tonight as Delaney's phone goes to voicemail again. I stare at the front door of Tarnley's Pub, wondering where in the hell she is.

She's never late, and we had a meeting tonight. Desperation claws at my throat, and I pull my phone out again and tap on her contact information.

"You've reached Delaney! Sorry I can't get to my phone right now. Leave a message, and I'll call you back as soon as I can! Bye!" Her voice sounds so happy, a direct contrast to the fear steadily taking me over.

I need to talk to her, to ask her why the fuck she thinks she has to die in order to save her sister. I shove the cell back into my pocket again and head down the street in search of her. It's a Friday, so it's entirely possible she got hung up with supernaturals misbehaving.

After all, she is a hunter, and there's not a damn thing that will ever alter her belief that duty comes first. Not even whatever it is she feels for me.

When she'd asked me to kill her—I close my eyes and swallow hard as I head down the street. I won't think about it that way because she promised me she'd find another way.

Swore to me that she'd fight for herself instead of lying down and dying. Still, there's a huge part of me that is screaming, a voice repeatedly telling me that I'm a fucking moron for believing her.

That same voice is insisting that something is wrong. Very wrong.

The stench of the enemy fills my lungs, and I stop in my tracks, turning my face up and inhaling.

Wolves. A shit ton of them, and they don't belong to our pack.

"Delaney." Her name leaves my voice in a whisper as I sprint down the street, my legs moving even as my body goes into a shift.

Within seconds, I'm on four legs and racing down the street, not giving two shits if any humans see me. They don't fucking matter.

Delaney matters.

A scuffle just ahead pulls my attention. I come to a stop just outside an alleyway as a male hunter faces off with three wolves.

He's not Delaney so I move on, letting my instincts

draw me to her. Up ahead, copper tinges the air and I howl as the scent of her blood assaults my senses, spurring the predator in me into overdrive.

My mate lies on the ground, surrounded by wolves, her blood spilling all over the asphalt.

I throw my head back and howl, agony, grief, and terror stealing every bit of sanity from my brain. I lunge toward the nearest wolf, ripping his throat out without a second thought.

Another attacks. I dig my claws into its side as I drop it to the ground and tear into its body. Blood drips down my snout, falling to the ground as I slaughter my mate's attackers.

One by one they fall.

Because they touched what is mine.

Only when the ground is littered with bodies do I whimper and walk toward her. She doesn't move, but I can hear her heartbeat. Faint, but present. Hope tries to push through the grief, but when I nudge her leg and she doesn't move, panic claws its way right past the faith that she's going to come out of this.

Her caramel eyes flutter open, and she stares at me, eyes widening when she looks past me and sees the bodies surrounding us. Then, her eyes meet mine.

I shift quickly and kneel at her side, my throat so fucking swollen it's painful to speak. "Del, shit. We have to get you out of here." I slip my arms beneath her body and start to lift her. She shakes her head, eyes shutting tightly as if the movement is painful.

And why the fuck wouldn't it be? There's so much blood I don't even know where all of it's coming from.

"Please, leave me." She coughs, expelling the same crimson that's dripping from the corner of her mouth.

I shake my head as tears blur my vision "No. Not like this." The words are like sandpaper on the inside of my throat.

"I told you it has to happen."

I shake my head again. No. You promised me. I want to scream at her, to shake some fucking sense into that thick-headed hunter brain of hers.

"Please, finish it."

I glare down at her, pissed the fuck off she lied to me. "No."

"Please, Cole. Please, kill me. Put me out of my misery. I'm so tired."

Never did I think whispered words could be so jagged, but she guts me with her plea. I gather her in my arms, pinning her against my chest, but I make no move to stand. "You can't die, Del. You can't ask me to deliver that blow. I won't fucking do it."

"If you don't, I'll die anyway. Please, I can't live like this anymore."

I drop my forehead to hers as tears slip down my cheeks. I can hear her heartbeat slowing, the werewolf venom and injuries combined too much for even her hunter abilities to heal. I'm losing her.

My mate.

My other half.

I guess this is my punishment for falling in love with a hunter.

Fuck this. *She won't die like this. She can't die like this.*

Kill her. *A voice tainted with venom fills my brain.* Kill the hunter now, wolf. I command you.

"I can't." *My vision blurs, and I release Delaney, pushing back away from her as my body begins to shake, my wolf trying to claw free. Desperation kicking in, I try to restrain myself. The voice begins to chant in a language I can't even begin to fucking understand.*

My body begins to shift, but for the first time in my life, I fight it, knowing that if I complete the change, I'll lose Delaney.

She'll die in this alley if I can't gain control, and that's not something I can live with.

Kill her, *the voice commands again.*

No! *But even as the word goes through my mind, my body completes the shift, and I'm standing before Delaney, no control over my predator.*

All he sees is bloody prey while I see the woman I was born to love.

To protect.

I shake my head, trying to shove the voice out, but it's

no use. *My wolf lunges toward her, teeth wrapping around her throat.*

No! Please, no! *My internal voice might as well have been as silent as the voice who ordered me to commit the most heinous act of my life.*

And as Delaney's blood fills my mouth, I'm helpless to do anything but watch her eyes roll back in her head. My wolf drops her with the horrified shock spreading through me as I realize what just happened. The hold over me snaps, and I shift back.

"Del! No! Please, no!" I fall to her side, clutching her body against mine. Blood pours from the wound in her throat, and I try to stop it, placing my hands around her throat in an attempt to halt the bleeding even as I know there's no hope now.

My world falls away, and all I can see is Delaney.

I cry out, throwing my head back and howling into the empty sky, a tortured cry from a broken man.

Her heart slows to a stop, and I scream again, my grief filling the night air.

"Delaney!" a man calls her name, so I lay her down gently and press a kiss to her forehead.

"I'll love you forever, Delaney Astor. Please, please, forgive me." I cry out, leaving my tears on her cheek as I lunge to my feet and race down the alley until I reach a ladder. I quickly ascend, looking down on the scene as a man —the hunter I saw earlier—runs in and slides to his knees.

"Del? Del!" he shakes her. "Wake the fuck up!"

She doesn't move though.

Because I killed her.

I killed my mate.

———

"Are you even listening to me?"

I glance up at Bestiny and shake my head. "No. What did you say?"

She glares at me before turning her attention to Josiah. The other pack members in the room watch expectantly, probably waiting for me to lose my shit and storm out. It's pretty much become my MO over the last few years when someone pisses me off.

Much like Bestiny is doing now.

"Everything okay, Cole?" Josiah asks, and I nod.

"I'm just tired of listening to bullshit."

"I didn't realize the opinion of the pack is bullshit," Bestiny snaps.

"A pack you didn't even belong to until I helped bring you in a few months ago. And what, now you suddenly speak for them all?" I snort. "You don't get a say yet because you haven't earned it."

"I haven't? We fought that night the witches and vampires came. I lost two of my pack to that fight, and for what? So you can fuck a witch?"

I lunge to my feet, stopping less than an inch from her. "Watch your fucking mouth."

"Or what?" Bestiny arches an eyebrow. "You going to do something?"

"I will."

Bestiny has always been a handful. She's mouthy, crass, and jealous. My guess is her animosity toward Delaney is not coming from a place of fear, but rather the latter of those three things. She's pissed because she knows I don't want anything from her.

I made the mistake of falling into that trap once, back after Delaney died, when I was trying like hell to forget. But that mistake was quickly remedied. Bestiny knew it was never anything but fucking, and still, she'd tried every damn trick in the book to get me back into bed.

This is her being pissed off. But what bothers me the most, though, is that she's dragging the pack into it. And it terrifies me to think Josiah might actually take that into consideration and make us leave.

"Knock it off, you two," Josiah orders.

Bestiny smiles at me, the expression dripping with venom as she backs away. "I'm only looking out for what's best for the pack," she says sweetly.

Thankfully, Josiah isn't stupid. "I can appreciate that *if* it's what you're doing. Make no mistake, though, Delaney Astor is a part of this pack. Shifter or not. She has done more for us than you can even begin to understand. Hell, her father protected us when other hunters would have come in and killed or driven us away. She has earned our protection just as I would protect any one of the wolves in this pack."

"You're making a mistake, Alpha," Bestiny shoots back. "More will die if those witches come back."

"If those witches come back, we're better prepared this time," he assures her. "And she's not staying in the new village. She and Cole are staying in his cabin back on the old grounds."

Bestiny's jaw twitches, and I don't hide my grin, knowing good and damn well Josiah dropped that in there on purpose. A reminder that I am off the menu.

"Yes, Alpha," she growls and steps back.

Z moves forward, blocking Josiah from the rest of the pack. "Anything else that needs to be brought to the Alpha's attention?"

When no one makes a move toward us, Z nods and turns toward Josiah. "Alpha," he says, bowing his head slightly before turning to me. "Beta."

"Dismissed."

Chairs scrape against the wooden floor, and murmurs fill the cabin as the pack members who'd attended today's meeting get to their feet and head out into the early afternoon sun. We rarely have full attendance, but today was damn close. At least one member from nearly every family was here today, and I can't help but worry it's Bestiny's doing.

She's convincing, which is how she managed to get so many shifters to keep the peace in her bar. But I never thought it would carry over into a pack that's known me my entire life. And the fact that it has is concerning.

As soon as the pack is gone, Josiah turns to me, and Z crosses both arms, facing me, too.

"What?" I glare up at both of them.

"Care to explain what that bit was with Bestiny?"

"She needs to keep her damn mouth shut when it comes to Delaney."

"I agree," Josiah tells me. "But, that being said, you're the beta of this pack, and you need to behave as such."

"I will as long as Bestiny stays the hell away from my mate."

"I'm pretty damn sure Delaney could kick her ass." Z grins. "I'd pay to see that fight."

"Delaney has fought enough, she doesn't need this, too."

"You need to stay calm, Cole. I promise you that Delaney can stay on pack lands as long as she wants. Nothing will change that."

"I appreciate that." Pushing up from my chair, I roll my shoulders. "I need to go take care of some shit. See you both later."

Not bothering with the stairs, I jump down off the stage in our community hall and head for the door.

The sunshine outside is a direct contrast to my pissy fucking mood.

Between dreaming of Delaney's death last night and dealing with Bestiny all fucking morning, I'm more than ready for tonight and what I have planned with Delaney.

Or rather for her.

So with that in mind, I pass my bike and head straight for my truck. As soon as I slide behind the wheel, I do what I can to leave my shitty mood behind and focus only on my mate and my need to show her just how fucking much I care.

CHAPTER SEVENTEEN
DELANEY

Duffel bag in hand, I step onto the main floor of my gym. To my surprise, it's empty. Apparently, I beat both Rainey and Elijah here. Smiling, I drop my duffel to the floor and head to the treadmill for a quick warm-up walk.

As I start up the belt, I let my mind wander back to Cole and the sex we had nearly all night. The image of him above me—I can't stop smiling.

If I were to die tomorrow, I know the time we spent together would be the only thing on my mind.

A muffled gunshot echoes from below me. I freeze up, the misstep nearly sending me over the back of the treadmill.

Rainey. Logically, I can almost guarantee it's my sister in the range, but I grab my blade and head toward the door that will take me down to the basement shooting range. One step at a time, I descend until I reach the thick door at the bottom.

Another gunshot, followed immediately by another. I shove the door open.

Rainey turns toward me, earmuffs covering both ears, pistol aimed downrange.

Elijah stands beside her, arms crossed.

"Missed me again!" Fearghas appears downrange.

"What the fuck are you guys doing?" I gape at Rainey—who now looks incredibly guilty, her cheeks flushed. Then, I turn my attention to Elijah, who shrugs.

Fearghas appears beside me. "We're just having some fun."

"You let her shoot at you?"

"I wanted to prove that I'm faster than a bullet."

Disbelief and shock are pretty damn much all I can feel at this point. "Are you *kidding* me, Rainey? You're a cop! Aren't you supposed to know better?"

"He's wearing a vest," she defends.

I roll my eyes as Fearghas slams a fist against the plates in his bulletproof vest. "You guys are morons. And you!" I point to Elijah. "You are supposed to be the rational one, aren't you?"

"Tell me you've never wanted to shoot at a fae before."

I look between the three of them and shake my

head. "And what would have happened if she'd landed a headshot?"

"I wasn't aiming for his head," Rainey insists. "Just his chest. Maybe a leg."

"A leg? That was not agreed upon."

Spinning to Fearghas, I shake my head. "There was an *agreement*?"

Fearghas nods. "We're not complete imbeciles."

"You all could have fooled me." I turn back toward the door. "Whenever you all decide to stop shooting at my best friend, I'll be upstairs, doing what we actually came here to do—train."

"Technically we were training!" Rainey calls after me as I push through the door and head up the stairs.

By the time I reach the top, Fearghas has shed the vest and is already waiting for me. Wearing sweats and a tank top, he leans against the wall.

"You can be such a party pooper."

"Excuse the hell out of me for not wanting you to die."

He snorts. "A bullet is not going to be the way I go, H.W., I can assure you that."

"You're not bulletproof, jackass." I step back on the treadmill to finish my quick five-minute warm-up.

"Maybe not, but I proved that I'm faster than one."

"Debatable," Rainey argues, as she and Elijah join us in the room.

"I swear, Fearghas. I'm going to pump you full of lead just to end this ridiculous conversation."

"You can use my firearm," Rainey offers.

"I'm good, thanks."

She heads for the water cooler and fills a paper cup. "We will probably be facing fae at some point. It's not a bad idea to know how to kill them."

"We know how to kill them."

"Yes, but now we know they can dematerialize faster than a bullet, so we need to make sure they don't see it coming."

I can see her point, but the idea of losing Fearghas is entirely too raw. He's my best friend, someone I'm pretty damn sure I couldn't live without. I touch the stop button and walk slowly until the belt comes to a complete stop.

Then, I head for the mats and stretch. "Can we please refrain from shooting Fearghas in the future?"

"I can try." Rainey grins, and the fae smiles right back.

At least their relationship seems to be better now.

"Who would have thought I'd be big brother fae to the Astor sisters. I feel awfully lucky."

"You should," Rainey says. "We're pretty fucking awesome."

Unable to keep the smile from my face, I stretch my hamstrings for thirty seconds then straighten. "We going to sit around and chat about how cool we are all day, or are we going to train?"

"Was she always this much of a ball buster?" Fearghas asks Rainey, who nods enthusiastically.

"When she was teaching me to fight, we'd go until the walls sweat."

"Walls can sweat?"

"They can if you work hard enough," I answer Fearghas with a wink and then turn back to my sister. "You kick Elijah's ass. I'll take Fearghas."

The fae appears in front of me. "Bring it, Astor."

———

Two hours and countless sweat droplets later, I'm finally walking up the steps and into Cole's cabin. Every muscle screams in agony, but I feel better than I have since before I opened the damn box. I have a purpose again, and while it's changed drastically, I finally feel like I'm doing something.

Shoving the door open, I step into Cole's living room and freeze in my tracks. Candles line nearly every flat surface, their flames casting a romantic glow over the space. Cole's in the kitchen, and he glances up at me, wearing a smile on his handsome face.

"Hey, gorgeous."

"What is that spectacular smell?" I ask as I move

farther into the room and inhale the aroma of what-ever he's cooking.

"That would be twice baked potatoes and mari-nating steak." He grips the back of my neck and pulls me against him, crushing his mouth to mine. His tongue slips past my lips, sliding against my own, and I moan, my hand fisting the front of his button-down-shirt.

When he pulls back, I'm damn near breathless. "What was that for?" My eyelids flutter open, and I stare up into his hazel eyes.

"I missed you today."

"I missed you, too."

He kisses me quickly, then threads his fingers through my own and pulls me down the hallway and into the bathroom. Steaming water topped with bubbles fills the bathtub, and I see that he's put more candles in here.

My eyes fill at the gesture, so romantic I practically melt into a puddle. "You did all this?"

"Who the hell else would?" He grins, his hands slipping down my sides. Gripping the bottom of my shirt, he pulls it up over my head and tosses it to the floor. Then, he kneels at my feet and slips his fingers into the waistband of my pants.

I swallow hard, placing both hands on his broad shoulders as he pulls them down, stopping at my shoes. He makes quick work of the laces and continues removing all of my clothing, one piece at a time.

The slow seduction is so damned arousing I don't even care that I probably smell like sweat.

He straightens and kisses me gently. "I love you, mate." The words are barely above a whisper but echo through my mind as though he'd shouted them.

"I love you, too."

Cole's smile spreads, and he guides me toward the bathtub, holding my hand as I lift my leg and climb in. Hot water burns my skin for a moment, but my sore muscles weep with relief as I sink lower into the tub.

"Are you going to join me?"

"Not this time. I have dinner to prepare. Relax as long as you want."

"What did I do to deserve this?"

"You were born." He kisses me again, then stands and leaves the bathroom. Sinking lower into the bubbles, I can't help but wonder how and why we stayed apart for so many years before.

Even though I'm more relaxed than I've ever been, I don't wait for the water to grow cold before I wash and get out. After slipping into leggings and a long, black shirt, I head back into the kitchen where Cole sprinkles croutons onto a salad.

"You could have stayed in longer." He offers me a wine glass.

"I wanted to be out here with you." After sliding onto a barstool, I take a drink. "How was your day?"

"Much better toward the end."

"The meeting not go well?" I've discovered that the pack meets nearly every morning if someone has something to bring to Josiah's attention. And lately? It's been every morning.

"We don't need to talk about it." Cole smiles at me briefly before covering the salad and pushing it off to the side.

"We can if you need to."

"I don't need anything but you." He leans across the counter and kisses me again before he takes a drink of his own wine. "How was your day?"

"Not bad. Rainey shot at Fearghas."

He arches an eyebrow. "What did he do to piss her off?"

"Nothing. She brought him a bulletproof vest, and they tested to see if he could dematerialize faster than a speeding bullet."

Cole snorts. "And?"

"He can."

"Too bad." He winks at me, and I roll my eyes.

"You would have jumped on that opportunity, wouldn't you have?"

"Of course not," he insists. "I'd never do anything that you didn't want me to."

"Uh-huh, sure."

We both know he's lying. Had he been given a chance, he wouldn't have hesitated before pulling the trigger.

Cole heads for the patio door, plate carrying two raw steaks in hand. I watch him as he passes by the window, studying his profile as he puts the steaks on the grill. Every time I see him, I swear he gets even more attractive.

Someone knocks on the front door, so I leave my wine and head over to open it. "Hey—" I trail off when I see there is no one there. A breeze moves past me into the house, and I start to turn back inside. Before I shut the door, though, my eyes drop to the mat, and all the air rushes from my lungs. A bloodied, dead raven sits on the mat, its eyes missing, feathers twisted in horrific angles.

Rage burns hot through me, obliterating any other emotion, and I rush farther outside, stepping carefully over the bird before running out into the dark. "Where are you, you coward?" I scream into the night, blood pounding like a heavy drum in my ears. "Come out, you son of a bitch!"

The door to Rainey's cabin opens across the way, and she rushes outside, gun in hand, Elijah behind her.

"What is it?" she yells, as she rushes down the steps and toward me.

"Who did it?" Cole's question is barely above a

whisper, the edge in his tone betraying anger, unlike anything I've ever heard come from him.

"I don't know, I didn't see them." Spinning in a circle, I search for anything out of the ordinary, but all I see are the dark outlines of trees.

"Did what? What happened?" Elijah demands.

"Someone left a present for me on the doorstep," I snap before turning on my heel and heading back toward Cole's cabin.

The moment I see the dead bird for the second time, my anger intensifies. An innocent creature dead because someone wanted to send a message and was too damned pathetic to face me. "Fucking coward." Kneeling beside the corpse, I slip my hands beneath the bird's body, lifting it gently. When I meet Rainey and Elijah's gazes, I see the same horror reflected in them that I know are in mine. I shift my focus to Cole. "The body is still warm."

CHAPTER EIGHTEEN

COLE

Those five words are all I need to completely lose my shit. Shifting without hesitation, I drop my clothes in tattered shreds around me. Without forethought, I take off into the night, racing through the trees in desperate pursuit of the motherfucker who left that on my doorstep. As I run, I inhale deeply, searching for the scent of anyone who shouldn't be here. Of any recent scents that don't match those of the members staying in the old village.

The lingering scents of my pack begin to fade the farther I get into the trees. Something I'm thankful for as it will make it easier for me to identify the culprit—if this is the direction they went. It's the way I would go—quicker escape—but that doesn't necessarily mean anything.

My instincts heightened, I follow my nose, letting

the predator lead the way. If any of my pack left the damned bird—let's just say I hate to think of ripping the throat out of someone I'm supposed to be helping protect.

But I will with no hesitation because they threatened what's mine.

Leaves crunch from behind where Rainey, Elijah, and Delaney follow, but I focus only on the hunt.

When I find whoever did this—the ground gives way. Before I can fully comprehend what the hell is happening, I'm tumbling down. Frantic, I claw at the dirt, desperately trying to keep myself from tumbling down into the pit, but even my claws are no match for the steep fall.

I slam into the ground, and pain spears my body as white steals my vision. Warmth trickles down my side, matting my fur, and I don't dare to shift. There's no telling if whatever the hell is sticking out of me will tear out a vital human organ if I do.

Fire burns my veins, an inferno that tells me whatever the fuck I landed on was probably coated in wolfsbane. One other time I've been infected with it, and I nearly died.

I attempt to move, but sharp pain shoots through me again, the bleeding coming faster, so I stop and lie perfectly still. The pit is deep; I can barely make out the night sky above me. It's hardly large enough for my wolf, and I can't help but wonder how I never came across it before.

These woods are more familiar to me than my own cabin. Which means it is probably a new addition.

"Cole!" Delaney calling my voice is a beacon. Carefully lifting my head, I howl. The sound is muted compared to my normal call, and I can only hope she's close enough to hear me.

My vision begins to fade while my blood burns in my veins. My entire body feels like it's on fucking fire. Lungs ache as I suck in breath after breath, not knowing if each one will be my final.

"Cole!" *Closer now.*

I howl again. Seconds pass before I see her above me, peering down into the hole.

"Cole! Oh my God, Cole!" She starts to move closer to the edge, but she slips. Elijah's hand on her arm keeps her from falling down here with me.

"You're going to die if you go down there," Elijah warns, moments before a light flashes above me. Closing my eyes against the beam, I whimper.

Rainey appears beside them. "Motherfucker." She pulls out her phone.

"Who are you calling?"

"Fearghas. He's the only one of us who can get down there and back without dying."

"Cole? We're calling Fearghas!" Delaney calls down to me, her voice cracking. "Hold on, okay!"

"We need you," I hear Rainey say as she moves farther away from the hole.

My vision swims again, coming in and out of focus. My wolf's strangled breathing grows even more so as more and more blood pours from the wound in my side. I can feel my heart rate slowing, each second becoming more and more crucial.

Fearghas appears beside me, face grim. "Haven't you ever been told not to run off the leash?"

Never in my life have I ever been happier to see the fae. He reaches down and places a hand on my hip, the other beneath my head. Based on the strain of his jaw, the worry in his eyes, I'm in bad fucking shape.

"This is going to hurt, Cole."

I whimper in understanding as lightning shoots through my body. From my nose to my tail, it burns through me, singeing every inch of me as we appear outside the hole and he lowers me to the ground. Delaney is at my side, her hands on my face.

Using the last of my energy, I shift back. Bones crack as my body morphs back into man, the process taking a hell of a lot longer than it should have.

"Wolfsbane," I choke out.

"We need to get him to Bronywyn, right now."

"On it." Fearghas touches Delaney's shoulder and my arm. A moment later, we're outside her hospital where rocks bite into my bare skin.

Not that I can fucking feel much past the pain in

my abdomen. Ice coats my skin as my body begins to shake and numb simultaneously.

"Don't you dare die on me, Miller," Delaney warns.

"Not. Sure. I. Have. A. Choice," I choke out.

"I swear I'll follow you into the veil and kick your ass."

Fearghas reappears with Rainey and Elijah. The ex-vampire covers my waist with a blanket. Then, he lifts me and carries me as though I'm a small child, and not a grown-ass man, into Bronywyn's hospital.

Just before we reach the threshold, my shaking stops, and I can feel nothing.

Not Elijah carrying me.

Not Delaney's hand on my head.

Not a fucking thing.

My eyes close of their own volition, my body too tired to keep up the fight. And as I slip away, I hear Delaney call out for me.

———

"Delaney Astor." Josiah reaches for the young huntress, taking her steady hands in his own. "I am so sorry for your loss."

She tips her chin up, but her bottom lip quivers despite the outward show of strength. "Thank you, Alpha." A purple bruise mars her left cheek, a crusted cut on her swollen lip.

I do my best to remain calm, to not frighten her when really what I want to do is track down her attackers and slit them from naval to throat.

"You can call me Josiah, kiddo."

She nods.

"What can I do for you?" He releases her hands and I study the way she clenches them both into fists at her sides. I can see that she's trying like hell to keep herself steady, and I have to be honest; she's doing a damn good job for someone who lost their parents and became a surrogate mother to her younger sister all in the same day.

"I was hoping that you could help me train."

"Didn't your father start?"

"Yes, but I want to learn more."

"I will do anything for an Astor, you know that."

"Thank you."

"May I ask what that bruise is on your cheek?"

She swallows hard. "I killed some vampires last night."

"How many did you come across?"

"I didn't come across them. I hunted them down and killed them."

"If you need help hunting, why come to me after your fight?"

"They killed my parents," she explains. "And they didn't deserve to breathe for even a day when my parents no longer can."

I'm impressed, even as terrified as I am that she went out—alone—and took on a nest. To have been able to take out Melanie and Steve Astor—there had to be a good number of them to get the drop on those two.

So how did a nineteen-year-old huntress manage it?

"How did you kill them?" I ask, needing to know.

She turns her caramel eyes on mine, and a piece of my soul slips into place. As though part of me has been waiting for her, for this moment of recognition. "I waited outside and sliced off their heads as they came out. One by one."

"You did it alone."

"Yes." She juts her chin up as though challenging me to say something. I'm far too dumbfounded to look away. The strength in this girl—it's mesmerizing.

Josiah clears his throat. "Delaney, this is Cole Miller, I don't know that you two have met properly."

"Hi." Her heartbeat changes when she looks at me this time, a subtle shift that's barely noticeable.

Do you feel it too? I want to question, to figure out just what this bond means.

Too soon, she turns back to Josiah. "Can you help me?"

"Of course. I told you I would. You and Rainey are more than welcome to come out here and stay—"

"Rainey can't know about any of this," she interrupts.

Josiah cocks his head to the side. "Any particular reason?"

"I don't want her to have any part in any of this. It's important to me that she gets a normal life as long as she wants."

"But she's a hunter, Delaney. There will be no normal life for her."

"Maybe not, but this is my fight right now. Can you agree to that?"

"Of course."

"Thank you. When can we start?"

"How about now?" I ask, cracking my knuckles. I don't know why, but making sure Delaney Astor is strong enough to keep herself alive has just become my one and only priority.

———

I come out of the memory slowly, the world piecing together around me like a twisted puzzle with missing pieces.

But when the single most important piece comes into view, I focus only on her and let the others come as they need.

"Del?" My voice is hoarse, but she looks up at me, her tear-stained cheeks red.

"Thank God." Her hand grips mine; that much I can see, but I can't feel it.

And that's terrifying.

My heart begins to pound, the overwhelming feeling of being trapped my biggest fear. "Why can't I feel—" I try to move, but nothing happens. "Delaney, why can't I move? What the hell happened?"

"Easy," she says softly. "Bronywyn had to put a spinal block on you in order to repair the damage. You were already out, and she was worried if they put you fully under, you'd not be able to come out given the wolfsbane." Her voice cracks, and she shuts her eyes.

"Wolfsbane," I repeat, trying to recall exactly what happened. "I fell," I say, the memory coming back. "What did I land on?"

Rage momentarily hardens her expression. "Someone sharpened tree branches and buried them in the ground, then tipped them with wolfsbane."

"So it was a trap?"

She nods. "And I'm willing to bet that the bird was a diversion."

"How would they know I'd run that way?"

Her jaw tightens. "That's just it. Elijah and Rainey searched the rest of the woods. There were a dozen other similar traps, all laid out so no matter which way you ran, the odds are high you would have come across one of them."

"Who the fuck would do that?" I try to move my arm, to run it over my face, but it might as well be nonexistent. I'm pissed that I got hurt, but even more furious at the risk to the rest of my pack. We all go run those woods—kids included. Whoever did that could have trapped a kid. An innocent."

"We're going to find out," she growls. Green sparks

her fingertips, and her eyes shine bright with power. "And we'll make them pay."

"I'm going to start charging every time I save your sorry ass."

I turn my head—the only part of my body I can move—and glare at the fae. "Thank you."

"That's what I do it for—the appreciation. How you feeling, wolfman?"

"Like I was impaled on a poisoned tree branch."

"Original," Fearghas says as he walks around the room and plops down in a chair beside the door. "We haven't figured out who baited your little game, but we will."

"It has to be someone in the pack," Delaney insists. "Otherwise, Bronywyn's wards would have gone off."

I hate the idea that someone I know could have done this, especially given my earlier concern that a child could have wandered into the trap. However, I'd be a moron not to consider every possible angle—especially given the pack's recent distaste for Delaney. I may be a lot of things—but a moron is not one of them. "Have you called Josiah?"

"He and Z are keeping an eye on the pack, and they have men going out to fill in the holes. Rainey asked them to let her know if anyone's behaving suspiciously."

"That's good." I cough, annoyed by the oxygen in

my nose that's really fucking cold and drying out my sinuses. "When am I going to be able to walk again?"

The door opens, and Bronywyn strolls in, tablet in hand. "That's going to depend on how long this wolfsbane takes to get out of your system. The block was removed right after I closed your wound, but your body is going to need time to recover."

"I feel fucking useless."

"You nearly died," Delaney says from beside me, her bottom lip quivering. Her shirt is torn at the sleeve, her arms and neck smeared with dirt. She looks completely and totally exhausted, and I know the last thing she needs from me is complaints.

I've already caused her enough grief.

"I'm okay," I promise her.

"I gave you something to counteract the effects of the poison, but it will take some time to work through your body. Wolfsbane embeds in your muscles, which is why it takes even longer. I'm actually surprised you managed to shift."

I turn my face back toward my mate. "I had incentive to survive."

"Sweet." Bronywyn's reply is dry as she checks my vitals and turns away. "Back in a bit."

The door shuts behind her, and I glance over to where the fae was sitting. He's gone, leaving Delaney and me alone. "I think it's safe to say I had a much different evening in mind for us."

Delaney laughs, but there's no humor in it.

"Are you okay?" I ask her, wishing I could squeeze her hand or, at the very least, feel hers on mine.

"No. I'm pissed the hell off. Someone used a raven to draw us out. And they damn near killed you."

"We'll find them."

"We will," she promises. "And I'm going to show them what Astor's do to those who fuck with the people we love."

CHAPTER NINETEEN

DELANEY

I shove open the door to the pack's community cabin, marching right past the dozens of eyes trained on me. All chatter stops abruptly, and I don't bother to hide my anger. Best they sense it now than say or do something that will set me off.

More than likely they're trying to decide why I'm here, but I don't give two shits. I owe no one in here an explanation. In fact? I'm willing to bet my life that someone in this room is the same person who drew Cole out.

"Delaney, what can we do for you?" Josiah asks softly from his chair on the stage. Z stands beside him, and the moment he sees my expression, he straightens. The move is so slight I doubt anyone else noticed it.

On the other side of Josiah, Willa grins at me,

offering a nod to let me know she understands.

"I have something I'd like to bring to the pack's attention."

"You aren't a shifter. You have no business here, witch."

Turning, I pin Bestiny with a glare that promises an ass-kicking unlike any she's ever had. At this point, I'm more likely to rip her fucking tongue out so she can't say another damn word in my presence. "I've known this pack a hell of a lot longer than you, *bartender*. So keep your damn opinions to yourself before I make you."

She snarls, lunging toward me. I throw up my palm in warning, grinning when the green flame has her backing off. *That's right, bitch. I've got more than that up my sleeve.*

"Easy, there's no need for violence." Josiah stands and crosses both arms, looking every bit the alpha. I've known him long enough to know that while he prefers peace, he's also a force to be reckoned with.

A male shifter steps forward and grips Bestiny's arm.

"I'd suggest keeping her on a leash," I snap.

"You'll pay for that," Bestiny warns.

Grinning, I snuff out the flame. "I certainly hope you'll try." Then, I turn back to Josiah.

"Someone here tried to kill Cole last night."

Shocked murmurs erupt behind me.

"You think someone here did it?" Z questions, and I nod.

"It makes the most sense. Their scent would have likely blended into the background, and they would have known Cole well enough to realize he'd go running after them."

"No one here wants to kill Cole. You, on the other hand—"

I don't even spare Bestiny a glance. I'm not entirely sure she's not guilty. Josiah's eyes narrow on her behind me.

"I've already explained it to you once, Bestiny. Delaney Astor and her sister are like family to me and mine. Should you make a move against either of them, I will consider that a personal attack on me and react accordingly."

"Yes, Alpha," she chokes out.

This time, I do cast a smile over my shoulder. *Eat that, bitch.*

"I can't think of anyone here who would want Cole dead," Josiah says with a sigh. "Though, I do think it needs to be looked into."

"If any of you motherfuckers tried to kill Cole, I will personally rip your throat out." Z's warning is met with complete silence. I can't blame them for being afraid; he worries me. Who the hell would want to come up against six and a half feet of tattooed muscle?

"Where is the bird that was left on your doorstep?"

I reach into my bag, pull it out, and lay it at Josiah's feet.

"A raven."

"Yes."

"That's no coincidence," Z snaps.

"No, I don't believe it is." I step to the side so the rest of the pack can see the mutilated bird.

Josiah growls and stands. "This is a direct threat against Delaney and Cole. If any of you know anything about who might have been behind it, now is your chance to come forward, or risk facing the consequences right alongside the guilty party." His voice carries through the room, a deep rumble that commands.

No one moves.

Well, no one but Bestiny, who shifts her gaze to me. In her eyes is pure hatred, the kind that could absolutely have caused her to lash out at Cole. Unfortunately, I don't have enough evidence to pin it on her, but I damn well will figure it out.

"Cole is lying in a hospital bed," I announce. "Someone not only impaled him, but they poisoned him with wolfsbane."

Eyes widen, and I search for anyone who's not overly surprised. Especially Bestiny. She doesn't shift her focus from me, and her expression never changes.

"I have never done a damn thing to hurt any one of you. In fact, when the witches attacked, I could have run. Could have disappeared and never looked back. Instead, I stayed behind, and I fought. The result? I was captured and nearly killed by someone who should terrify you all a hell of a lot more than my presence here should." I cross my arms. "I know you're worried for your families. If you truly want me to leave, I will pack and go. I have no problem finding somewhere else to hole up until this whole thing is over." I shift my gaze over the pack, resting my attention on Bestiny. "But let my next words sink in. Make a move against Cole or me again, I will fucking kill you. And for the record? That's not a threat, it's a promise."

"You can't speak to our pack this way," Bestiny growls.

"I'm not. You aren't part of this pack," I reply sweetly, hoping she gets the message.

Without giving a chance for a response, I step down, leaving the bird on the stage, and head out into the sun.

I still need to train and then get back to the hospital to see Cole. But first, I want to pack because there is no way in hell we're coming back here again. Not after last night. All that did was show me that losing Cole is a possibility, and there's no world where I want to risk it a second time.

"Hey, Del! Wait up."

I stop and turn to see Jack jogging toward me from the community building. "I didn't see you in there."

Dressed in jeans and a black hoodie, he comes to a stop beside me. "I have to hide out in the rafters. The pack's not overly keen about a hunter hanging around."

"I know the feeling."

We start walking again, and I climb into the driver's side of Cole's truck. Jack gets into the passenger side.

"How's Cole?"

"He'll survive, but barely." I start it up and pull away, heading back down the road toward the old pack village. Minutes pass in silence until Jack clears his throat.

"I can't fucking believe someone pulled some shit like that."

"I can. They're pissed and blaming me for the attack on the village."

"An attack that wasn't your fault," he reminds me.

"I know that, but they're grieving, and looking for someone to blame is easier than not having anything to hold on to. If they want to be mad, fine, but hurting Cole? That crosses a fucking line."

"Hurting either of you does."

After parking in front of Cole's cabin, we both climb out and head up the steps. I shove open the door and step aside, letting one of my oldest friends in. "I just can't believe they'd go after him."

When Jack doesn't reply, I cross both arms and

study him. He looks around the space, careful not to make eye contact with me. "You know something."

He clicks his tongue and turns toward me. "Cole's been arguing with the pack ever since the attack. They want you gone, and he's been pretty fucking adamant that's not happening."

"Josiah?"

"You heard him in there. He considers you family, and that man will never push his family aside. Not even for the pack."

"Cole alluded to them being angry, but he never told me how bad it was."

"It's been pretty damn bad ever since the attack. Let's just say Cole's not making any new friends. Willa said he's always been pretty short-tempered, but lately, she's noticed it getting worse."

"He feels backed into a corner." A feeling I know for a fact Cole does not handle well.

"I can't blame him. He wants to keep you safe."

"I can keep myself safe."

Jack grins. "No offense, Del, but you haven't got the greatest track record there."

I glare at him, knowing there's no heat in his words. "I kept myself alive for over thirty years, thank you very much."

"You did. But if I were Cole, there's no way in hell I'd risk losing you again. Not after having to come to terms with killing you in the first place."

"This whole thing is fucked up." I walk into the bedroom, and Jack follows. Grabbing a bag, I start shoving some clothes for Cole inside. "We spent so many years being good, obeying The Accords, wasting time. And now, finally, I have the chance to be happy, and not only do I have to worry about a psychotic witch who wants to drink my blood, but I also have to be concerned about a jealous fucking shifter with an ax to grind."

"So you're thinking Bestiny?"

"I am. You?"

He nods. "Chick's got some issues, and according to Willa, she's got it bad for your boy."

I clench my hands into fists and close my eyes, breathing deeply as magic surges through my body, the challenge to my happiness something my power apparently wants to deal with on its own. "Are you staying out here?"

"At least until someone starts leaving dead birds on my doorstep."

"Then keep an eye on her for me."

"Where are you staying?"

"The apartment in my gym. Cole won't be happy about it, but at least he'll be alive. And according to Bronywyn, due to the wolfsbane in his system, it'll more than likely be a few days before he can shift."

"Which makes him even more vulnerable."

"Exactly." I shove a pair of tennis shoes into the

bag, zip it up, and sling it over my shoulder.

Jack places his hands on my shoulders, and I stop to stare up at him. "It's going to be okay, Del."

"I hope so."

"I know so."

"You've always been so optimistic."

"I'm getting back to that side of me."

After taking a deep breath, I nod. "We'll keep on going about things the way we are, and hopefully, Lucy stays away long enough for me to get my shit together, or for us to find an alternative to my plan."

"Yeah, have to say I'm rooting for the latter on that one. I get that you think you can be an absorb-all sponge for the power, but I'm not so sure about it."

"You and me both. Let me know if Bestiny acts any more like a bitch." Moving past him, I head for the front door, stopping on the porch as I take in the six shifters standing below me. Bestiny's in front, and I don't instantly recognize any of the others, which means they probably came here with her.

I drop my bag.

"Hey, Del," Jack says, coming to stand beside me.

"Yeah?" My gaze never leaves Bestiny, though.

"Bestiny's acting like a bitch again."

I snort. "Sure seems that way."

"What the hell are you doing here?" Jack demands.

"We have no beef with you, hunter. Get on with your day."

"You're a fucking moron if you think I'm going to do that." He withdraws his silver blade, palming the hilt while I cross both arms.

"You come to have a play date? Or did you just run out of birds?"

She smiles widely. "I have no idea what you're talking about."

"Yes, you do. It's just us out here, Bestiny, go ahead, be honest. Didn't you ever hear about the boy who cried wolf?" I taunt, stepping down the steps. Jack moves down beside me.

"We finally found a pack, and you're not going to take it from us."

"You're right. I won't do a damn thing. Your bad attitude is going to get you alienated." I shift my attention to the men behind her. "You all want to play, too? Or do any of you have any of your own common sense?"

"Josiah's not here to save you. We could kill you both and bury the bodies. No one would ever find you. And from what I've heard, you both used to fuck. Maybe people will think you ran off together."

"Not a fucking chance," Jack snarls.

"You do realize that even if I'm gone, Cole won't have a thing to do with you. He doesn't care much for gang bang leftovers." I grin at her and then nod toward the men behind her.

Every single one of them snarls, baring extended

fangs. Bestiny throws her head back and laughs.

"Maybe not. But at least he fucked me while I looked like myself. Tell me, how does it feel knowing he's really fucking whatever bitch had that body first?"

It doesn't matter that the first time Cole and I were together I was glamoured. Her words snap my restraints, and I lunge toward her.

The pack moves toward us, and Jack engages.

My shoulder slams into her gut, knocking her back to the ground. Rearing back a fist, I slam it down into her jaw repeatedly. "The only reason Cole had anything to do with you was because I was dead. How does it feel to know you will always be nothing but second best?"

She bucks, tossing me up.

Jack grunts.

I flip up and fling a blast of energy at the two shifters trying to sneak up on him from behind. Unfortunately, the distraction is long enough for Bestiny to sweep my legs out from under me. I fall backward, my back hitting the ground with a pained thud.

One of the male shifters, not pre-occupied with Jack, rips me up from the ground and pins my arms behind my body.

Bestiny slams her fist into my gut. My lungs burn while my stomach churns. Since I'm unable to protect my face, she hits me in the jaw then pulls back to grin at me.

"Not so fucking mouthy now, are you?"

I spit blood to the ground. "Now that you had to have your boy toy hold me down for you?"

She gets in my face—no doubt to hit me with some ridiculous retort—but before she can open her mouth, I slam my head into hers. A move that gives me an instant headache, but I don't hesitate as I throw my entire body forward, blasting the male shifter with magic at the same time.

He flips over me and lands on the ground, stunned. I rush toward Bestiny again. She starts to shift. "No, you fucking don't." I blast her with power, and she twitches, falling to the ground beside her buddy. Her body convulses, once, twice. I fall to my knees beside her and rear back a fist, slamming it down into her nose.

Bone crunches. She reaches up and grips my arm as I raise her up off the ground.

"Delaney!"

I turn to see Josiah, Z, and Willa rushing toward us.

Beside me, Jack kicks a shifter one last time before wiping his blade on his jeans and shoving it back into the holster. "They attacked us."

I throw Bestiny to the ground at Josiah's feet and use the back of my hand to wipe the blood from my face. "I will kill her if she stays around me."

"You are no longer welcome here, Bestiny. You will

be held accountable for your actions today and put to death should the pack see fit. Grab her," he orders Z.

Reaching down, Z hauls her up and slaps iron cuffs on her wrists.

"Came prepared?"

"We saw them leaving and assumed they'd be coming here."

"What the hell took you so long?" Jack asks, as Willa wraps an arm around his waist. Other than a split lip and a cut on his forehead, he looks like he dealt out more damage than he received. Which is pretty damn impressive seeing as how a handful of the shifters shifted before he got to them.

"We ran into a bit of an issue," Willa replies. "Your speech did quite a bit of damage," she tells me with a grin. "I don't think I've ever seen everyone so riled up."

"I just wish they'd taken me more seriously." I gesture to the dead on the ground.

"I have no doubt they will now," Josiah replies. "I am so sorry they attacked you. I truly hadn't considered her to be a danger until you said you believed it was someone in the pack. I don't know how I missed it."

"You read them, dad. They shouldn't have been able to deceive anyone."

"I still should have known. Are you okay?"

Nodding, I head back up the porch and grab the bag. "I'll be fine. Though, I don't think I need to train today." My head throbs, and my freaking right knee feels swollen.

Definitely no training today.

I head toward the truck and toss my bag inside. Since Fearghas is out looking for the ley lines, he's busy, and I don't feel like explaining to him why I look like I was just in a ring. He'll likely dematerialize behind Bestiny and snap her neck.

And honestly? The idea of the pack she tried to turn against me deciding her fate is too damn good to pass up.

"Do you want to see our healer?" Josiah offers, but I shake my head.

"No, thanks." I glance at Jack as I shut the door. "Thanks for helping me kick ass."

"Just like old times." He grins.

"Just like old times," I repeat. "I'll call you guys with any Cole updates."

"Let him know we're thinking about him," Josiah calls after me as I turn the truck on and cast one last glare at Bestiny, who's currently kneeling in front of Z, her eyes trained on me. If they let her go, I know she'll come after me again.

I also know I won't hesitate to kill her next time. She's already gotten the ass-kicking; next time, I won't waste the energy.

CHAPTER TWENTY

COLE

S itting in this fucking bed in this fucking room is fucking suffocating. Monitors beep beside me as I tap my fingers along with the beat. At least I can finally move.

The urge to rip the cables off of me, to run outside and breathe fresh air, is nearly enough to have me doing just that. But I promised Delaney I'd stay put, and I'm tired of breaking promises to her.

I'd promised to keep her safe, and I'd failed.

Promised her a normal night, and I failed.

Over and over again, I'm letting her down. So, if there's a chance I can keep from doing it this time, I'll do it. I take a deep breath and do my best to calm my racing heart. She should have been here already, right?

She'd said she was going to the gym for an hour

and then coming by. I check the clock on the wall. It's been almost three since we spoke.

"This is bullshit." I shove the covers back and swing my legs over the side. Cables connected to my bare chest pull against my skin, but I reach up and rip them off.

The monitor's alarm blares in the room. Within seconds, the door swings open, and Delaney rushes in, eyes wide.

As I take in the bruises on her face, the blood crusted to her lip, I lose my fucking mind. Gripping the tubes in my arm, I rip them out and rush to her before she can get to me. My legs are weak—shaky—but at least I can use them again.

I'll need to walk in order to kill whoever hurt my mate.

"What happened? Who hurt you?"

"What the hell are you doing out of bed?"

"Who. Hurt. You." Reaching up, I gently cup her cheek and run my thumb over her swollen lip. "I'll fucking kill them."

"I already took care of it."

"Who." It's not a question.

She glares up at me. "First of all, don't order me around. Second, it was Bestiny, and in case you're wondering, I kicked her ass until Josiah came and arrested her."

"She's not dead?"

Delaney shakes her head. I start to shove past her, but she stops me with a hand on my arm. "Please, sit back down. I brought you shoes."

"I'm going to kill her."

"I'm guessing the pack is voting on just that. And if you really want to deal out that blow, I'm sure Josiah will let you. But right now, I want you to sit the fuck down so Bronywyn can check you one last time before we leave."

As if waiting for her cue, the witch comes in and walks straight to the monitor, silencing the alarm. "Next time, hit the bell button so you don't freak out all my other patients." She turns to Delaney. "What the hell happened to you?"

"Cole's jealous ex-girlfriend thought she was going to take a bite out of me."

"Did she?"

"No. But not for lack of trying."

It's not until Delaney presses a hand to my chest that I realize I growled. The warmth of her palm against my skin helps to calm my racing heart.

I close my eyes and suck in a deep breath, urging the rest of my nerves to chill the fuck out. Since the wolfsbane is still blocking my shift, it already feels like a part of me is missing. And to not be able to defend Del? That's a hell of a lot more than I can handle.

I let her guide me back to the bed and take a seat, but instead of letting her pull away, I tug her down with me, pulling her across my lap and against my chest.

"I'm pretty sure Bronywyn can't check you over while I'm lying on you." But she relaxes against me despite her objections.

"I'm just reading his heart monitor. He's fine. Maybe avoid large pits in the ground in the future."

"Thanks for the tip."

She disappears without another word, leaving me alone to hold Delaney. "What happened today?"

"I might have threatened an entire pack of shifters."

"You did *what?*"

She pulls away from me, placing her feet on the floor in front and standing in between my legs. "Bestiny left that bird; I'm sure of it."

"And you thought to threaten the rest of the pack, too?"

She shakes her head. "I wasn't entirely sure it was her until *afterward*. I told them you were injured and in the hospital. That I knew it was someone in the pack who'd done it, and I promised to kill without hesitation if they made another move against you or me. A promise I broke, by the way, because I wanted to kick Bestiny's teeth in."

I can't help but gape at her. There's zero doubt in my mind that Delaney was a ruthless hunter, and now she's a powerful witch. But to threaten an entire pack of shifters? I can't help but be impressed. Especially as my mind drifts back to the fearless nineteen-year-old who took on an entire vampire clan alone.

"You can't fucking threaten an entire pack, Del. Not without me."

"Noted. And you have to stop trying to shield me. When there's a problem, you need to tell me."

"A problem with what?"

"Jack told me how much you've been fighting for me to remain on pack lands, Cole. I know the rest of them don't want me there."

Fucking hunter. "Josiah does."

"Josiah needs to do what's best for the pack so they don't put together a coup and toss him out."

"That won't happen." Just the thought of anyone challenging my alpha puts my back up. They wouldn't dare, especially not with Z back in town.

"Either way, I deserve to know if there's a problem about me."

I'm not even entirely sure why I kept it from her. Probably because I was worried she was going to do something stupid and try to leave when I wasn't looking. Still, I know her biggest thing is trust. And if we're going to remain together, she has to be able to count on me.

"Deal."

"Great." She opens the duffel and drops to her knees.

"I don't think this is the right place."

Through thick lashes, she glares up at me and pulls out a pair of socks. "Not until you're at full strength."

"I'm feeling pretty fucking strong right now." I may still have some lingering aches, and I may be pissed the fuck off, but the sight of Delaney on her knees in front of me is more than enough to have my cock hardening. "I can put my own shoes on," I say, hoping to distract myself and get her up off the floor.

"I want to do it."

She continues slipping my socks on, followed by my shoes. After she finishes tying them, she straightens and reaches into her bag for a sweatshirt. "As much as I love seeing your ink—cover up so I don't have to kill anyone who eye fucks you on the way out. Bronywyn has a large patient load tonight."

Arching an eyebrow, I do as she says, my lips quirking up in a grin. Delaney's in a mood tonight, and I have to be honest—it's hot as hell.

But then, she glances up, and I see the split lip, the bruised cheek, and I get pissed the hell off all over again. I should have been with her, not laid up— useless—in this hospital bed.

"I can't fucking believe she went after you."

"Yeah. She and her merry band of misfits tracked me down at the cabin."

The blood drains from my face. "How the fuck many of them went after you?"

"Seven including her. Though, Jack took the brunt of the attack."

"The hunter was with you?"

She nods. "He went back to the cabin with me."

Jealousy creeps up into my brain, but I shove it down. "I'm glad you were not alone."

She straightens and puts both hands on her hips. "I don't fucking believe it. You're jealous."

Shit. "I didn't say I was jealous. I said I was glad you weren't alone."

Eyebrow arched, she studies me. "You can't lie to me, Cole."

"It's a bit difficult to swallow that a man you used to sleep with followed you back home when I was sitting idle in a hospital—yes."

"Do you not trust me?"

"Of fucking course, I trust you. It's more about my not being there to help you fight when you needed me."

She narrows her eyes on my face.

It's true, though. I don't worry about Delaney being with other men—but knowing I wasn't there when she needed me is going to eat at me for a long fucking time. Because it could have been so much worse. If Bestiny had managed to kill her—fuck—I don't know what I would do.

"Jack and I are just friends."

"Yes, I know that. Can we fucking go now?"

She hesitates a moment before nodding. "But we aren't going back to your cabin."

"Wait—what? Where the hell are we going?"

"My gym. There's an apartment inside. Rainey and I lived there for a while."

"That's not safe enough."

"Your place was supposed to have been safe, and look what happened."

Pride wounded. "Point taken."

She wraps an arm around my waist, so I sling one over her shoulders and leave the room behind. I won't argue about staying at the gym. Honestly, it makes my life a hell of a lot easier. And while I was more than willing to fight for her to stay before, Bestiny changed the game.

"Are you sure you're okay?" I ask as I climb into the passenger side of my truck.

"I promise." Delaney smiles and kisses me gently before shutting my door and walking around to the driver's side.

I feel fucking useless, completely and totally vulnerable, and I hate it.

She fires up the truck and pulls out of Bronywyn's massive estate, heading back toward the city. Closing my eyes, I lean back against my seat and listen to the sound of the engine and Delaney's heart beating.

———

"Cole?"

Someone shakes me softly, and I open my eyes, rubbing them to clear the rest of the sleep. "Shit, sorry. I passed out."

"It's okay. We're here."

"How long was I out?"

"About fifteen minutes."

"Feels more like fifty."

Delaney chuckles and climbs out of the truck. Before she can come around and open my door, I do it and step down. My legs feel steady; it's the exhaustion that's driving me nuts. I get small bursts of energy—like the one triggered by the sight of Delaney's split lip—but other than that, I'm pretty fucking out of it.

I follow her up to the small door of a windowless building and wait while she unlocks it. As we move inside, I take in the open space. The weights, tread-mills, weapons—it's impressive as fuck, and I can't believe I've never been in here before.

"What is this place?"

"My gym. I had it specially outfitted after my parents died. It was Rainey's and my safe haven. There's an indoor range in the basement and an apart-ment in the back."

"How have I never seen this before?"

She shrugs. "You never really wanted to be alone with me."

"False," I reply immediately. "I wanted nothing

more than to be alone with you. I just didn't think it was the best idea since my idea of being alone with you was fucking until neither of us could walk."

"And look how much time we wasted."

Her comment is not anything I haven't already considered, though I don't miss the pain buried in the words. Her mood shifts, and even as my instincts are dull, given the wolfsbane, I can still feel the change.

"Have I told you today how much I love you?" I ask and reach for her.

Delaney smiles and walks into my arms, resting her head over my chest. "I love you too, Cole. Seeing you in that pit—" Her heart rate speeds up.

"It all worked out okay."

"Because Fearghas was able to get you out. If he hadn't shown up, I don't know that we would have gotten you out in time."

"I'll be sure to thank the bastard again when I see him next."

She grins up at me. "You could start by not calling him a bastard."

"I could." I sway slightly. "This wolfsbane is a bitch."

"Come on, let's get you into bed."

"Are you coming with me?"

"Absolutely. Though, we will only be sleeping. You need to rest so that shit gets out of your system."

"That puts a damper on my plans to seduce you."

She chuckles, the sound music to my ears. "Come on, wolfman."

Delaney leads me through a door and across a tiny office. On the other side of the office, she pushes a panel, and we make our way through the secret entrance, into a small, one-bedroom apartment.

A large mattress sits in one corner. It looks freshly made, making me wonder when Delaney had time between threatening an entire pack and kicking the shit out of Bestiny.

"Rainey helped me get it ready. Well, she and Fearghas. He brought in the mattress."

"That was nice of him."

"I know you hate him, but he's a good man."

"He's all right." Truth be told, I respect the hell out of the fae. Not that I ever plan to admit that out loud. It's far too much fun to hate him.

"Are you hungry?"

"Not particularly," I answer honestly. Exhaustion roots in me, and my eyes grow heavier and heavier by the second. "I'm hoping one more day of this shit, and I'll be back."

"Let me get you some water. Bronywyn said the more you drink, the faster the wolfsbane will leave your system."

"Then hook me up to a hose," I joke, as I take a seat on the edge of the bed. I remove my shoes and stretch out.

"Here." Delaney holds a straw to my lips, so I drink deeply, letting the cool water enter my system and hopefully carry the wolfsbane the fuck out of it. As soon as I finish the cup, she sets it aside and covers me with a blanket.

"You're not leaving, right?" I ask, barely able to hold my eyes open now.

She smiles softly and presses a kiss to my forehead. "No. I will be here in the gym, I promise."

Nodding, I close my eyes again and let myself drift away to a place where Delaney and I don't have to fight for our lives—or our souls.

CHAPTER TWENTY-ONE

DELANEY

After re-racking the weights, I head for the pull-up bar. Cole's been asleep for nearly forty-eight hours. Which I expected, but it still makes me so nervous I'm heading back to the apartment to make sure he's still breathing at least a dozen times a day.

Rainey's at work. Apparently, there has been an increase in human deaths and disappearances—something that's pissing me off because I'm responsible for it. I turned the supernaturals back out on the city, and I can't wait to put Lucy down so I can go back to hunting.

Skin slick with sweat, I pull myself up, enjoying the feeling of strength that's come out of working out. I'm nowhere near where I used to be, but one day, I'll be

The door opens, so I drop back to the floor and turn as a sand-colored wolf stalks out from the office. Seeing him on four legs is the most thrilling thing I've seen in weeks.

It means the wolfsbane is gone.

He shifts back and rolls his neck, the bones cracking as he smiles at me, completely naked. "I'm back, baby."

"It's about time. I was about to come give you a sponge bath."

He grins at me. "I can go back to bed." Eyes hungry, he stalks toward me.

My blood heats, my pulse hammering as my body warms to a touch I haven't even felt yet. "I'd really rather you not."

He stops just in front of me, mere inches from my face. "You expecting company today?"

"No. Fearghas is out—" I'm cut off when Cole's mouth slams down onto mine. He kisses me with a feverish need that pulsates through my body, and I wrap my arms around his neck as he lifts me, carrying me back to the pull-up bar and pressing me against the back bar.

His hands grip my thighs, and I release him, reaching up and gripping the top bar as he steps back and strips my leggings from me. There's no calm in this storm, just a wild hurricane, and I can't wait to get swept up in it.

Cole steps between my legs again and grips my hips, angling me so he can slide inside. I moan, head falling back as he fills me completely, my body slamming against his as he fucks me with all of the passion born of our fear.

Our breathing is ragged, and I drop my arms to grip him again as he spins us and pins me to the wall mirror. Holding me with his body, he rips my shirt up the middle and slides his hands over my chest, cupping my breast.

Rolling my nipple between his thumb and finger, he drives me up to the edge of bliss, and I'm helpless to do anything but fall.

———

"Okay. I don't think I ever considered how sexy gym equipment could be," I say, as we lie breathless on the sparring mats.

"Your fucking pants did it for me."

"Glad I opted for them rather than sweats."

He snorts. "I'd want to fuck you if you wore a paper bag and bunny slippers."

"And now I need to buy myself a pair of bunny slippers and test this theory."

Cole rolls over onto his side and runs a hand over my forehead, brushing the strands that came loose from my braid aside. The way he looks at me—it sets my soul on fire.

"I love thee with a love that shall not die, till the sun grows cold and the stars grow old."

His quoting of Shakespeare brings tears to my eyes as I stare up at him. "When I saw you, I fell in love, and you smiled because you knew," I repeat back to him. It's one of my favorite Shakespeare quotes of all time. Cole grins and leans down to press a gentle kiss to my lips.

Then, he pulls away and yanks me onto my feet. "The last thing I want to have to do is kill a fae because he saw you naked."

I laugh and shake my head. "Way to go from quoting Shakespeare to threatening murder in under ten seconds."

"I'm a man of many talents."

———

Three hours later, we're walking into Tarnley's Pub. There are a handful of supernaturals off in one corner, while Rainey waves at me from the back of the room. I grip Cole's hand and pull him toward my sister.

We slide into the booth and he wraps an arm around my shoulders.

"Glad to see you back on your feet," Elijah says to Cole.

"Glad to be back on them."

"How are you feeling?"

"Back to normal," Cole tells Rainey. "I'm a little bummed Delaney kicked the shit out of Bestiny and I wasn't there to see it."

"You and me both," Rainey replies with a pointed look at me.

"Next time I get into a fight, I promise to start a phone tree."

"It's called a group text now, old lady," Rainey retorts.

"Technically, I'm a month younger than you."

At my response, Rainey throws her head back and laughs.

Fearghas appears beside the table. "Hey there, fam," he greets. Grabbing a chair from a nearby table, he flips it around backward and sits on it, resting both arms over the back.

"Where the hell have you been?" Rainey demands.

"Looking for some lines that seem to take pleasure in evading me."

"You still haven't found them?" I ask, and he shakes his head.

"I'm closing in on them, though. I can feel it. There are a shit ton of trees to go through. It's been a hell of a long time since they surfaced last."

"Surfaced?"

"They can go dormant at times—or at least seem

that way. More like they're damn near impossible to find."

"Well, at least that means Lucy hasn't found them yet."

"True point. Everyone drinking?"

"Whiskey, please," I ask.

"Same."

"Make that four," Rainey adds, gesturing to Elijah.

"You've got it." He disappears only to reappear near the bar. From where we're sitting, Tarnley looks less than pleased, and that amuses me. Not because I don't like the vampire, but because I find it humorous that someone who is truly as likable as Fearghas finds such joy in annoying the shit out of others.

"How are things in the city?" Cole asks, and I turn my attention back to the table.

"Not great," Rainey replies. "Deaths and missing persons are steadily climbing. It's taking everything for Paloma to keep the city calm and the media at bay. They want to call for another serial killer—or rather the same one who's resurfaced."

"Vampires?"

She nods. "And succubae, based on what I'm seeing. Men going totally postal and killing other men. My partner brought one guy in yesterday, and he nearly took a chunk out of the other guys in the holding cell."

"Maybe letting them come out wasn't such a good idea."

"You did what you had to do." Cole places a hand on my thigh beneath the table.

"But at what cost?"

"Their lives won't mean anything if Lucy gets those lines open and turns this place into a total shit show."

I sigh, knowing he's right but still feeling incredibly guilty over the innocents lost. It's a shitty situation to want to go out to a club for a girls' night and end up dinner for some bloodsucker.

Fearghas appears back at the table, tray of whiskeys in hand. He sets them down then takes a seat and raises a glass. "To the wolf. May he never be impaled on something again."

I snort, and Cole grins beside me. "Aww, that's so nice of you fae. You were worried."

"I was worried Delaney was going to lose her mind."

We all cheers to that and take a drink. It's well past time we had a semi-normal night, and this one is shaking up to be a good one.

Or, at least it was.

The lights flicker.

When they come back on, Lucy is standing beside Fearghas, her black fingernails digging into his shoulder. "Well, well. Isn't this cozy?"

We start to stand, but she tightens her grip, and Fearghas's eyes shut tightly.

"Move and the fae is going to lose his shoulder."

"What the fuck do you want?" I growl.

"What I've always wanted. My power."

"You have no business here, witch," Tarnley warns as he blurs around the counter. The other supernaturals stare up at her, terror evident in their wide eyes.

"You have no words in this play, vampire." She snaps her fingers, and Tarnley crumples to the ground.

I start to shove past Cole in the booth, but when Fearghas groans and sways in his chair, I stiffen, fear for my friend outweighing the desperate urge to rip her head off. "What the fuck are you doing to him?" His cheeks grow pale, so damn pale, that he looks far too close to death.

"Iron nail polish. Get your nails deep enough into the skin, and it can be excruciating. Isn't that right, Fearghas? Oh, before I forget, your sister says hi." She turns back to me, and it takes all of my strength to shift my focus from the blood blossoming on Fearghas's button-down shirt.

"You're going to want to let him go." A feminine voice carries through the room, and I stretch up to see a red-faced Eira standing only a few yards away.

"Go,' Fearghas chokes out. "I'm. Fine."

She completely ignores him. "Let him go, witch."

Lucy chuckles. "Or what? Are you going to make it rain on me?"

Eira grins, a humorless smile that turns even my blood cold. I never would have pinned her as a killer before, but now? With a simple expression, she looks more bloodthirsty than any of us. She snaps her fingers, and all the liquid in every glass floats up, joining together in the center of the room, one massive drop. "Do you know that it only takes a few drops of water to drown a person?" she asks. "And there is no power in your possession that can stop that from happening."

"This isn't your fight, siren."

"You made it my fight when you put your hands on the fae."

Lucy bends over and places her lips right over Fearghas's ear. "Your sister was right, then? You are screwing a siren. Good pull. Too damn bad Sheelin is going to mount her head on a trophy wall. I bet she'll keep you alive long enough to watch the life drain from the siren's eyes."

Fearghas groans and fights against her hold. I palm my dagger, ready to pounce the moment Fearghas is safe.

"You should all know that I'm coming for you. Every single one of you bastards will die before this is all over." She turns to me. "It could have just been you and Bronywyn, but now? Now I'm coming for you all."

She snaps her fingers again, and the lights go dark. When they come back on, she's gone.

Fearghas slumps down in his chair, and both Cole and Elijah lunge to their feet, and Rainey and I follow closely behind. Liquid crashes to the floor as Eira rushes toward Fearghas. She stops in front of him, bending down to check his wound.

With the wave of her finger, she pulls his blood up and out of his shirt. Then somehow, she uses it to knit a temporary bandage. It's as if she hardened a portion of it, freezing the blood in place to stop the bleeding.

Impressive as hell, that's for sure.

"Better?" she asks, and he nods.

"You should have stayed out of it."

She shakes her head. "There's no way in hell I'm letting her bully us."

"She's gone." Cole comes to stand beside me again. "Apparently, she doesn't need a portal anymore."

"Fae blood," Fearghas growls. "Sheelin must be providing her fae magic to absorb."

"Seriously? She would do that?"

Fearghas meets my gaze. "There seems to be no limit to my sister's treason."

"We need to find those lines and end this fucking thing," Elijah growls.

I glare back at the door, almost wishing she'd walk back in here again, but also knowing there's no way I'm ready to face her yet.

Not without the ley line power, and until I get it, we're all sitting ducks. "It's time to find them," I agree. "Then we put her down."

CHAPTER TWENTY-TWO

DELANEY

The faucet squeaks as Cole turns the shower off moments before he appears in the doorway, a towel draped over his hips. Beads of water drip down his chest, sliding over the ink before disappearing into the towel.

Lucky fucking drops if you ask me.

"Find anything?" he asks, and I shake my head, shifting my attention back to the book in my lap.

"Unfortunately not. With how little we know about the lines, I won't be surprised if I don't find anything to give us information on another way to capture the power."

"Are you sure we need to do it at all? Why don't we do something similar with her as we did with Heather?"

I close the book, set it aside with a yawn, and lie

back on the mattress. "Chances are that Lucy has prepared for just that. I wouldn't be the least bit surprised if she has more up her sleeve than her mother ever did."

"So, you think even killing her will be met with consequences?"

"I think killing her without having a magical bonus might be. She's resourceful, and if she finds a way to come back, we risk having already shown our cards and pissing her off."

"Then why not take you last night? Why threaten us instead?"

"Who the hell knows?" The mattress dips as Cole lies beside me. "It feels like we're constantly playing defense even as we're fighting to remain on the offensive side. She just shows up and is two moves ahead of us." I think back to her fingers buried in Fearghas's flesh. To the pained look on his face and the fear that she was going to do just as she threatened to do.

"She won't win this," he tells me as he reaches down and interlinks his fingers with mine.

Turning my head, I meet his gaze. "I know she won't." After a brief moment, I sit up on the bed and get to my feet. "You up for coming with me to see Rainey?"

Cole sits up slowly, propping himself on both elbows. "I would, but I need to head out and see Josiah. Figure out what they're doing with Bestiny.

Any chance you'll come with me? We can swing back by and see Rainey afterward."

"You're offering me a chance to rub you in her face? Why would I ever pass that opportunity up?"

He chuckles and sits up all the way, extending both arms out to me. I go to him, moth to a flame, and he wraps his arms around my waist. "You are simultaneously the best and worst thing that's ever happened to me."

"The worst?" I chuckle. "That seems harsh."

He pushes me back just enough to look up at me through thick, dark lashes. "Your death was the worst thing," he clarifies. "But your life—it's the best possible thing that could have ever happened."

I smile down at him. "You're a charmer, that's for damn sure."

He flashes white teeth in a smile that's more carnal than humorous. "You bring it out in me."

"That's what all the boys say." I wink at him and start to pull away, but he grips my arm and yanks me back down, flipping me over and covering my body with his. He growls low and deep against my ear, his hot breath against my skin making me breathless.

Will I always react this way to him? I sure as hell hope so.

"No other boys better be saying a fucking thing to you, *mate*."

"No one but you," I clarify.

He pulls back and grins down at me. Then, he licks the bridge of my nose and digs his fingers into my ribs.

Laughter erupts between us as I squirm in a desperate attempt to get away from the tickling. My phone rings, the shrill tone ending the moment. "Saved by the ringer." Cole kisses me then climbs off.

"Hello?" I answer, still out of breath.

Cole glances back at me and rips his towel off, giving me an incredible view of his muscled ass right before he disappears into the bathroom.

"Why are you out of breath?" Rainey asks curiously. "Wait, don't tell me. I'm good."

"Then why did you ask?"

"Curiosity will not be what kills this hunter," she replies. "Or makes her hurl."

"When did you start talking about yourself in the third person?"

"When are you coming up here?" she asks, ignoring my question.

"Cole and I are going to swing by the pack lands to see what Josiah is doing with Bestiny. Then, we'll swing by." I check the clock on the wall. "So probably about two-ish?"

"Perfect. Bring skittles and coffee."

"You've got it."

"See you then!" She ends the call, and I toss the phone down as Cole steps out dressed in jeans and a black t-shirt. He shrugs into his leather jacket and turns to me.

"Ready?"

"Almost." I grab my jacket and throw my hair up in a bun and retrieve my phone from the bed. Then, I turn to face him. "Ready."

———————

We arrive just as the pack is filing into the community center. Cole takes my hand and shoves through, pushing past them and up toward the stage where Josiah and Willa sit, Z standing behind his alpha like a statue. Josiah looks more exhausted than I've ever seen him with dark circles beneath his eyes and a slump to his shoulders.

I hate that I'm probably part of the reason for his stress.

When they see us, Willa lights up and waves us up to the stage.

"I can stay back here," I whisper to Cole, who shakes his head.

"You're my mate. You will be with me."

As soon as he finishes speaking, Jack emerges from the back and comes to stand behind Willa's chair. He nods at me, looking just as uncomfortable with this shift as I am.

Cole takes his seat at Josiah's right hand, his place

as pack beta. I come to stand beside his chair, and Z smiles softly at me. "Good to see you, Delaney."

"You, too."

Josiah stands, and the room quiets as the rest of the shifters take their seats. "I am calling this meeting to let you all know of the changes our pack will be making, as well as to allow you to have a say in the fate of Bestiny and the two remaining shifters who attacked Delaney and Jack." He pauses, and no one speaks. "As is customary in our pack, the mate of my daughter—Jack Keller—and the mate of our beta —Delaney Astor—will be prevalent in our meetings."

Jack's jaw hardens as whispers break out amongst the crowd. I stand straighter, determined to be seen as Cole's equal. He doesn't look at me, but I know it's because he's searching the crowd just as Josiah is.

A woman raises her hand.

"Yes, Melanie."

"They are not shifters."

"No, they are not. But just as we cannot control the mating bond, we cannot control who our wolves choose. For a long time now, those who have mated with other factions have been cast out, killed, and otherwise alienated. That will no longer be the case."

Z crosses his arms as Lauren steps out from behind with their son, hand on her swollen belly.

"This is our new family," Josiah says. "If you have

an issue with this, then you are more than welcome to leave the pack."

Holy shit. He is literally choosing us over the rest of the pack. What made him decide this? What changed since Z? I glance at Lauren, hoping for an answer, but she only smiles softly as Kai goes to stand in front of his father.

"This is the new way of our pack. Inclusion, not prejudice."

A man stands. "With all due respect, alpha, you're asking us to turn our backs on The Accords. The very guidelines you have pushed us to follow since the beginning."

"I am. And I know some of you will be uncomfortable with this, but I implore you to look deeper. The Accords knew nothing of what would come should we mate and reproduce with other factions." He gestures back at Kai, who steps forward with his father. "Tell me, does this young boy look dangerous to you?"

All eyes shift to Kai. I can't help but smile as he juts his chin up and straightens, looking every bit his father's son.

"This child was born of a shifter and a witch. And because of The Accords, Zander and Lauren have been in hiding for over two decades. I am no longer going to allow our pack members to be alienated because of who their bond chooses."

"What of the councils? They will punish all of us!"

"Anyone who remains in my pack will be shielded from the councils. I will ensure your safety as it is the only thing that matters to me. I am choosing to take a stand. Once again, I implore you to do the same."

More chatter. While I can't make out each word, I know Cole can. He doesn't move in his seat, giving me no indication of what the others are whispering.

"Now that that's settled, should you choose to leave, I ask that you do so now." To my complete surprise, no one moves. This is their home, their pack, and the fact that they are standing by their alpha shows a hell of a lot about the character of the people in this room. "We need to determine the fate of the shifters who attacked Delaney Astor and Jack Keller."

A woman with bright red hair stands. "If the mates were wolves, we never would have even considered. They should be put to death for harming our own." With a curt nod directed at me, she sits.

A man stands this time with dark, shoulder-length hair and soft eyes. "Bestiny tried to manipulate us into blaming Delaney for the attack on our people. She worked within our pack to turn us against each other; then took it upon herself to threaten and attack the mates of the beta and alpha second. She must be put to death for her actions." He takes a seat.

One by one, a handful of shifters stand and say as much.

Josiah holds up a hand. "With the raise of your

hand, who believes Bestiny and the two shifters who remain should be put to death for the crimes against our own."

A sea of hands fills the air. Not one seat is left out of the vote. It's unanimous and feels a hell of a lot like an olive branch in accepting me. Maybe Cole and I will be able to return here after all, and I know that means more to him than he's let on.

"Very well. We appreciate your votes. You may all be excused."

Chairs scoot back, and voices carry through the community center as the pack stands and leaves the room. As soon as they're gone, Josiah slumps back down in his chair, a sigh leaving his lips.

"What's wrong?" Cole demands, getting to his feet so quickly I nearly miss it.

"This has been exhausting."

"Why did you do that?" I ask, my voice barely above a whisper. "They didn't want us here." I look up at Jack, at Lauren, and their tight-lipped expressions tell me they know it, too.

Josiah reaches for my hand and I offer it. He covers it with his other. "Do you know I was there when you were born?"

I swallow hard. "I didn't know that."

"You were delivered on our lands because your mother was here with your aunt and uncle—your birth mother."

"I had no idea."

"You couldn't know," he says sadly. "Because after your birth parents were killed, you had to all but disappear." He sighs. "You were here, though. My mate delivered you into this world." He laughs. "You came into this world ten weeks early and had to fight to survive."

My eyes fill, and Cole's hand presses against my lower back.

"You are my family, Delaney. And you will have a place in this pack for as long as you want. You're a fighter, a warrior, and a damn perfect mate for Cole. Do not let anyone chase you away." He glances up at Z and Lauren. "I should have told you both the same."

She reaches out and places a hand on his shoulder. "You're going to make a pregnant woman cry."

He laughs. "Let's not do that." Standing, he turns to Jack. "And you, Keller, are just as much a warrior as my most fearsome fighter. You saved my daughter when even I could not, and for that, you have more than earned your place in this pack. You will make a great alpha mate when the time comes."

Jack looks taken aback—and, if I'm not mistaken, slightly embarrassed—but he nods. "Thank you."

"You're welcome. I should have shoved The Accords aside decades ago, but I suppose it's better late than never."

"What happens to Bestiny now?" I've always

known that each faction has its own way of carrying out violations, but I've never actually seen it done before.

He sighs and runs a hand over his face. "This is the first execution we've had in at least three decades. Z used to carry them out."

"I'll do this one," Cole offers, jaw tight. "It's my fault she went after Delaney. Her blood will be on my hands."

Even as he says the words, I feel a shift in the air surrounding him. This death will weigh on him, heavier than anything he's had to bear.

"I can do it," I offer, and all eyes turn to me. "She attacked me; I can carry it out."

"Delaney—" Cole starts, but I hold up a hand.

"It's me she has a problem with, and me who should have ended it when she attacked me in the first place. If the pack wants her to die, I will do it."

"Her death will weigh on your conscience," Z tells me. "I can tell you that from experience. No matter how badly they deserve it, it will eat away at you."

"Then it definitely should be me." I look to Cole. "Please?"

He opens his mouth, probably to argue, but immediately shuts it and nods. "If you want her blood on your hands, then I won't stand in your way."

"Then, it's settled. We will call you when it's time." Josiah turns away and heads down the stairs, but before he reaches the bottom, he glances back at us. "I love you all. You are my family, and I am forever grateful you have each other." With a tight smile, he finishes his descent and disappears into the sunlight.

"Is he okay?" I ask the group. They all look nearly as confused as I feel.

"I haven't noticed anything," Z offers. "But I'll talk to him. Willa?"

"I'll come." She kisses Jack and strolls across the platform to me. "You shouldn't feel bad for carrying out her execution. It's how things work in this pack, and she nearly killed your mate."

"You know it was her?"

Willa nods. "We found a bottle of wolfsbane oil in her cabin."

Any guilt I might have felt vanishes as I recall how helpless I felt standing at the top of that hole, staring down at Cole as he bled to death. "Thank you for telling me."

"You're welcome." She leaves, Z trailing behind.

I glance back at Cole, who's watching me carefully. "Are you sure you want to carry that out?"

"I've taken lives before," I remind him.

"You have. But only in an active fight. It's a whole different ball game when you're executing someone in cold blood."

"I don't find her nearly killing you and me seeking retaliation cold blood."

Cole grips my chin, tilting my face up to his. "You are not a cold-blooded killer, Delaney. You've only ever killed in the name of your bloodline. If you go through with this, it's going to change you."

"It has to be done."

CHAPTER TWENTY-THREE
DELANEY

It's nearly three before we are walking through the front door of Rainey's precinct. She glances up from her desk and smiles, waving us over. Cole's hand linked in mine, we move through the room.

I've only ever visited her here twice before. Mainly because cops make me nervous. After all, a good portion of their unsolved homicides were me. Tarnley's clean-up crew took care of a good chunk of them, but there were some that got away from me—literally —only to die somewhere else.

I was always terrified someone was going to recognize me. That they would point and yell, "She did it!" and then my legacy would be over.

"Skittles for my addict sister," I say as I reach into the pocket of my jacket and hand them over.

"Thank you very much." She takes them and, like the fiend she is, tears into the bag and immediately starts eating them. "This is my partner, Detective Allen. Allen, this is my friend, Jane, and her boyfriend Cole."

I swallow hard, knowing why she has to introduce me as Jane, yet still hating every damned minute of it.

Cole squeezes my hand gently, our bond letting him feel my dislike at the public façade I have to maintain. It might raise some questions if Rainey's sister was suddenly raised from the dead.

"Nice to meet you both, you can call me Walker." He reaches out for my hand, and I offer my own. The moment our skin touches, a jolt shoots up my arm as though I just grabbed hold of an electric fence.

His eyes widen, and I know he felt it, too.

"I thought your kind was extinct?" Cole asks, quietly.

Walker's eyes widen further, his skin paling.

"What kind?' Rainey demands, looking from her new partner to Cole.

"How did you—"

"You know what I am," Cole replies. "I know what you are. If you're worried about her, she's not in the business of hunting psychics."

Rainey spits coffee everywhere, earning her amused glances from other officers in the precinct. She smiles awkwardly at them before heading for the nearest conference room. "Let's go."

We follow, with Walker falling into step behind her, and looking incredibly awkward about it. Which is amusing since the guy is probably about two hundred pounds of muscle, and nearly at Cole's height, while my sister might as well be fun-sized.

She shuts the door and whirls on her partner. "You're a psychic? As in, can read the future?"

"That's not how his kind operates," Cole says as he leans back against the table. "Is it?"

"I don't mean anyone any harm," Walker says, putting both hands up. "I keep my nose out of everyone else's business and just want to make the city safer."

"Cut the bullshit," Rainey snaps. "You've known what I am this entire time?"

He nods.

"Why the hell didn't you tell me?"

"Cut the guy some slack," Cole tells her. "Supernaturals have nearly slaughtered the psychics into extinction."

"Why?"

At my question, Walker turns to me. "Because they feared what we can see."

"Which is?"

He turns back to Rainey. "Not nearly as much as they thought we could."

"Psychics work on feelings, don't you? Rather than specific visions."

"How the hell do you know so much about us?" Walker crosses his arms and faces Cole.

My mate isn't even mildly intimidated. "I knew one of your kind once. Saved her from a vampire clan back in the seventies. Samantha something. We had a good chat over some coffee before going our separate ways."

"You're the wolf that saved my sister."

"If her name was Samantha, yes. But I don't remember ever getting a last name."

"Was it here in Billings?"

"No. It was in Whitefish."

Walker nods. "That's my sister." He extends his hand. "Thank you."

Cole eyes it for a moment then takes it. "She was innocent, and I was in the area."

"I feel like every damn time I believe I have a handle on this world, another new supernatural pops up."

I chuckle, nodding at Rainey. "At least, the ruse can be over." I turn to Walker. "I'm Delaney Astor, Rainey's older sister."

"I thought your sister died?"

"She did. Then became a bird. Then came back. It's been a long few years."

"What was the jolt? I'm assuming you felt it, too?"

"Jolt?" Now Cole looks jealous. It makes me smile.

"My kind and your kind are linked. Different branches, but the same tree if you will. That was your magic recognizing mine and vice versa."

"Then why don't I feel that with other witches?"

"Because they are your kind. You recognize them instantly," he replies. "My people have been fighting to stay hidden. We've warded our lines for generations." He pulls up his left sleeve and shows me a huge tattoo on his forearm.

Black ink climbs from his wrist up to his elbow in an intricate design I don't recognize. Lines and circles collide in a sort of organized chaos that draws the eye. "That's a ward?" I ask, my fingers itching to touch it because my power senses the magic embedded in his skin.

"It is. Tattooed on me as a baby by my father. Every person in my family has had this mark put on them at birth. It keeps us from being sensed by other supernaturals."

"Which is why I couldn't sense you."

"Yes."

"Why the hell would you stay in Billings?" Rainey asks. "This place is crawling with supernaturals."

"I felt a shift in the energy the last time I was here. Then again, a few months ago. Something big is coming, something evil. And I want to stop it."

Rainey snorts. "You're a bit late for what's coming, we already know who and what it is."

"What the hell do you mean? The shift hasn't fully happened yet."

Those six words chill my bones. Is Lucy's rise not what he felt? "You're saying that the reason you're here—the evil you sensed—it hasn't happened yet?"

"That's exactly what I'm saying."

Rainey and I exchange glances before I look to Cole. He's lost all amusement, his expression tight.

"What did you mean by I'm a bit late?" he questions. "What's going on?"

"A hell of a lot, Allen. A hell of a fucking lot," Rainey replies. "How much time do you have?"

———

Eira's club is busy tonight with supernaturals belonging to factions I've never seen up close and personal shaking their asses to some beat I don't recognize.

Cole is just behind me, lurking close enough that I can feel the heat of his body against my back. Since Fearghas didn't come around at all today, I thought I might find him here. Cole was less worried about him, but when I'd offered to come alone—well—you can imagine that didn't go over super well.

We push through the rest of the dance hall and into the dining room. A hostess smiles widely at me, but I don't listen to a word she says as I scan the room for the fae. My gaze drifts over a woman wearing all black in the corner, her eyes greedily watching someone across the room. Following her gaze, I spot my target in the corner, lounging in a booth and looking less than comfortable.

Hell, if I'm not mistaken, he looks pissed.

"We're here to see him." I point and move past her, Cole right on my heels.

"Delaney," Fearghas greets without looking up from his glass of whiskey. "Isn't this a surprise?" He pops the last word, completely unamused with the fact that I'm here at all. I slide into the booth across from him, and Cole follows, his hand dropping to my knee.

"Where the hell have you been all day?"

"Here, there, a bit of everywhere, really," he replies dryly. "What do you want to drink?" He still doesn't look at me, and he drops a hand to the table where he begins drumming his fingers.

Concern pushes past the anger. Something is off. "What's wrong?"

"Nothing. Why would anything be wrong?"

"Fearghas."

"What can I get you two?" A woman asks as she

glides up to the table on legs that might as well have been stilts. Based on the gills at the back of her ears, and the shimmery incandescent skin visible beneath her pink miniskirt, I'd say she's a mermaid.

Another lore the books get wrong. Sirens and mermaids are completely different species. Where Sirens have control over the water, mermaids are basically fish shifters. Or rather, half-fish shifters.

"No."

"Excuse me?" she asks, and I glare at her.

"No. We don't want anything right now. Thank you."

With a curt nod, she turns away.

"You didn't have to be so rude," Fearghas snaps. "I do come here often, and would prefer for the staff to not think my acquaintances are savages."

He didn't say 'friends.'

"What in the hell is going on with you?" Cole snaps, as he leans across the table.

I turn around, scanning the room for Eira, but don't see her. The same woman is eyeing Fearghas, though, and when she sees me looking at her, she runs a forked tongue over her lips and winks.

The hairs on the back of my neck stand on end as a shiver of fear runs up my spine. *Dark witch.* What the hell is a dark witch doing in Eira's club?

"Answer my fucking question," Cole demands.

"Nothing, wolf boy. All is dandy in my world. And

why wouldn't it be? It's not like it's ending any time soon, is it?" He snorts and lifts the glass to his lips. "Oh wait, it is."

I am completely unable to do anything but gape at him. "Who in the actual hell are you, and where is Fearghas?"

He smirks. "Really, Delaney? That's the best you've got?"

Cole's up so damn fast it doesn't even register he's no longer beside me until he has Fearghas by the throat and is slamming him against the wall behind the booth.

The room falls completely silent around us.

"Let me go, Cole," Fearghas warns, his eyes glowing green.

"Then drop the shit," Cole growls back.

I get to my feet and rush over to them, placing a hand on Cole's arm.

"Fearghas?"

At Eira's voice, the fae's gaze shifts past Cole's shoulder and to her. His eyes change, a subtle constriction of his pupils. "What's going—" But before I can finish the sentence, we're in the lobby of my gym. Cole drops Fearghas, who slides down to the floor.

"Care to tell me what the hell is going on with you?" I drop to my knees in front of him.

"I don't—" He shakes his head, blinking rapidly as though he's desperately trying to clear a bad dream.

"I'm not entirely sure what's wrong with me." His eyes meet mine, and then he glances back at Cole before his eyes trail around the room. "What the hell are we doing here?"

I stare at him. "What the hell do you mean? You brought us here."

He shakes his head again. "I did?"

"What's the last thing you remember?" Cole questions, gripping my arm and pulling me to my feet and back to his side.

Slowly, Fearghas stands. "Walking into Eira's, taking a seat at the table. That's about it." He pinches the bridge of his nose.

Dark witch. "We need to get back to that club," I growl, clenching my fists at my sides.

"Why?"

"There was a dark witch there. I bet that bitch was messing with Fearghas."

"They can do that?" Cole questions. "I thought fae were supposed to be all-powerful, unaffected by most magic."

"We are." He shifts his attention to me. "There was a dark witch in Eira's club?"

"Yes."

He disappears.

"Dammit, Fearghas!" The cell in my pocket rings, so I pull it out, too damn annoyed to check the readout before answering. "Hello?"

"Delaney, so nice to hear from you."

Ice chills my blood. "Lucy."

"Don't bother going back to the club. She's already gone. What you should realize, though, is that I've been lenient on you. Something that could very quickly change should you not do exactly as I say."

"Fuck off." I hang up on her, ignoring the shrill tone when it goes off again.

Fearghas reappears in front of us. "She's gone."

"No fucking shit, Sherlock. We just got the message," Cole snaps back.

"What the hell do you mean you just got the message?"

"Lucy called."

He pales ever so slightly. "She did this?"

I nod. "And she promised to make things a whole lot worse if I don't do what she asks."

"Which was?"

"I told her to fuck off."

Fearghas gapes at me for a moment before throwing his head back and laughing. Why? Who the hell knows? It's not like this situation has even a sliver of amusement. "What the fuck are you laughing about?"

"You Astor's are cocky, that's for damn sure." His laughter dies down. "And as unfortunate as my next words are, I'm starting to think your original plan may have been right. We may have to have you open the lines."

"Seriously?" Cole lunges for the fae who disappears then reappears a few yards away.

"Think about it; Lucy needs Delaney. It has to be because our favorite hunter witch here is the only one with the power to open those lines."

"She may have the power to open them, but it'll kill her if she does!"

"And what if it doesn't?"

Both men turn to me.

"What if this power boost is exactly what I need to put her down? It could be what pushes our side to the winning one."

"Or it could kill you."

I turn to Cole. "If I don't try this, we could all die."

"I can't watch you die, Delaney. Not again. You can't ask me to go through that twice."

"I'm not. But we knew this decision was on the table, and I think it's well past time we face the music."

Cole's jaw hardens, a muscle twitching on the right side as he shakes his head angrily. "There has to be another way. We still have to find the fucking lines."

"We will." I can feel it in my soul that this is the right decision. That opening these lines will be the one way we can beat Lucy at her own game. She may have a seat on the immortal council, may have control over supernaturals and have fae magic at her disposal.

But I'm about to take on something a hell of a lot more ancient.

Deadly.

And I'm going to rip her apart with it.

CHAPTER TWENTY-FOUR

DELANEY

"Bronywyn?" I call out as I step into her house. It's immaculate, polished marble floors, bright tapestries...the woman has impressive taste, that's for damn sure.

"Up here!" she calls out.

I head toward the stairs and take them slowly, letting my hand trail over the smooth, mahogany handrail. This is one of the only times I've ever been in here and haven't either been dying myself, or had someone I cared for on their death bed, so I spend a moment to really take in the home of the witch I owe my life to.

The upstairs is nearly as pristine as the down-stairs. Tables with vases overflowing with flowers line the landing. Only one door is open, so I peek inside to find the woman I'm looking for seated behind a massive desk.

Her blonde hair is piled up on top of her head, and she appears to be dressed casually in a cropped sweat-shirt. I knock on the door jamb, and she glances up, smiling softly. "Delaney, what can I do for you?"

I hate that I'm about to erase what is surely one of Bronywyn's rare good moods. "Lucy came to see us the other night."

She stands so quickly the papers on her desk fall to the side. "Where?"

"She came to Tarnley's pub. Night before last."

Her face pales. "What happened? Is he—"

"He's fine. She didn't kill anyone, though she did nearly take a chunk out of Fearghas's shoulder."

"Son of a bitch."

"Eira actually showed up and scared her off. Or, at least, that's what I'm guessing happened."

"Not surprised there. Lucy is anything but stupid, and Eira is one hell of an enemy. It's the whole reason she has to stay in hiding. The council would capture her in a heartbeat if they thought she was breaking The Accords and giving them any reason at all to act." She pinches the bridge of her nose. "What the hell did she want?"

"To warn us? I'm not entirely sure. Like I said, I think Eira showed up and put a damper on her plans."

"So she's watching us."

"We knew she would be."

"But why hasn't she acted yet?"

"Honestly? I think she needs us to lead her to the ley lines. If her tracking Jane told us anything, it's that she's beyond patient."

"You don't think she's found the lines." It's not a question, but I shake my head anyway.

"Fearghas hasn't even found them yet, and he's actually been there. The bigger issue now is that Fearghas thinks Sheelin is giving Lucy fae magic."

Her eyes widen. "She's sacrificing her own kind?"

"That's how it seems. Lucy managed to appear and disappear without a portal this time." I hesitate a brief moment before piling on, "It gets worse."

"Worse than Lucy nearly ripping Fearghas apart?"

I nod. "Cole and I went to see Fearghas at Eira's club last night. We hadn't seen him since Tarnley's. He was different—moody and irritable."

She snorts. "That's different?"

"There was a dark witch there, and it seemed as though she had some kind of hold on him."

The other witch pales, her hands clenching into fists. "How? That shouldn't be possible."

"It shouldn't be," I agree. "He saw Eira, and it broke the trance. When we got back to the gym, Lucy called and let us know it was her. She said she's going to make our lives much more difficult if I don't do what she says."

"Which was?"

"I told her to fuck off before she could tell me."

Bronywyn's eyes darken, a storm rolling in as her power snaps in the air around her. "We have to stop her."

"That's why I'm here. It's time to face what neither of us wants to."

"And what's that?"

"I need you to do exactly what Lucy was going to do to me, but this time, I want to use the extra space in my body to channel the ley line magic."

"I told you—there's a higher probability that you're going to die than survive that."

"We have to do something. Every day that passes, she's gaining more and more power."

"What happened to waiting it out? To letting the supernaturals distract her while we find another way?" She gestures to the papers all over her desk. "I'm trying to find another route, any other route."

"I know you are, and I appreciate that." The fact that the witch and I have become friends makes this entire thing even more difficult—for both of us. I'm essentially asking her to kill me, or damn near almost kill me, anyway.

"It's been days, Delaney, we need more time."

"We're out of time, Bronywyn. Lucy is going to make her move soon, I'm sure of it. And I, for one, don't want to be caught unaware."

"And if she is using us to lead her to the ley lines? What's to stop her from tracking us there and killing everyone?"

Honestly, that's the worst-case scenario and something I've considered. "It's risky. But so is doing nothing. We take as many preparations as we can and hope for the best."

"We know nothing about those lines, Delaney. Not a damn thing. That magic could kill you on site."

"It could, but it's unlikely." I bite down on my bottom lip, trying to decide if I should mention the other reason I'm here. "What if more than one witch opens them?"

At that, her eyes widen even further. "I hadn't considered that."

"With the vacancy in our blood, we could do it."

"You mean the two of us."

I nod. "You're the only other witch I would trust. Except Lauren, but with her being pregnant, that's a no go. There would be two of us. We could potentially take the power on, and it would be less likely to overload us."

She considers. "Possibly, but it's still risky. I wasn't born with the extra power boost that body was. How much time do you think we have?"

"I'd say days, and that even feels lenient. If she makes a move before we're ready, we're screwed."

"And you're willing to risk your life? Everything you've built with Cole?"

Swallowing hard, I try not to focus on losing him forever. "It means nothing if we're dead anyway."

"How does he feel about this plan of yours?"

"Not great," I admit. "But I think he knows telling me not to do something never works out."

She chuckles and sits back behind her desk. "You two are doing well then?"

We both know why she changed the subject, but I don't mention it. Potentially sacrificing your life for the greater good more than earns some small talk. "We are. He's back to normal, and I feel—happy. For probably the first time since my parents died."

"I'm really glad."

"How are you doing?"

Bronywyn sighs, and I catch a glimpse of the terrified woman from the cell. "I'm managing. I'll be better as soon as this is all put to rest and things go back to normal."

"You think they will?"

"They will go back to something. Whether it's the normal we're used to or some twisted version of it, who the hell knows at this point?"

I plop down in the seat across from her desk. "Have you spoken to Tarnley?"

"Not since the night of your plan."

"What happened that night? When you two came

out from the back of the bar, you both looked pretty damn worse for the wear."

"What Tarnley and I have—it's complicated. We're friends, sometimes, enemies a hell of a lot of the time. I just told him it was time we both moved forward."

"Have you two—"

"No." She leans toward the desk, resting both arms on top. "When I've fallen in the past, it's been hard, fast, and damn near immovable. It took me decades to get over Elijah, and we both always knew what it was going to be."

I can understand that, the need to feel loved and seeking it. Hell, I fell for Cole the first day I saw him.

"I can't risk myself again, and now that Lucy is back..."

"You're worried she'll target Tarnley."

"I know she will. The joy she gets out of hurting people I love, it's sickening."

The warlock Lucy mentioned when we were back in the cell comes to mind. I couldn't even imagine suffering that kind of pain. "You love him."

"Of course I do. I have for quite some time now. Ever since he came to me and asked for a way out of his mate bond."

"Well, take it from someone who sat on her feelings for three decades. We may be immortal, but that doesn't necessarily mean we have unlimited time."

She shakes her head. "Maybe once all of this is

done, we can see if there's anything there. But not until Lucy is stopped."

I smile at her. "Want to go out for drinks later?"

"Drinks?"

"Yeah, girls' night out. I'm thinking Eira's club with Rainey and Willa."

"You are inviting me on a girl's night out? After asking me minutes ago to risk my life for the greater good."

She looks honestly surprised—perplexed, really. And that makes me even more grateful I asked her. Bronywyn is not a woman with a lot of friends. She's gruff and can honestly be a massive bitch when she wants to be.

But I've learned over the little bit of time I've been back that her walls are nothing more than shields erected to keep her from feeling too much.

"I am. What better time is there? We may not have a tomorrow, but we sure as fuck have tonight."

She chuckles. "Okay. Yes. I think that could be fun."

I grin at her. Truth be told, I'd fully expected her to argue more than that. "Great, I'll come pick you up at seven?"

"How about I come get you? I can use my driver."

"Even better."

CHAPTER TWENTY-FIVE
COLE

"Remind me again why I can't come with you?"

Delaney bends over, her tight dress stretching even further over a perfect ass. I groan, knowing she's putting on a show to drive me fucking wild.

"Because you have a dick, and this is a girl's night out," she replies as she straightens and turns to face me. I sit on the edge of the bed, cock hard like a fucking teenager seeing a pair of tits for the first time.

It's pathetic.

"You can't be serious. You're going out looking like a piece of meat, and you won't even let me tag along to lurk in the background?"

"No, I won't." She walks toward me and comes to stand between my knees. I place both hands on her hips and lie backward as she climbs onto the bed and straddles me.

"This is not making you leaving any easier." To demonstrate what she does to me, I arch my hips up and press them against her pussy. The thin layer of cotton and the barrier of my jeans doesn't mute her response. Cheeks flush, her lips part slightly, and I grin up at her.

"No." Her tone is soft, weak, but I get it. She needs time with her sister, Willa, and Bronywyn—for whatever reason that is. And when we don't know how much time we have left, any normal nights are a gift.

"I think I'll go out with Elijah and Jack then. Maybe hit up Tarnley's pub and see where the night takes us."

"It had damn well better bring you back here."

I stretch my arms back and fold them behind my head. "You never really know."

"You are an asshole, you know that?"

"I do. It's something I'm reminded of almost daily." Gripping her hips, I flip her over onto her back. Having her in my arms is a hell of a lot more than I ever thought I'd deserve. Fuck, it *is* more than I deserved, and yet here she is.

As much as I hate that we wasted so much fucking time before, I'm more than grateful for the moments we get now.

Leaning down, I press my lips to her ear,

enjoying the sharp intake of breath. "When you get back, I'm going to peel this dress off of you, bend you over this bed, and fuck you until neither of us can walk."

She moans softly as I run my hand up her thigh and beneath the skirt of her dress to cup her ass.

"So fucking sexy."

"You're driving me wild."

"I just want you to remember what you're coming back to."

"There's no world in which I could forget you, Cole."

I take her mouth and hold her tightly against my body, letting her feel everything through the kiss. Delaney is my entire fucking world, and when she's not with me, it's as though a piece of me is missing.

The last thing I want to do is smother her, but letting her walk out tonight feels like a huge mistake.

A knock on the door has me pulling back, but Delaney remains where she is for the breath of a moment, her eyes fluttering open and meeting mine.

"I know you're in there!" Rainey calls out. I sit up and pull Delaney with me, giving her a moment to tug her dress back down before I open the apartment door.

Based on Elijah's glare, I can see he's not overly thrilled with this outing either. And I can see why; both Rainey and Delaney are dressed to catch attention.

"Call me if I need to kill anyone," I say as she and Rainey head for the front.

"Me, too!" Elijah calls after them.

Delaney tosses a wink over her shoulder and heads outside to the massive limousine waiting for them.

"Tell me you're as uncomfortable about this as I am," Elijah groans.

"Absolutely. But I'm pretty sure they'll relieve us of our balls if we follow."

"You're probably right. I'm headed to Tarnley's in a bit if you're interested."

"I'll meet you there. Want to get a quick work out in."

"Sounds good, mate." Elijah heads outside, shutting the door on his way out, and I turn back toward the apartment to get changed.

After pulling on some basketball shorts and tennis shoes, I head out into the main part of the gym—straight for the heavy bag in the corner. The amount of steam building up in me, the rage at our current situation—shit, it takes everything I have to keep my wolf at bay.

He wants blood, and I sure as fuck can't blame him. Because I want it, too.

Quickly, I wrap my knuckles and take my stance. My fist impacts with the bag, sending it swinging backward. I continue slamming my knuckles into it, hit after hit, then spin and land a kick to the side.

In my mind, the bag stands for every obstacle in our way—every enemy—every moment we were apart when Lucy took her.

Minutes pass in a blur as I let out all of my anger. One final hit, and the bag explodes, sending sand falling onto the floor and coating my shoes.

"Son of a bitch."

"That really wasn't nice, Cole. What did that bag ever do to you?"

My back stiffens as I turn to face Lucy, who's seated in the corner. "What the fuck are you doing here?"

"Relax, wolf. I came to have a little chat with you." She stands on heels that put her close to my six-four and strolls across the gym, her fingers running over all of the pictures of Delaney and Rainey hanging on the walls. "How sad is it that such sweet sisters have faced so much turmoil."

"What the fuck do you want?" I ask again, my body shaking with the urge to shift right here and rip her throat out. Which, I would do if I thought I stood a chance at succeeding. I'm pretty fucking sure—even as much of a hit it is to my pride to admit it—that she would see it coming and evade.

"There's a way to keep your sweet mate from feeling any more pain, Cole. No more misery for her. The two of you can live in peace for the rest of your pathetic lives."

"Are you going to concede? We accept."

She barks out a laugh. "I genuinely like you, wolf. In another life..." She peruses me in a way that makes my skin crawl.

"Not a fucking chance."

"Tell me, have you all found the lines yet?"

"Why the fuck would I volunteer that information?"

She grins. "That's a no then. No worries, I'm closing in on them, and when I do, there will be no reason for me to let your mate stroll free anymore."

"Oh, is that what you're doing? *Letting* her live free?"

"I'm giving her time to experience life before I bleed her dry and use her blood to open the lines, yes."

A snarl leaves my lips. "You'd better come up with a new plan because there's no way in hell I'm letting you anywhere near her."

"I've proven to you that I can take out your fae, that your biggest tool against me is no longer relevant." She grins at me. "If I want her dead, wolf, there is no way you can stop me." She sounds almost amused by my threat, which only pisses me off even more.

My fangs slide down, the restraints on my body beginning to erode away.

"Of course, it doesn't have to go that way." She heads toward the water cooler, gets herself a paper cup, and fills it with water. Turning back to me, she rests an elbow on the top of the five-gallon water jug. "I could be persuaded to leave her alive when I'm done —if my demands are met."

"And what demands would that be?"

"Naturally, I want the ley lines opened. That power belongs to me. I want the fae to leave Billings—hell, I want you all out of my city."

"And the humans? What of them?"

"They would continue going about their lives, not knowing anything else was going on. At least, those who managed to survive the onslaught of super-naturals."

I shake my head angrily. "I won't stand for the deaths of innocents. Neither will Delaney."

"Well, it's their lives or yours, pet. There really aren't any other options."

"You're forgetting one massive one. You know, the one where we fucking kill you."

She arches an eyebrow, regarding me with complete and total amusement. "You are such a fun little thing. Perhaps I'll keep you once Delaney is dead."

I growl and lunge for her. She's gone in the blink of an eye, reappearing a few yards away.

"My patience is wearing thin, wolf. Not too long from now, I will find those lines, and when I do, I'm coming for Delaney. Your best chance of keeping your mate is to convince her to help me open the lines then get the hell out of my city." With that, she's gone, leaving me standing alone in the gym.

I rush toward the bedroom and grab my phone, ready to call Delaney and warn her. But before I dial, I stop. She can have tonight. This one, normal night out with her sister. Tomorrow, we can deal with the bull shit.

———

Tarnley's pub is fairly busy tonight, tables packed with shifters and vampires alike, all keeping to their own factions. Meanwhile, I'm crossing the room to join two hunters. Elijah and Jack glance up at me as I slide in beside the ex-vampire.

"We were just discussing the shit storm we've found ourselves in," Jack says dryly. The hunter and I have come a long way since nearly killing each other. I find him much less irritating than before. Which is probably a damn good thing since he's one of Delaney's closest friends.

I try not to think too hard about the fact that they used to see each other.

"I can one-up that. Lucy paid me a little visit."

"When?"

"About an hour ago. Popped up and promised to leave Delaney alive after she's done using her as long as we all agree to help her open the lines and then disappear and leave her city."

"Her city?" Jack scoffs. "Witch has an ego the size of this continent, that's for damn sure."

"She honestly believes that we would do that?" Elijah questions.

"Apparently. She can dematerialize like a fae, has the powers of a witch, she's a pretty damn formidable opponent. That's for fucking sure."

"Del will never go for that."

"I know." I glare at Jack, who tosses his hands up.

"I didn't mean anything by it."

"I know you didn't." I let out a long sigh and pinch the bridge of my nose. "I can't lose her." I'm not particularly close with Elijah or Jack, but somehow, voicing my fear, having a chance to air it out with two people who understand, it's helpful in terms of muting the war inside of me.

"You won't," Jack promises.

Elijah is smart enough to remain silent. Both men know as good as I do how unlikely it is Delaney will walk away from this. Not when her blood is what can open the most powerful hot spot in the country.

"We may all die," Elijah finally says. "There's no guarantee that any of us walk away from this. All we can do is fight our hardest and hope for the best."

"That's motivating," Jack retorts.

"It's the truth," I offer. "We all know it. Denying it won't do anything but set us up for failure."

"Well, excuse the fuck out of me for trying to be glass-half-full-guy."

"That's a shitty superhero name," Elijah jokes.

"That would be Rainey's influence, I'm guessing?" Jack asks with a laugh.

"We've been watching a shit ton of movies lately. So, yeah, I'd say so."

"Well, while shittiest superhero award might be in my future, I'd still rather stay fucking positive. Which is a difficult stance when the entire world is working against you."

Jack and Elijah break off into a conversation, and I let my mind wander back to all the time Delaney trained on pack lands. She's strong; that much has always been apparent. Resilient, sure. But is she strong enough? Resilient enough to beat Lucy?

Or is it far more likely this is one fight we won't be walking away from?

CHAPTER TWENTY-SIX

DELANEY

Music thunders through the speakers in Eira's club, the bass making my heart feel as though it's hammering against my chest.

I move along to the music with Willa, Bronywyn, and Rainey all dancing around me. Tonight has been therapeutic, completely and totally amazing.

I can't even remember the last time I went out dancing. Shit, I'm pretty sure it was for Rainey's twenty-first birthday.

"I'm getting hungry!" Willa calls out over the music. Bronywyn and Rainey nod in agreement, so we shove through the dancers and head for the private dining section of Eira's club. We approach the hostess stand and are greeted by a smiling woman bearing a large feather tattoo on her forearm.

"How many?"

"Four," Rainey replies.

"Right this way, please." She guides us through the nearly empty dining hall toward a back booth, finally stepping aside so we can all slide in."

"Your server will be right with you."

"Thank you."

The woman bows her head and turns away as we open our menus.

"This has been a wonderful evening," Bronywyn says. "Thanks for inviting me."

"We're so glad you came." Willa smiles at her.

It's damn near impossible not to like Josiah's daughter. She's one of the kindest people I think I've ever met.

"Well, well, well, aren't you ladies a lovely sight on this fine evening?"

I glance up as Fearghas strolls over, wearing a full suit. "Are you okay?"

Moss green eyes meet mine before he slides onto the oversized bench seat beside me. "Why wouldn't I be?"

"You nearly had your shoulder separated from your body the other night. Then had a dark witch fuck with your brain." Rainey's crass response earns a grin from the fae.

"Both problematic evenings, but I'm better now."

"Problematic? Lucy threatened to rip your shoulder off."

"Which didn't happen." He claps his hands together. "What are you guys out doing tonight?"

"It's girls' night out," Bronywyn tells him.

"Ah, that sounds fun! I'll get out of your way. Anyone gives you any trouble, I'm just over there."

"Lurking here again, I see."

He grins at me. "If I'm not with you or searching for those damn lines, you can damn well bet I'm here. I told you. Long game." With a wink, he disappears and reappears at his table across the restaurant. The fae raises his glass in a cheer then turns his attention to the rest of the room.

"How often is he here?" Bronywyn questions.

"He practically lives here. He's got it bad for Eira."

Bronywyn snorts. "She's not overly open to relationships from what I know."

"She cares for him, too," I say as I see her walk out from an office and head straight for the fae, a smile on her face. "They're both just running scared."

"Can't blame them at this point. Having more to lose, it's terrifying."

I get what Bronywyn's saying. When it was just my life on the line, decisions were a hell of a lot easier. But now that I have Cole, that Rainey is wrapped up in all of this, too, the women at this table as well, it's just a lot.

The stakes are higher than they've ever been, and the cost is so much more than I can bear to pay.

"Hey." Rainey nudges me. "Get out of your head. This is supposed to be a fun night. No shop talk."

I snort. "It's hardly shop talk when we're discussing what could be the end of the world as we know it."

"Fair point, but we deserve tonight." Rainey wraps an arm around my shoulders, and I lean into her.

"Got it. No shop talk."

"Okay," Willa says, leaning across the table. "I know what Rainey literally just said, but how about you kicking the ever-loving shit out of Bestiny?"

A smile stretches across my face. "That felt really good."

"It's about damn time. I can't stand her. I told dad when he said they could come out that it was a mistake. There's just something off about her, something that doesn't quite mesh with the persona she put off at first."

"She's gone now, right?" Bronywyn questions.

"Technically, no. She's still on pack lands, but she's in holding until Delaney deals out the execution."

Bronywyn and Rainey both whirl on me. "*You're* going to execute her?" Rainey exclaims, and I nod.

"Seemed fitting since it was me she tried to kill and Cole she nearly did."

"Execution...that's out of your wheelhouse," Bronywyn adds.

"I don't think it is. Not this time." I feel no guilt at what I am going to do, not after Willa told me they know it was her who lured Cole into that pit.

"When are you supposed to do it?" Even my sister looks uncomfortable with the idea. And she has a tendency to be even more ruthless than I ever was.

"The elders have to come up with a date. The pack votes, but it's them who work with my father on the final say," Willa tells us moments before her eyes flash black. "I wish I had gotten there sooner. Then, the bitch wouldn't have had the chance to nearly take bites out of you and Jack."

"I wish I'd just killed her then," I admit.

"Well, I just can't believe she had the balls to come after you like that," Rainey says with a shake of her head. "Fucking moron."

"She had backup," I explain. "My guess is that she didn't think I was going to fight back."

"I'm surprised she got a hit on you at all. With your power, you could have taken her out in an instant."

"I didn't even really use it. I wanted her to hit me so I had the chance to slam my fist into her face."

"What I don't get is why didn't they all shift?"

"A few of them did," I tell Rainey. "But I'm not

entirely sure. She's had it out for me ever since we met."

"Because she wants in Cole's pants again." Willa shakes her head. "And I heard what she said to you, by the way. Fuck her."

"What did she say?" both Bronywyn and Rainey ask at the same time.

"She alluded to the fact that Cole is sleeping with someone who doesn't look like me, and that they were together while she was in the body she was born into."

"Fucking cunt."

"Rainey!"

"What? I call it like I see it, and she is a cunt. A soon to be dead cunt."

Chuckling, I shake my head. "You're not wrong. But I made sure to remind her that the only reason he slept with her, to begin with, was because I was dead and he was trying to get over me."

"Good for you. I would love the chance to kick her ass, too," Rainey tells Willa. "You know, if you accidentally leave the door unlocked while passing by, with me walking behind you."

Willa laughs. "Noted."

"Anyone else realize just how dark life has gotten when we're sitting around on a girls' night, casually discussing an execution?"

"I'd say, at this point, an execution is a hell of a lot

easier to discuss than the impending potential supernatural apocalypse," Rainey replies.

Before any of us can respond, a man wearing a black button-down and black slacks comes to stand at our table. He's young, maybe early twenties, though there really is no telling when it comes to supernaturals. "Hello, ladies. What can I get you all tonight?"

All eyes turn to me. *Guess I'll go first.* "I'll take a water and a filet—medium rare—with mashed potatoes."

"You've got it."

He looks from me to the others, and as they rattle off their orders, I reach into my clutch and withdraw my phone. Cole's name is sitting on the home screen, so with a smile, I unlock it and read his text.

Life is so boring without you around. Listening to Elijah and Jack argue over superheroes.

I grin as I read his text again before replying: *That sounds like fun. We just ordered dinner. Then, we're headed back onto the dance floor. Fearghas is playing babysitter even though we asked him not to.*

After hitting send, I wait a beat to see if he's going to reply. When I see the little bubble pop up telling me he's replying, my heart does a stupid somersault.

Not fair! Why does the fae get to be there and I can't?

The fae is sitting in his own booth on the other side of the dining hall. He was already here when we arrived. He's being Eira's stalker again tonight.

Creepy. I'm still pissed that he gets to be there, and I'm stuck here.

I'll be home soon.

Can't wait. If you beat me there, leave the dress on.

I shove my phone back into my pocket and lift my head to meet three pairs of amused eyes. "What? What did I do?"

"You get this stupid grin on your face whenever you're talking to Cole." Rainey demonstrates what I can only describe as a lovesick puppy.

"I do not look like that."

Bronywyn nods. "I'm afraid you do."

Willa throws her head back and laughs, and just like that, girls' night is back on.

———

Exhausted, and up well past my bedtime, I wave at the limo as it pulls away from the front of the gym. I'm still smiling, even as I turn around to open the door. But before my hand reaches the handle, it's flung open, and I'm pulled inside, then slammed back against it as Cole's mouth devours my own.

I drop my clutch, sliding my hands up his arms and gripping onto his biceps as he pins me with his body.

After a few moments, he pulls back, both of us

breathless from the best fucking kiss of my life. "What was that for?"

"I missed you."

"I should go out more often."

He pulls back. "No, you really shouldn't."

Something in his tone has me worried. "What's wrong? Did something happen?"

Cole forces a smile. "Everything's fine." He bends over and picks up my clutch, then reaches for my hand. "You have a fun night?"

"I did. Are you sure everything's okay?'

"It was a long night." He opens the door to the apartment and steps aside so I can come through.

"Cole, what happened?"

After shutting the door behind me, he sighs and runs both hands over his face. "Lucy came to see me after you left."

All the blood drains from my face moments before my blood begins to pound. "What do you mean? Are you okay? Did she hurt you?"

"She came to offer us a deal."

I toss my clutch onto the bed and cross my arms. "What kind of deal?"

"The kind where she lets us all walk away from Billings after she gets what she wants out of the ley lines."

"Are you kidding me? She thinks we're going to help her?"

"She said that if you help her open the lines and we all leave—Fearghas included—she'll let us go."

"That manipulative bitch!" I begin to pace, running through all of the different reasons as to why we can't trust a single thing that comes out of her mouth.

"I know you won't take it," Cole says softly. "But I'd be lying if I pretended that there wasn't a part of me that wanted you to."

"We can't leave the city defenseless like that. And, not to mention, the rest of the world if she gets enough power. Lucy won't just stop here, Cole. She'll take on the entire supernatural world. And if she does that— the rest of the world is screwed right along with us."

"I know that." He reaches for my hands, and I accept, letting him guide me to the bed beside him. "A world without you is not something I ever want to experience again. And I know that's selfish, that thousands of lives—if not more—will be destroyed if she wins. But you're the only one I care about. Can you understand that?"

I shift to face him. "I know that, Cole."

"The rest of the world can go to hell for all I care."

"That's not the type of person I am."

His face falls, though I imagine he knew it was coming. Cole knows me, probably better than anyone else does. Even Rainey. He knows that guarding the humans and keeping the supernaturals in check is what I live for.

"Then, I guess we need to make sure we win."

I kiss his cheek and stand. After starting to unzip my dress, I pause and face him again. "Can I ask you something?"

"Of course."

"Does it bother you that I don't look—you know —like me?"

Cole hesitates a brief moment. Then, he stands and crosses the floor to me. He reaches forward and cups my cheek. "Love looks not with the eyes but with the mind, and therefore is winged cupid painted blind."

What did I say about Shakespeare? I could melt right here, right now. Straight into a puddle at his feet.

"You are all I see, Delaney Astor. All I've ever seen. And no matter what you look like on the outside, the love I have for you will never fade. I swear it."

Tears fill my eyes. I hadn't realized just how much Bestiny's comment had bothered me. Not until Willa brought it up at dinner again tonight. The truth is I don't feel like I look different. When I look in the mirror now, I no longer see Jane. I see *me*. So, to know Cole is seeing me, too...it's important and feels like the final piece of my life falling back into place.

"I love you, too."

CHAPTER TWENTY-SEVEN

DELANEY

"You surviving back there, H.W.?" Fearghas calls over his shoulder as I step over yet another fallen tree.

"I'm fine." A little out of breath, but being out in the crisp, morning, Montana air is therapeutic, and a nice change from the scents of the city.

"What about you, wolf boy?"

Cole growls. His large, sandy wolf walks beside me, his head coming up to nearly my breast. He's massive and so incredibly beautiful. Reaching over, I run my fingers over his soft fur, and he casts a curious glance my way.

He'd insisted on shifting before we started walking, thinking he might be able to sense the lines easier that way. I smile then pull my hand back and face the

"You're moving awfully slow for a predator."

I roll my eyes. "Stop taunting him, Fearghas."

The fae grins over his shoulder then appears beside me. "Just trying to give him motivation for picking up the pace. We are racing against the witchy clock."

Cole drops his snout to the ground then looks back up, ears forward as we walk through the forests of Montana. According to Fearghas, he's already searched the area where the ley lines used to be and most of the surrounding area. This last part is kind of our last-ditch effort before moving to an entirely new place.

Birds chirp overhead, their happy songs giving me the chance to pretend we're on a nice nature walk and not searching for what could lead to the end of the world as we know it. Sun shining above, it's easy to pretend. Especially when Cole sidesteps closer, his fur brushing against my hand.

The backpack on my back is starting to weigh on me, so I shift it.

"Here." Fearghas grabs the handle and hauls it off my back, slinging it over a shoulder.

"Thanks." Rolling my own, I stretch.

"So what's the plan if we find the lines today?" Fearghas asks.

"We guard them until Bronywyn has a chance to

finish figuring out the fastest way to relieve me of my blood."

Cole growls.

"I agree, wolfman. It is a stupid plan."

"Will you two knock it off? Please. There's not many other options available to us."

"That's because you're impatient."

"I'm not impatient. I just don't like sitting around and waiting for the shit to hit the fan when there's something that can be done about it."

"Even if that something is potentially life-ending?"

"It's not going to be life-ending."

"You don't know that."

"We don't know that it will be."

"Then we can all agree that we shouldn't move forward with this plan until we know whether or not you're going to end up dead. I know you have a flawed perspective on the reaper, H.W., but typically when someone dies, they stay dead. You got lucky. I doubt you will a second time."

Cole snorts beside me, and I glare at him.

"What is this? Gang up on Delaney day?"

"Only when you're being a martyr."

"If it makes either of you feel better, I did ask Bronywyn to take on some of the power with me." As soon as I finish talking, I pick up the pace even as both men stop abruptly behind me.

So far, Bronywyn is the only one I've told of my plan to have her carry some of the burden. Not because I was purposely keeping it from anyone but because I wanted to give the other witch enough time to consider my proposal. But I woke up this morning to a text from her, bearing a thumbs up and a *let's do this*.

Fearghas appears in front of me, forcing me to stop. "Wait a fucking minute. You asked Bronywyn to help you open the lines?"

"I did."

He glares at me. "You do realize that power can corrupt, right? And she's not the most levelheaded of our merry band of misfits."

"Bronywyn is a good person, Fearghas. And if she can help me channel the power—potentially saving my life, by the way—then why shouldn't we try?"

"Because the last witches who opened these lines were all killed. And let's not forget the greedy bitches who warded the damn things up in the first place. They all went crazy, and I murdered them. You know, in case you forgot that I'm not just a pretty face."

"You didn't like me taking in the power alone, so I solved that problem. Now, I'm not."

"I didn't say run off and find another sacrificial lamb for the slaughter," he snaps.

Bones crack behind me, so I turn to see Cole glaring at me, completely naked, arms folded across his inked chest. "Why didn't you tell me you asked her?"

"I wanted to give her the chance to say yes or no before I told anyone."

Cole's hazel eyes narrow further, his muscles tense. He's pissed. I get it. We promised no more secrets, but this one had less to do with me and more to do with Bronywyn. The last thing I wanted was for them to pressure her into agreeing.

Though, now I see that wouldn't have been an issue.

"You should have told me."

"I know."

Cole shifts his gaze from me to Fearghas. "Could it work?"

I turn, but Fearghas's back is to me. "I'm not talking to you until your dick has been put away." He starts to walk, but Cole clears his throat.

"You're going the wrong way."

I turn toward him, eyes wide. "You found them?"

Cole nods.

Fearghas pops up beside him. "Well, where the bloody hell are they?"

"Now my dick being out doesn't matter?"

"Not interested in spending any more time talking about your cock, wolf. Where are the damn lines?"

Cole chuckles. "This way." Shifting back in a blur

of skin and fur, he heads off to the left, paws padding softly on the ground.

Fearghas and I follow silently behind until Cole comes to stop beside a small, grass-covered mound. Cole shifts back and holds out a hand for the backpack on Fearghas's shoulder. After plopping it onto a boulder, he reaches in and withdraws a pair of sweats and tennis shoes, slips them on, and turns to face us.

Cocking his head to the side, he studies us. "Can you feel it?"

Fearghas nods.

I close my eyes and try to sense whatever it is he's talking about. Even a subtle shift in the air, but there's nothing. "Feel what?"

"You can't sense the energy?"

I shake my head.

"Probably because of the wards," Fearghas replies. "I guess we're extending our adventure underground. Think you can conjure us up some light?"

"I can try."

"Great. Let's go."

He moves forward and shoves some vines out of the way to display an entrance to a cavern. It's pitch-black inside, and I swallow hard. Damn, I hate dark, small spaces. Cole reaches out and interlinks his fingers with mine, the touch calming my frayed nerves as we start walking toward Fearghas.

I duck my head and climb inside, close my eyes,

and take a deep breath, picturing exactly what I want my magic to do. I can all but see the tiny lights floating above my palm as my power drifts to the surface, buzzing intensifying with each passing heartbeat.

When I open my eyes, I'm nearly as surprised as Cole and Fearghas to see the lights floating in front of us. Tiny, green, fairy lights that bob and weave just above our heads illuminate the cavern enough that we can see a few yards ahead of us.

"Way to go, H.W."

"Thanks."

We start walking deeper into the shadows. The tunnel weaves around, turning a corner, then another, leading us deeper and deeper into the ground.

"Were these underground before?"

"No. But as I said, they move. Could just be that they've shifted deeper into the earth after all these years."

"How do we know that we've foun—" I can't even finish the sentence when a current so strong slams into me that it knocks me backward and to the ground. What feels like hundreds of bricks on my chest weighs me down, making it impossible to move and damn difficult to even breathe.

"Delaney!" Cole drops beside me, but I can barely hear him over the roaring in my ears.

My magic is screaming inside of me, electricity

buzzing along my skin. But I'm not afraid. No, I feel strong, liberated.

I've *never* felt this powerful. The weight dissipates, and I suck in a breath as I shove past Cole and to my feet. He yells my name, but I hear nothing but the thundering of drums. Feel nothing but the current, the pull, the need I have to get to the end of the tunnel.

Because if I can get there, I can win.

I start to run, pumping my arms as fast as they'll go, ignoring the voices behind me.

Fearghas appears in front of me, and I slam into him, full-speed, knocking us both to the ground. Cole grips my arms and yanks me backward, away from the power.

"No. Let me go. It's just ahead."

"Del! Stop!"

I stop moving and turn to him. His eyes wide, he's regarding me with fear. "What?"'

"Look at yourself."

I glance down at my hands and nearly jump out of my own skin. They're glowing green with power snapping around my fingers and climbing up my forearms. But even as shocking as that sight is, I know I have to continue. "I can feel it, Cole. It's calling to me."

"Of fucking course it is. It wants to be used. That's what makes it so fucking dangerous." I whirl as Fearghas pushes to his feet. His chest where I made contact is singed, his skin smoking.

"Oh my God, Fearhgas, I'm so sorry."

"I've had worse."

"What the hell happened?"

"This is a hotspot. The lines are close enough they're fucking with you. We need to get out of here."

"What? Why? We finally found them."

"Yes, and now we know where they are and that we can guard them. You need to leave until you're ready for whatever the hell it is you think you're going to do. Opening them now will kill you for sure."

He reaches forward and takes my hand then places a hand on Cole's shoulder. Before I can argue, we're standing in the main part of my gym.

"I'll take the first shift." Fearghas disappears, and I suck in a breath, feeling my magic receding like the ocean after a tide.

"You okay?"

I glance up at Cole. "That was intense." The smile on my face spreads as I remember the way it felt to have that much power at my fingertips. "I get why she wants them, Cole. The power, the complete and absolute strength, it was intoxicating."

He regards me with wariness, unlike anything I've seen. "Maybe it's best we hold off then."

"What do you mean?"

"You lost control in there, Delaney. Shit, you knocked Fearghas clean out. Not that I haven't ever wanted to do that, but you get the point. That's a lot of power you're dealing with. What if when you open it, you're not the same?"

Which is something I hadn't considered. I'd been so caught up in the power either killing me or not, I hadn't put any thought into the damage it could do if it didn't kill me. "Do you think it might?"

"Before today, I would have said no. But your one goal was to get to it, and you didn't give two shits who you blew past to get there."

"I stopped, though, when you touched me."

"You did."

"That has to mean something."

"I'm sure it does. You jolted me pretty fucking good, too." He shows me his palm.

"Cole," I whisper as I walk toward him. His shifter blood is already healing the burn, but I singed nearly all the skin off his left hand when he'd grabbed me. What if he'd tried to tackle me like I did Fearghas? Would I have killed him?

"I'm fine now. But you need to make sure you're ready for all possible consequences of this plan. Because I don't believe it's going to go one hundred percent smooth."

"Things rarely do for us."

He snorts. "That's the truth."

"I'm sorry I burned you."

"Wasn't your fault." He glances up at the clock on

the wall. "I need to go meet Josiah. Are you going to be okay?"

"Yeah. I'm going to go head over to the precinct and take Rainey lunch."

Cole reaches for me, and I go to him, wrapping my arms around his waist and pressing my ear to his heart. He kisses the top of my head and gently strokes my back. "Please, don't keep shit from me. I promise not to go off and interfere. I just don't like to be kept in the dark."

Probably because I kept you in the dark about the voices and then took off and got myself killed. "Understandable, and I promise. As long as you continue to do the same."

"Deal." He kisses the top of my head one last time then pulls back and heads for the apartment door.

"What's the meeting about today?"

"Not entirely sure. He said he wants to meet before the elders give the execution a date."

"Do you think they'll change their minds?"

Cole strips off his shirt and tosses it into the laundry bin. "No. The elders almost always side with the pack."

"Do you think they will this time?"

"Not after she and her friends attacked you and Jack without provocation. I'm sure there will be a few, but the majority will rule to have her put to death; I can almost guarantee it."

"I know I volunteered to do it, and I stand by that. But it sucks that I feel mildly bad for her."

Cole turns to me. "She tried to kill you."

"Because she's in love with you."

"That doesn't make it okay."

"I know it doesn't, but it still sucks. I mean, I know how amazing you are, so blaming someone else for loving you, too, seems a little fucked up."

"It has nothing to do with her feelings for me, and everything to do with the fact that they attacked you, Del. I won't stand for that, and neither will anyone else. She is responsible for her actions."

"I know that. But if they give you the choice between execution and exile, please push for exile."

He purses his lips together a moment but finally nods. "But if she comes for you again..."

"She gets put down. I know. I worry that the pack only voted for that because they were afraid of what Josiah would say. And now that I've had time to think, I believe that if we take the stance of exile, the rest of the pack will stop fearing me. I would like to go home at some point."

Cole smiles and steps toward me. "Home?"

"Your cabin is home to me," I admit. "I think it probably always has been."

"The pack doesn't hate you, Del. I can promise you that. They're just nervous about what's to come."

"Well, hopefully, one day soon, we can move back and start our life together."

"Yeah? What does our life look like?" He wraps an arm around my waist and tugs me toward him.

"Lots of sex."

"I like it so far."

"Maybe some kids at some point."

"Love it."

"And happiness." I meet his eyes, hoping he can see the truth of my words reflected in my gaze. "We're going to be so happy one day. You'll see."

CHAPTER TWENTY-EIGHT

DELANEY

"Bronywyn?" I call out as I walk through the foyer.

"In my office!" she calls out. I head up the stairs, excited and terrified about what she found. After agreeing to help me open the lines, she's spent the last four days, researching her ass off, trying to find any way to test the link before we actually give it a go.

Here's hoping she found it because I'm well past ready to get on with a life not involving Lucy. Any day now, we're a go. We have the lines in sight with Cole watching over them right now.

We could literally leave here, head there, open the lines, and take Lucy out. Damn, wouldn't tomorrow's sunrise be even more magnificent if it rose on our

After reaching the landing, I walk the short way down to Bronywyn's office, not bothering to knock.

She's not seated behind her desk this time but standing by the window, book in hand. Blonde hair piled on her head, she's wearing black leggings and a cropped white t-shirt. Pale pink glasses frame her eyes, and she pushes them back up her nose when she looks up at me.

"We need to test our power." Slamming the book shut, she tosses it into an armchair off to the side.

"Test our power? What do you mean?"

"We need to make sure our magic is compatible. While there is no actual research on the ley lines themselves, there has been plenty done with witches sharing magic. It's possible, but if our magic is not compatible and we attempt to take on that much, it will kill us both."

Definitely would rather avoid that. "How do we test that?"

She bites down on her cheek, glances at her desk, and then looks back at me. "Take my hand, and close your eyes."

I do as I'm told.

"I need you to focus on me, on the pressure of my hand in yours. Picture threads of your magic spreading down through your body and extending into mine."

The buzzing grows louder as I call to it. I can feel it

slipping to the surface as though water was rushing over my skin.

"Anything?"

"No." Bronywyn pulls her hand away. "Though, that doesn't mean anything. All of the books I read suggested that only in times of high stress does it genuinely work. Otherwise, our power remains bound to us. Of course, if it's stolen—"

"Which is what will happen if Lucy has her way."

Bronywyn's mouth flattens into a tight line for a moment. "Let's hope it doesn't come to that."

"What do you propose we do?" My cell rings, so I reach into my back pocket to check the readout. "Hey, Rainey, what's up?"

"I'm seriously considering a massive supernatural slaughter," she growls into the phone. "We just found an empty vampire nest with six dead bodies, and now the media is all up our assholes."

"Fuck." I lift my gaze to Bronywyn, an idea taking form. "Maybe it's time we remind them they still have to obey The Accords."

"You saying that you're up for a hunt, sis?"

"That's exactly what I'm saying. Meet me at the gym at nine."

"See you then."

Ending the call, I shove my phone back into my pocket. "I have an idea as to how we can test whether or not we're compatible."

Bronywyn quirks an eyebrow. "I'm listening."

"You up for going hunting tonight?"

"Hunting?"

I nod. "Rainey's precinct got called to a building that was a vampire nest. They found half a dozen dead humans."

She mutters something under her breath and shakes her head angrily. "Dumb fuckers. They're going to get us all killed."

"You up for it?"

"I've never actually been hunting. All of us tend to stay to ourselves." She bites down on her bottom lip. "Plus, I can't very well be healing supernaturals if I'm the one killing them."

"We only take out the uncontrollable ones. Those who would rather break The Accords than follow the law and live peacefully. It's all about keeping the balance."

"You do realize you're not a hunter anymore, right?"

"Not by blood. But my soul still belongs to the hunters, and until I die, I plan to continue fighting to uphold the rules."

"The same laws you're breaking by being with Cole?"

I see her point, and I honestly can't blame her for being wary of joining on a hunt. But, I also know my soul, and hunting—keeping the city safe—makes me happy. "Being with Cole isn't killing innocent humans."

She sighs and nods. "I guess it will give us that high-adrenaline scenario where we can effectively test it out."

"Exactly." I smile. "Does that mean you're in?"

"It does." She crosses the room and slumps down in her seat. Right now she looks nothing like the centuries-old witch and more like an exhausted woman in her early twenties. It makes me sad to see her so down, and I'm pretty damn sure the vampire is to blame.

Truth be told, it makes me want to march down to the pub and kick his ass. Maybe a bit of head trauma will help him see straight.

I take a seat across from her. "You okay?"

"Honestly?" She laughs. "Not entirely sure at this point. Jane coming back into the picture then dying— then you coming back, Lucy following closely behind... it's all a bit much."

"I'm sorry."

"Don't be." Bronywyn shakes her head. "Honestly, I like you, Delaney. And I really, really didn't think I would."

Laughter bubbles up in my chest. "I feel the exact same way about you."

She smiles. "It's weird, right?"

"Definitely." We fall into a companionable silence

for a moment as she stares up at the ceiling tiles mounted above our heads. "Does any of this have to do with a certain vampire?"

"Tarnley is a whole different issue and, as I said before, one I honestly don't want to even consider visiting until all of this is over. Can you tell me what a hunt is like? What should I expect?"

"Well, we'll meet at the gym and head toward the nest to do some recon. Vampires tend not to move far if they have a successful hunting ground, so I'm guessing we'll find them nearby. After that, it's go in, eradicate, and dispose."

"Does Tarnley's company handle the disposal?"

I nod. "Though Rainey was doing it by hand, for a while."

She arches an eyebrow. "Really?"

I nod. "She didn't have a whole lot to do with this world until after I died, so Elijah filled in quite a few of the blanks after he came around."

"She makes him truly happy."

"They make each other happy," I counter.

"I'm glad. Elijah deserves someone like her. She can help keep his ass in line."

Chuckling, I nod. "She most definitely can."

Bronywyn is quiet a moment before nodding. "Hunt, eradicate, dispose. I can do this."

"You can. By the way, I've been meaning to ask

you; where the hell did you learn to fight hand-to-hand like that?"

Color blooms on her cheeks, making me grin. Bronywyn is *not* someone you'd expect to be embarrassed about anything. "A few decades ago, I had a fling with a human pit fighter. He taught me quite a bit, and I discovered that I loved the thrill of not just relying on my magic. It's come in handy a few times over the years."

"You're damn good."

"You're not bad yourself. Especially for someone who spent two years as a bird."

"I'm a bit rusty," I admit. "It's been a hell of a lot harder than I would have thought."

"What has?"

"Coming back from the dead. Becoming human again. I always felt human on the inside if that makes any sense, but going from bird to human so rapidly, it was a shock."

"I can imagine."

"Being able to fly was pretty damn handy though."

She sighs. "That's the one rumor about witches that I truly wish was true."

"Broomsticks?"

She nods.

"That would be pretty fucking epic."

CHAPTER TWENTY-NINE

DELANEY

The heat of Cole's body pressed against my back staves off the cool March air. He presses a kiss to the top of my head, and I tilt it over my shoulder to give him access to my mouth. To go from never being allowed to touch him to this has been even better than I ever could have imagined.

"You ready for tonight?" he asks me, his chest vibrating against my back as he speaks.

"I am. It will be an interesting experiment if anything."

"You two can do it."

Curious at his change in attitude when it comes to my plan, I pull away and turn to face him. He leans back against the front wall of my gym and crosses his arms. "What's with the change of heart?"

"I spent all day with those lines. They mess with your head. It was damn near impossible to keep my wolf under control."

"So the idea of Lucy getting her hands on them—"

"Not something I even want to consider. Besides." He reaches for me, and I lean against his chest, resting my head above his heart. "If you've taught me anything, it's that I should never underestimate an Astor."

"That's the damn truth."

Headlights shine over us as a car turns down the street and pulls into the spot right next to Cole's truck. Bronywyn climbs out wearing jeans, boots, and a black sweatshirt. Her hair is braided down her back, giving her a major "Buffy the Vampire Slayer" vibe.

I snort when I remember that Jane once referred to us all as the Scooby Gang.

"Hey," she greets as she hits the lock button on her sedan, and comes to stand beside us.

"You ready?"

She shrugs. "I will be."

"Then, let's get going." I take Cole's hand, and we start down the street. Bronywyn falls into step beside me.

"We're walking?"

"It's only about three blocks from here to where Rainey discovered the vamp nest," Cole tells her.

Even with us going hunting tonight, he's in a

pretty damn good mood. I smile up at him then avert my eyes forward after he winks at me.

It's absolutely ridiculous that the gesture sends my heart racing.

"Do we just bust in there? Or do we look around first?"

Bronywyn's nervous. I can feel it rolling off of her, so I offer a smile, hoping it will put her at ease. For me, this is just getting back to normal. Granted, with completely different abilities than before.

Even for Cole, this is business as usual, since his pack helped us out policing the outskirts of town.

"We'll check out the outside of the building first before going in. Typically, they leave something behind that we can use to identify which clan they belong to."

"You track all of the clans?"

"We used to. The system got a little rusty after I died, but Rainey knows the majority of them. Good news is that Elijah wiped out the Gale Clan last year, so that's one less we have to worry about."

"Though more could have risen," Cole offers.

"This is true." We move across the street and head down the final stretch before reaching the run-down house where the dead humans were discovered. The streetlights end here, the rest of them burnt out or shattered on purpose.

Honestly, it could be either. Even without realizing

it, most humans avoid supernaturals. A basic survival instinct, to be sure. Which is why most of them target intoxicated humans, those whose inhibitions are not quite all there.

Up ahead, I can see shadows moving. By count, I'm guessing it's Rainey, Elijah, Jack, and Willa. Another shape takes form beside Rainey, and she jumps before slamming a fist into him. *Fearghas.*

I grin. Sneaky bastard is going to get himself shot.

As we grow closer, I can hear the murmurings of conversation, idle chatter about the state of the bodies and who she thinks is responsible.

"I'm honestly not sure, which is concerning. Hey, guys."

"Hey. You don't have any idea which of the clans is responsible?"

"No. And by the body count, I'm a little worried the vampire council has something to do with it. The bodies we found weren't drug addicts. They were normal people, each snatched from their jobs or while they were out running errands."

"Fuck."

"Exactly."

Tarnley blurs past me, displacing the air, which brushes stray strands of my hair off my shoulder, and finally stops beside Bronywyn. "Happy to see I didn't miss anything."

My new friend doesn't even spare him a glance,

which is unusual for her since typically, she's demanding why he's following her around.

"Shall we?"

"Let's do it." Rainey shoves open the door, and we move inside with only her cell light to guide us.

Once we're away from potentially prying eyes, I do just as I did in the cavern the other day and open my palm so tiny, green lights can float up toward the ceiling and guide us.

"That's cool as shit!" Rainey exclaims as she shuts off her phone light and sticks it into her pocket.

"Thanks."

"Look out world! H.W. is getting the hang of things."

I grin at Fearghas as heat creeps into my cheeks.

The house carries the stench of death. It burns my nostrils and makes my stomach churn as I move farther into what I'm guessing was a living room at one point. Now, it's nothing but an empty shell, the floor host to massive gaping holes that lead beneath the house. I shiver. Freaking creepy for sure.

"I can't hear anything below the house," Rainey says. "And I checked it earlier when I was here. Nothing but dirt. Still, we need to keep our eyes open."

Everyone fans out with Rainey, Elijah, and Fearghas heading toward what I imagine used to be a kitchen, Jack and Willa heading up the creaky stairs, and Cole, Bronywyn, Tarnley, and me moving cautiously around the stairwell and toward the back of the house.

"I can still smell the dead," Cole says after lifting his nose to the air.

Forcing myself to tune the sound of my own racing heart out, I listen to the other sounds around me. Since my instincts are already impacted by the fact that I'm no longer a hunter, it's more important than ever that I pay attention. I could rely on Cole, but he may not always be at my side. There could very well be times when we'll be apart, and I need to be able to find a way around my current weakness.

It could very well mean life or death, and I have so much to live for now.

Something slams into the side of the house, shattering what remains of the right windows. We all spin toward the source of the noise.

"What the hell was that?" Jack calls down.

"I don't kn—" I'm cut off when a full series of slams and clinks surround the house, hitting on all sides. My body reacts causing magic to pool to the surface as we race back to the front of the house.

"Motherfucker!" Rainey exclaims.

We emerge in the living room to see her and Elijah slamming their shoulders into the front door. Fearghas is dematerializing to different parts of the house, his eyes wide with panic.

"I can't get out."

I scan the room, studying faces to make sure everyone we came in with is still here. "What happened?"

My sister's eyes meet mine in the dim light of the lights still hovering above. "Someone blocked us in here."

Warmth drains from my body, and a chill ices up my spine as the sound of heavy drums fills my ears.

Panic surges through me, and I spin in a circle, searching for an exit anywhere in the house. My lungs burn with the force of my breathing as I try to cling to even the smallest shred of hope. Hope that is very quickly extinguished when I realize that every single window and door is blocked with wood, locking us inside this carefully planned death trap.

I turn to Cole and see the same fear plastered on his face. "Get upstairs!" he roars, and we spin on our heels, the thundering of boots momentarily joining the death drums. Or rather, the skittering movement of the nightshades headed straight for us.

Cole moves to the side, and I join him, unwilling to leave him downstairs while he shifts. Willa's wolf comes to stand at the top of the stairs, dropping her head down and baring her teeth as Bronywyn, Tarnley, Elijah, and Rainey join her and Jack upstairs.

"Let's go, Cole!" I yell as I head up the stairs. He bounds up, joining me as we reach the top and rush into the room.

I'm nearly there, a step away, when the floor creaks and falls out from beneath me. The entire world slows in that moment as I tumble down. Someone grips me, their hand on mine the only thing keeping me from falling.

And when I glance down at the floor below, it's all I can do not to scream.

Black shimmies across the floor, a dark, death-filled sea, pouring in from the holes beneath us. Hundreds of nightshades, their only motive to kill us. We might as well be on a sinking ship.

The stairs fall down to the ground, killing a few dozen of them, and I glance up at Cole, who's clinging to me. Bronywyn is beside him, golden magic pouring from her as she rips the house apart, creating a temporary barrier between us.

Cole yanks me up and sets me on the floor beside him. Wasting no more time, we rush into the room and slam the door. Bronywyn waves her hand, and the closet doors are ripped from their hinges and pinned against the door, a barricade that won't last long.

"That's not going to hold them for long," she echoes my thoughts aloud and reaches for my hand. "I have an idea. Just like we practiced."

Nodding, I do what I can to shove my fear down and focus only on my magic. It pulsates on my skin, primed and ready, so I imagine it flowing down into

Bronywyn. I use my concern as rocket fuel, knowing I can't do this alone.

If we stay in this house, we'll die.

Cole.

Rainey.

Fearghas.

Elijah.

Jack.

Willa.

Bronywyn.

Tarnley.

All of us, dead, and no one will be left behind to protect the city from Lucy.

The house begins to shake beneath us.

When Bronywyn squeezes harder, I do the same and all but physically push the power out of my body.

"Whatever the hell you're doing, keep doing it!" Fearghas calls out.

I focus even harder, imagining my life without those I love.

Power slams into me, and I groan as sweat beads on my brow. My legs grow weak, and I fall forward to my knees.

"Stop!" Tarnley roars.

I open my eyes.

He blurs forward and catches Bronywyn as she starts to fall forward.

"What the hell happened?"

Fearghas groans, his face growing red as he's slammed backward into the wall. "Fearghas!" I push to my feet and rush toward him, but before I can reach him, the sheetrock behind him cracks, exploding outward, and he's flung from the house.

"No!" I scream.

"Del!"

I spin as Elijah, Jack, Willa, Tarnley, and Bronywyn are lifted and thrown from the house moments before the wood flies back up and seals off the house once more.

Cole—back in wolf form—rapidly shifts his gaze around the room, searching for something. Rainey breathes heavily, blade in hand. The door flies open, and nightshades pour into the room, stopping in the center and glaring at us with beady, red eyes.

"What in the actual fuck is going on?!" Rainey takes her fighting stance while Cole drops his nose and growls.

Lucy appears in front of us, a sick smile on her face. "Long time no see."

I barely have time to process the fact that not only is she controlling the nightshades, but they are also able to survive beneath my green fairy lights. Something that should have been impossible.

"I should have fucking known," I growl, sensing power snapping along my arms.

"You probably should have. But we all know you've

been a bit distracted." She pins Cole. "And who could blame you." After eyeing him for a moment, Lucy claps her hands together. "Now, my pets are going to eat one of the two people you care most about. And here's the fun part; you get to choose."

Adrenaline pulsates through my body right alongside my magic. I hold up both hands as green power snaps between them like electricity. "You're not getting either of them." I step forward, and the nightshades inch closer.

Lucy pinches the bridge of her nose. "Look, we both know you can't beat me. And if you don't choose, I'll let them." She leans forward and drops her voice to a whisper. "If that happens, you're going to lose both of them."

There's no time for hesitation, no time to contemplate the ramifications of my actions. So instead of doing either, I stomp my foot, sending magic down into the ground. The floor crumples beneath Lucy and her pets. She screams and disappears as they scratch against the wood while tumbling down to the ground.

I spin and slam my palm into the wall. It opens, and I reach behind me and grab Rainey. I throw her out and turn for Cole as Lucy reappears beside him.

She growls at me and raises her hands.

The wall closes again, leaving us trapped once more. Cole backs up in front of me.

"You really don't fucking know when to quit, do you?"

"Neither do you!" I wave my hand, but she raises hers and blocks the blow.

Lifting her own palms, she brings the wood floor up right along with the nightshades. "Enjoy your meal, pets."

With a wave, she disappears, and dozens of night-shades rush straight for us.

CHAPTER THIRTY

DELANEY

"Get behind me!" I yell.

Cole moves to stand beside me, and I throw up both hands. Magic pours from me, creating a temporary energy barrier between us and the enemy. I hold it up, my hands shaking as the power pours from me.

I know there's no way in hell I can hold it for long, but I also know I'd rather fucking die right here than let these bastards get to Cole. They claw at the barrier, their arachnid feet tearing through the webbing faster than my magic can generate it.

My vision swims, but I use it as motivation and grit my teeth against the exhaustion.

"Drop it," Cole orders.

I glance over to see he's shifted back to human

"Not a fucking chance," I growl. Warm liquid drips from my nose, falling to the ground at my feet.

"You're going to kill yourself if you hold it."

"If I don't, they will kill you." My voice breaks beneath the weight of my fear. I can see it now, them tearing him apart all because I wasn't fast enough—strong enough—to save them both.

He reaches up and grips my wrist. "We can fight, Del. Drop the barrier and open the wall back up."

"I can't move that fast."

"Yes, you can. Trust yourself. I do."

I shake my head as my knees begin to shake. The weight of holding the power steady starts to bring me down, but still, I don't give up.

"If you hold it much longer, you won't have the strength to re-open the wall."

I glance back at him and nod. "Move."

He moves to stand behind me. Holding the barrier with one hand, I move my other toward the wall. The strength it takes is beyond anything I've ever experienced, and my arm feels like fucking lead.

Shaking, I manage to move it then divert some of the energy. A pulsating of power. The wall cracks, so I back toward it.

"Come on, Cole!"

Something thuds to the ground. I spin and scream.

Cole's body lies on the floor, eyes wide open as a nightshade tears at his side. Blood sprays me when the creature turns its beady eyes on me. I slam it with every bit of power I have. The house shakes again, and the creatures scramble back.

Whether in fear or because they were ordered to, I'll never know.

All that fucking matters now is Cole. The house shifts back and forth, the walls crumbling around us as I fall to my knees, tears streaming down my cheeks.

"No, no, no, Cole." I reach for him, pulling him into my arms and closing my eyes as the world around us falls to the ground, nothing but a pile of rubble and dirt.

The roaring is deafening for a brief moment before everything becomes eerily silent. I open my eyes as the dust settles around us. Lucy appears in front of me. "How sad."

"You fucking bitch!" I raise my shaking hand, a bluff to be sure. I have nothing left in me. And based on her satisfied smile? She knows it.

"This really is all your fault."

I turn my head as someone screams my name. Fearghas beats against an invisible barrier, eyes wide with panic.

Rainey is beside him with the rest of my friends, trying to get through to me but held off by whatever power Lucy is wielding over us. The entire house is gone, but not even the chilly air can reach where we kneel at the center of the rubble.

"Cole could have saved himself."

I glance down as tears slip from his eyes. He's unable to move, barely able to breathe, the pain in his paralyzed state excruciating. There's no cure, human or supernatural, that can save him. No spell able to reach him now.

And all because of her.

"He could have saved you all, but it seems you're all too stupid to know a good deal when you see one. So here's my new proposition." She kneels in front of where I hold Cole against my chest. "I can save him."

"You're lying. Nightshade bites are terminal."

"They are unless you're the witch who created them in the first place." She lifts her wrist and runs a sharp fingernail over her vein. Red wells up against pale skin. "One drop of my blood in his system will neutralize the venom and allow his body to heal as though it were nothing but a dog bite."

Hope surges through me, and I know I'll do any damn thing she wants. "Then do it."

Her grin spreads because she knows she has me just where she wants me. "You haven't heard my price."

"I don't care what it is! I'll pay it. Just save him."

"You will open those lines for me, Delaney Astor. You will give me whatever blood of yours I need, and then you and lover boy here, along with your pathetic group of friends, will leave this city and never come back."

There's nothing to consider. No price is too high to pay. "Fine. Save him!"

She reaches down with her wrist and runs the blood along Cole's lips. He convulses, and his eyes roll back in his head.

"What did you do?"

"Give it a moment." As she holds her wrist in place for a moment longer, I see the change in Cole. He relaxes against me and chokes.

She pulls back, and I roll him to the side. "Cole? Cole are you okay?"

"It will take him a while. He was just nightshade chow." She reaches forward and places a hand over his wound. It knits together beneath her fingers, stopping the bleeding. "If you do not follow through with my deal, your boyfriend here will die."

"I understand."

"Do you? Because up to this point, you've been pretty damned stupid in thinking you stand a chance against me."

"I. Understand," I snap.

"Good. Still, just in case," she says with a grin and reaches for Cole. The next heartbeat, they're both gone. Scrambling to my feet, I feel my bones turn to ice as I spin in a circle searching for him.

Cold whips around me as the barrier falls. Fearghas appears beside me.

"Where is he?" I scream, still scouring the destruction.

"Delaney!" Fearghas roars my name. I stop moving and meet his wide eyes. "We need to go now."

"Not without Cole."

"He's not here, and if we don't leave, there won't be a way to get him back." He reaches for me, and I jump back, knowing that if he touches me, we'll be gone before I can object. I rush toward where I think the back was, hearing nightshade bodies crunching beneath my boots.

Sirens screech in the dead of night, and Fearghas appears in front of me. He drops a shoulder and rams me with it, lifting and tossing me over his shoulder as the darkness is replaced with the bright lights of my gym.

I scream. "You left him there!"

"He was already gone!" Fearghas roars back at me.

Red-faced, I glare at the fae. Never in my life have I been so fucking pissed at him. "You had no right."

"No right to what? Make sure you weren't arrested for taking down an entire house?"

I turn in a circle and stare up at the bruised, exhausted faces of my friends and family. Fearghas stumbles, and I shift my attention back to him, anger popping like a soap bubble when I take in the slump of his shoulders and the pale complexion of his face.

"What's wrong?"

"I'm fine," he growls, and backs away from me.

"No, you're not. What is it?"

"Fearghas popped around, catching everyone," Rainey tells me. "He's the only reason we're all still breathing."

Grief and anger at myself overwhelm me, and tears spill down my cheeks. "I'm so sorry," I tell him. "I just —" I trail off, my voice cracking.

"I get it. What the fuck happened in there?"

"She tried to make me choose between Rainey and Cole," I manage, shutting my eyes tightly against the grief. I crumble to the floor, falling to my knees and covering my face with both hands. "She was pissed that I got Rainey out, so she sent the nightshades after us. I thought I had them—" I sob, shoulders shaking. "One got around and got Cole. Lucy said she could heal him with her blood if I promised to help her with the lines."

"Motherfucker," Rainey curses.

Fearghas kneels in front of me. "Please, tell me you didn't make a deal with her, Del. Please, tell me that you told her to fuck off."

I meet his panicked eyes. "I couldn't let Cole die," I choke out. "I had no choice."

Fearghas's eyes harden, and he shakes his head before disappearing from view.

"I couldn't let him die," I choke out.

"I know." Rainey kneels in front of me. "We'll figure it out, I promise."

"What if he's already dead?" I ask her.

"He's not," she assures me. "But Lucy will be soon."

CHAPTER THIRTY-ONE
COLE

Pain.

Endless, excruciating agony ricochets through my body like a stray bullet. It feels as though every single nerve in my body is aflame, my blood a raging inferno coursing through my veins.

I can't scream.

Can't move.

But I can see her.

Delaney hovers above me, tears falling from her caramel eyes, and in them, I see my fate. There's no walking away from it this time. All that happiness she spoke of? It was nothing but an empty promise that neither of us recognized. Hell, maybe we both always knew it would end up with one of us dead.

At least it's me this time.

Copper drips into my mouth, the tang unfamiliar. I

know it's not mine, which begs the question: Who the hell is bleeding into my mouth?

The blood soothes the pain though, extinguishing the fire little by little until finally, I begin to be able to breathe without pain.

Without agony.

But even as I'm able to do that, Delaney's face is stolen from view. When I open my eyes again, it's no longer my mate I'm seeing but the sneer of my enemy.

"What—" I start to sit but fall backward, vision swimming.

"I'd really try not to move right now," she warns. She crosses the room and kneels, then runs a long finger down my bare chest.

What a fucking time to be naked, am I right?

"I have to say, wolf, I'm impressed by what you have going on."

I swallow hard as her finger drifts lower, running past my dick and down the inside of my thigh. I never thought I'd wish for clothes, but right now I'd do just about anything for something to cover myself.

My wish is granted when she tosses a pair of sweats onto my chest. "As soon as you can, get dressed."

I manage to sit up—barely—and yank the sweats on with shaking arms. My entire body feels like it did after the first time I shifted. Beyond exhausted and so fucking sore it hurts to blink.

As soon as I'm covered, I lean back against the table I woke up on. There won't be any fighting my way out of this—not yet, anyway. "Why the hell did you save me?"

Lucy leans back against the wall and crosses her arms. "Because I need Delaney to stop being a fool and do as she's told. You seem to be the best option for controlling her. Though, it must have stung that she chose Rainey over you."

Not even a little. "Rainey is her little sister. I wouldn't have expected anything else."

She snorts. "I would have chosen you for your dick alone." She winks and gestures to my groin. It makes my stomach churn.

"Why not leave me to die? If you really don't care, why not just kill me now?"

"Your time will come, wolf. And when it does, your demise will be so much sweeter." Pushing off the wall, she strolls over to me. "Do you want to know why?"

I don't reply, knowing that sadistic psychopaths like her thrive on fear. I'll be damned if I show even an ounce of it.

She trails a fingernail over my cheek, dragging down and across my throat. "It will be so sweet because it's going to come with a side helping of Delaney's despair. Seeing that look on her face? The fear, the realization that you're gone, and finally the grief right before she dies...it will be well worth the wait."

I swallow hard and press up against her touch. "You're not going to fucking touch her."

Lucy chuckles. "Always the hero. You should have been the alpha. You're a hell of a lot stronger than Josiah."

The way she says it, the tone in her voice, settles into my gut like a rock.

"Aren't you wondering how your alpha is doing these days?"

"Leave my pack alone."

"See. I would have. If they had left me alone. But your alpha thought he'd call me up and offer me a deal." She walks over to a door and yanks it open.

Josiah's body tumbles out, his face bloody and broken.

"No!" Agony pulsates through me as my heart thunders while I scramble forward toward him. His skin is pale, his eyes open, and I know that when I touch him, his body will be cold.

"It really was sad. He didn't beg for his life, just for yours and Delaney's. He loved her quite a bit. You, too."

"I will slaughter you for this," I growl. My wolf tries to escape, but the nightshade venom killed all of my energy.

"You are more than welcome to try. I do love a good fight."

She laughs and turns on her heel. "See you soon, Cole. We have so much fun ahead of us."

After pulling open another door, she steps outside and slams it behind her.

Tears burn my eyes, blurring my vision as I gather a man who was like a father to me into my arms. Josiah was everything to me growing up, a hero, a role model...and now that he's gone—"Fuck, Josiah, what did you do?"

I shouldn't be surprised that he tried to fix everything. He was a man who would have sacrificed everything for those he loved. And as it turns out, he did. I run my hands over his eyes, closing them for the last time as my heart shrivels within my chest.

My life.

My alpha.

My home.

My mate.

Lucy has stolen it all. And when the time comes, I will make sure to return the favor. Or die trying.

CHAPTER THIRTY-TWO
DELANEY

Around me, people speak. All discussing what transpired less than two hours ago.

But I can barely focus on drawing breath into my lungs.

I have no way of knowing whether Cole is alive or dead. She could have killed him the moment they disappeared. Of course, she also knows that if she does, I won't help her. Not without proof that Cole is alive.

"Delaney?"

"What?" I shake my head to clear it and glance up at my sister who's regarding me as though I may snap and kill everyone at any moment. Probably a smart move since my magic has been unreliable at best ever

Some moments, I can't feel it; others, it's snapping around me like live wires in a thunderstorm.

"We wanted to know how you want to move forward."

"We don't have much of a choice. I won't risk Cole."

"I don't want anything to happen to him, either," Bronywyn says softly. "But we also can't give Lucy what she wants."

"Why not?"

"Because she will destroy Billings and kill thousands of innocents."

"Let them fight their own war." Completely deflated, I stand and head for my room at the back of the gym.

"Delaney. You don't mean that."

I turn to Rainey. "Don't I? Have we not already given everything to keep the city safe? Fuck, Rainey, I *died*. Our parents, grandparents…they all died. And for what? So we could live to face another unbeatable foe while the rest of the city goes on living their happy, uncomplicated lives? When the hell do we get to be happy?"

She folds her arms. "Hunting used to make you happy."

"Yeah, well, shit changes when you're knocked down one too many times. I'm tired of being knocked down and being expected to brush it off and get back up.

"It's what we were born for," Rainey tells me. "We were born for this, Delaney."

"Let the pain in," Bronywyn finally says. "Use it to strengthen you, but rolling over now will do nothing but result in all of us dying. Cole included. You're a dumbass if you think Lucy will keep him alive when she's done with you."

And there's the pessimistic Bronywyn we all know and love. Still, she's right, and I hate it. "Then, what do you propose we do?"

The door flies open, and Z storms in, Willa and Jack beside him. The female shifter's cheeks are red and wet with tears.

"What happened?"

"Josiah is missing," Z tells us.

Panic strangles me. "What?" Josiah has been the closest thing I've had to a father since ours died. Not once, in the entire time I've known him, has he up and disappeared. "Since when?"

"Last night," Willa whispers.

"How the fuck did no one notice he was gone?" Rainey demands.

Z glares at her, his already heightened emotions running short. "He was supposed to be at the meeting tonight, to address the pack and let us know what the elders have decided, but he never showed. Believe it or not, Hunter, we aren't up each other's assholes all the time."

Rainey doesn't reply, but a muscle in her jaw ticks. Elijah presses a hand to her back, and I shift my gaze back to Z.

"Bestiny claims to know who took him, but she won't talk to anyone but Cole."

"Who's gone," I tell him.

"That's what Willa said. I'm here to give you the chance to try and get it out of her. If I do, and she doesn't talk, I'm likely to kill her regardless of what the fucking elders want."

"And you don't think I will?"

"I think you'll have more creative ways of getting the information out of her, but I'm hoping you won't need them."

"She tried to kill me less than a week ago."

"Yeah, but you two share a common goal."

"And what's that?"

"Neither of you want to see Cole dead. So if you can leverage that, convince her that telling us about Josiah will save Cole, she might cooperate," Rainey finishes. "Not a bad plan."

Z doesn't turn his attention away from me. "I'm asking you to do this for a man who would have done the same, and more, for you."

"Of course. It's not even a debate. I'll do anything for Josiah."

He nods and turns, and I know that's my cue to follow him out to his jeep.

"Del."

I turn to Rainey. She and Bronywyn watch me expectantly.

"Cole is not gone for good."

"I hope you're right."

———

The drive to pack lands passes in complete silence, something I'm grateful for as it gives me time to process everything that's happened in the last few hours. I stare down at my hands clenched together. They look completely normal, other than the dirt smeared over my skin.

Shouldn't they be bruised? Battered? Show any signs of a fight?

"Some scars are not visible."

I hadn't even realized I'd spoken out loud. "If they were, humans and supernaturals alike would be a hell of a lot kinder to each other."

"I disagree. I think they would use those scars to manipulate and control. It's not in our nature to be kind."

"Do you truly believe that?"

"It's easier to be dismissive than to be inclusive," he replies.

"Some would argue smiling is easier than a frown."

"Lies."

"But you're happy, aren't you? With Lauren? Kai?"

"Beyond happy," Z replies. "But that doesn't mean the darkness doesn't creep in when we're not together. I've seen a lot of blood, Delaney. Lost a lot of loved ones. I don't intend to lose two more."

"You think they're still alive." It's not a question, mainly because I'm afraid to know what his answer would be.

He takes a deep breath but doesn't reply as we pull up to the village.

We climb out, and I note that there are no pack members out and about. "Where is everyone?"

"Josiah being gone has fucked with everyone's heads. A lot of them bailed, and the others are holed up at home. This way." He leads me between two cabins and out to a small mound on the ground. On top of the mound are iron bars.

"She's down there?"

Z nods. "Bestiny, get your ass out here."

"Is Cole up there?" Her voice is just above an echo.

"No."

"Then fuck you."

"Open it."

Z glances over at me. "Those are iron bars to keep her from shifting."

"Which means I can't use my magic, I get it. I won't need to. Open it, please."

Z shrugs and reaches down to lift the bars. He sets them aside and gestures in. "I can lower you down."

"No need." Bending my knees slightly, I jump. The impact is hard on my knees, but not harder than I'd been prepared for. Bestiny cowers in the corner, her face covered in dirt.

"What the fuck are you doing here?"

I march across the space and wrap a hand around her throat, lifting her from the ground. Slamming her back causes some dirt to fall to the floor around us. "Who did you see?"

"I'm not telling you shit. I told him I would only talk to Cole."

"Cole is gone. Possibly dead."

Her eyes widen. "What the hell did you do?"

"The person who took Josiah, who was it?"

"Where is Cole?"

"Answer my fucking question, or I'll take you topside and start stripping the skin from your body."

"You wouldn't dare."

"Wouldn't I? My mate has been taken, my friend missing. I think you'll find there's very, very little I won't do at this point."

Her cheeks redden, but she taps her hand on my wrist, so I let her go. "I saw a witch, dark hair, walking through the grounds last night with Josiah. She and

Josiah argued. Then, something hit the ground, and that was it."

"What did she look like?"

"As I said, dark hair...that's all I got. It's tough to see anything down here."

I'd bet my left tit that it's Lucy. What reason she had to take the alpha, I have no damn clue. "Thanks." I turn to leave.

"Wait!"

"What?"

Her gaze shifts from me, to the wall, then back to me again as she folds both hands in front of her. "Let me help get Cole back."

I snort. "Are you kidding me? You tried to kill me the last time you were out there. You damn near killed him."

"I swear to be on my best behavior," she growls. "Please, let me help. Cole is—"

"*Mine.*" I all but growl the word and immediately recognize the realization on her face.

"I understand."

"And how the hell am I supposed to trust you? You opened a pit in the ground and nearly had him killed."

"No. I left the dead bird on your porch, but I had nothing to do with the spikes in the ground. Why the hell would I do that where anyone could fall and get hurt?"

"They found wolfsbane in your house."

"I swear the spikes weren't me. That was planted in my cabin to throw you all off who really did it. And look how fucking great that worked." She gestures to the pit around her, cheeks reddening. "My problem, witch, has always been with you. You brought the other supernaturals here, you led this pack to slaughter by simply existing on this property. But I would never, not in a million years, do anything that would harm Cole."

"You tried to kill me," I remind her, yet again.

"You are not him."

"No. But I'm his mate. Losing me would have tormented him."

Her jaw tightens. "I could have made him happy."

"And therein lies my issue. How do I know you won't try to kill me again?"

"I suppose you don't. You only have my word."

I stare at her, trying to read the room. She's been beaten; anyone can see that. Her loyalists are dead. Still, I can't risk her getting into the pack's head. Not now when Josiah is nowhere near them. "Unfortunately for you, it's not up to me."

"The offer stands should you change your mind."

"Noted." I head back toward the hole and glance up as Z tosses a rope down. Hand over hand, I climb out until I reach the top.

"Well?" he asks.

"Lucy has Josiah and Cole."

"Why the fuck would she take Josiah?"

"I have no clue. But I intend to find out." I march past him and head for the trees. "Fearghas!" I yell the moment I'm inside. I know he's nearby; I can feel his presence, his magic. "I know you're there."

"What the fuck do you want?" It's not a question.

I turn to face him. Instead of his normal suit, he's wearing dark jeans and a navy sweatshirt. "What is your problem?"

"You."

"Excuse me?"

"For the last few months, I've watched you come to terms with being alive again, with figuring out who you are and how you fit into things. I watched you pine over a shifter who denied you over and over again out of fear. Then, I watched you—for a brief moment —be happy. I'd hoped that by being happy, you'd figure out sacrificing everything is *not* always the answer."

"She has Cole, Fearghas. What would you do if it were Eira?"

"I'd come up with a fucking plan! Not just roll over and accept the terms to some bullshit deal we both know she's going to rescind on."

"I'm not trying to give up," I tell him. "I want to fight for what we have. I just needed time to come up with something."

"Could have fooled me."

"Can we talk, then?"

He glares at me and reaches out a hand. I take it, and we re-appear in Cole's cabin. "The wards will keep anyone from listening."

"Good. Take me to the precinct."

"Why?"

"There's someone there who might have some answers."

Not looking overwhelmingly convinced, he grabs my hand, and we appear in the alley directly behind the Billings Police Department. "Here's hoping he's here. Rainey told me he works late."

"And just who are we here to see?"

As luck would have it, Paloma walks out of the station at that exact time.

"Paloma!" I call out and jog out across the street.

She stops and turns around. "What is it?"

"Josiah has been taken."

"What? When? Who took him?"

"Lucy. Last night. She has Cole, too." The words are venom on my tongue, but I repeat the thought over and over again, knowing that in it lies the strength I need to keep going.

"What do you need me to do?"

"Walker Alan, is he in there?"

"No, he went home a few hours ago. Why?"

"He's a psychic."

"A psychic?" they both repeat at the same time.

"I thought they were all dead," Fearghas says.

"I didn't even know they existed. How do you know this?"

"He told me. Can you tell me where he lives?"

"I can take you there," she offers, then withdraws her keys, hitting the unlock button of a navy blue sedan.

"I can get us there faster. Think of the location," Fearghas orders as he places a hand on her shoulder and one on mine. The air around disappears and is replaced with warmth.

I open my eyes and see that we're standing in the living room of an apartment and one that is so poorly decorated I'd be willing to bet we're in the right place. Just the small space we're standing in has 'single man' stamped all over it.

A pipe squeaks as the shower is turned off and Walker steps out from the bathroom, completely naked.

"What the fuck!" he yells, and we all turn around.

"I'm sorry!" I call out.

"Captain?"

"Detective Alan," Paloma greets, awkwardly.

"You can all turn around now."

The three of us turn, and I breathe a sigh of relief when I see that the detective has wrapped a towel around his waist.

"What the hell are you doing in my apartment?"

"My mate's been taken," I choke out.

His eyes soften. "I'm sorry, but like I told you before—my power doesn't work on demand."

"Cole rescued your sister once. I'm asking you to help me save him."

CHAPTER THIRTY-THREE

DELANEY

"You're telling me that this witch—the direct descendant of the original—has your mate," he trails off, turning to Paloma, "And your alpha?"

"Yes."

"But you're human."

"A human mated to a shifter."

"Fuck. This is a lot." He sinks down onto the couch and places both hands on his chin. "Sorry, I've been out of touch in this world for a while now."

I can appreciate his need to process, but we're running out of time. Hell, we've already run out of time. "We need you to tell us if you see what's coming —a double-cross—so we can prepare."

His eyes meet mine. "I told you my power does not work like that. I get feelings, not pictures."

"Then give me feelings. It's at least something to work with."

With a sigh, he stands and crosses the floor to me, bare feet padding softly on the carpet. Swallowing hard, he holds out both palms. "Place your hands on mine."

I do as I'm told, already prepared for the jolt. This time, it's less like a shockwave and more like a thump against my skin. His hands are warm beneath mine, and he closes his eyes, giving me the opportunity to search his expressions.

His eyes tighten, mouth flattening into a rigid line. I turn to Fearghas for clarification, but he doesn't even look at me—neither does Paloma—as both their gazes are trained intently on Walker. Minutes pass, but they might as well have been hours for the panic scratching its way up my chest and into my throat.

Another jolt, and I'm thrown backward. Fearghas catches me while Walker stares my way, eyes glowing brightly. The brightness fades, and the detective shakes his head.

"What do you feel?"

He meets my gaze, and I know by the defeated expression on his face his news is not good. "I feel darkness, Delaney. Death and pain are coming for you."

"What the fuck does that mean?" Fearghas demands.

"I don't know. It could mean someone around you will die, or they already have. Or it could mean—" he trails off, but I see the remaining words written all over his face.

"Or it could mean I'm going to die."

"Yes."

"Well, she already died, so maybe that's what you're picking up on," Paloma offers.

"I sense what's coming," he says. "Not what's already happened." He turns back to me. "I'm sorry I couldn't give you better news."

"It's not your fault." I smile tightly at him, wishing this trip had brought me different news but unable to deny it told me something.

That we may not win.

"Thank you for trying."

"What's your next move?"

"I'm going to get Cole and Josiah back regardless of the cost."

"Even if it comes at your life?"

"Yes."

"Let me help." He stands and heads for the bedroom. "I need fifteen minutes, and I'll be ready to go."

"Walker—"

He turns to me. "You came to me for help, so let me help."

———

The night is still in Billings, a direct contrast to the emotions warring inside of me.

I could go to Lucy, plead with her to free Cole. But then, I would surely be trading my life for his. Something I would do without hesitation, but he would never forgive me.

I could go to her alone and try to trick her, but I've already proven that I don't have the power needed for that kind of fight.

And last but not least on my plans to double-cross the evil bitch, are the ley lines. We know where they are, so opening them is a possibility. We could go there now, open the lines, and then confess that we know exactly where they are and lure her into a trap.

That last one feels like it will have the highest chance of victory, but if they kill me—Cole and Josiah are as good as dead.

So, here I sit, once again between a rock and a hard place. Except, this time half of me is missing.

"Hey."

I don't glance over as Rainey climbs up onto the roof of our parents' home. One I haven't been back to since I paid the final mortgage payment with their life insurance. I know she's not been back either, the structure carrying more than a few painful memories for us.

"I thought I'd find you out here." She takes a seat on the roof just above what used to be my bedroom window. It was my safe place, my solitude, and I spent quite a few nights as a teenager sitting out here and staring at the stars, wishing I could be anything but what I was destined to be.

After all, what teenage girl wants to be a killer when they grow up?

"It seemed the most logical place to go."

Rainey reaches into her pocket and pulls out a bag of sour patch watermelon. After a moment, I take it and tear into the bag. I may technically be fifty-six years old, but it sure as hell doesn't feel like it. Especially not now.

Shouldn't a fifty-six-year-old know what to do in this situation? Shouldn't they have all the answers?

"Contemplating life or death?" Rainey questions around a mouthful of skittles.

"Always seems that way, doesn't it?"

"There are some good days tossed into the mix."

"Few and far between."

She nods silently beside me. "I wish I could promise you that everything's going to be okay. Dad used to be able to do that, right? Even when we had those goblins break into our house when I was seven and terrified of the dark, he'd convinced me that everything was going to be okay and made a game out of hiding."

I chuckle, remembering that night well. The damn bastards had been paid off by a rogue group of vampires to take my family out. They'd failed, as had every other attempt up until the night Lucy had our parents killed in that alley.

"I wish they were here now," Rainey says softly. "It's silly, right? I'm fucking thirty-seven and still wishing my mom and dad would come save the day."

At her words, two black ravens float down and land softly on the roofline.

Seeing them fills my heart with such joy and pain I can barely stand it.

"And here they are. Right?" she asks me, and I nod. "I don't suppose you guys have any words of wisdom, do you? Any 'this is how you're going to win'?"

The ravens stand still as statues.

"Didn't think so."

"I think they would tell us to go with our gut, to fight like it was our last, and to stand tall even as the world wants to cut us down."

"Of course they would. That was mom's pep talk before every day of school." Rainey snorts and bumps against me. "Still as true today as it was then, though."

"Truth."

She sighs. "Cole is going to survive this."

"He's not the only life on the line."

"I know. But I have to believe you guys didn't go

through all of this shit, waste all of this time, only for destiny to take him from you now."

I turn to her, eyebrow raised. "Since when do you believe in destiny?"

"Elijah's made me a softie."

I grin because it's true. "Walker says death is coming for me. Pain. That doesn't exactly elude to a happily ever after."

"Not true. Death has come for you before. So has pain. Neither of those is a world-ender. It could just mean that—as awful as it is for me to say this—a happily for now is not headed your way. But neither death nor pain mean it's over."

"You were less agitating as a pessimist."

She snorts. "Someone had to play the glass-half-full part since you've packed it in."

"Can you blame me?"

"No," she admits. "But I can promise you that shit always looks darkest right before the sun."

Swallowing hard, I glance over at the ravens, who are watching me intently. Then, I turn my attention to the stars. "I can't decide how I should play this. Do I open the lines? Risk death to take on the magic I'll need? Or do I follow her plan and avoid any double crosses she sends my way?"

"Or," Rainey says. "We go with plan E."

"And what's plan E?"

"Elijah has an idea that may actually work."

I turn fully toward her, and the two black ravens walk across the rooftop to perch beside us. A sliver of hope blooms in my chest as I nod. "Hit me with it."

CHAPTER THIRTY-FOUR
COLE

Pain radiates through my shoulder as I slam it into the door, yet again. I wince as I move backward and take a seat against the wall. My eyes travel around the room, resting on Josiah's body for what is probably the hundredth time. I don't know why, but I keep expecting him to sit up, to tell me he has a plan.

My chest tightens, and I rub the palm of my hand against my sternum, urging the panic to dissipate.

I've been in tight spots before. Such is the nature of being a pack enforcer, but this has to be the worst fucking place I've ever been in.

Torn between grieving for my alpha and fearing for my mate, I feel split in two. On one hand, I know I have to keep fighting. Have to find some way back to Delaney, but on the other side, I can't help but believe that, this time, neither of us is walking away from the battle.

And that knowledge kills me.

The door opens, and Lucy strolls in wearing a black dress. Her lips are painted the same color and are turned up in a smile as she crosses the room to me. "Put this on." She tosses a garment bag at me, but I don't move. "Did you not hear me?" Hand on her hip, she studies me. "I said put it on."

"Fuck. You." I enunciate each word so that maybe it will get the fucking point across that I'm not her puppet.

Her sadistic grin spreads. "Oh, honey, we will get to that point someday, but it's not today."

The idea of sharing anything with this woman makes me nauseated. "I'm not your toy."

"You are my toy, and we have a date with some ley lines. I just got a call from your girlfriend, and we're meeting her out there."

"Delaney." Her name is a whisper of hope because, if I can see her, then maybe, just maybe, I can come up with a plan to keep Lucy from the lines and still make it back to my mate.

I stand and unzip the bag, proceed to strip down, and put the black slacks and matching button-down on without caring that Lucy watches my every move.

"You really are something, shifter, you know that?" She sighs. "In another life."

"In no fucking life," I retort as I slip into a pair of black boots.

She chuckles. "That's what you think. Come now." She walks over to Josiah, and I freeze.

"What are you doing?"

"We're taking him with us. I know how your kind like to mourn. Figure we should give his daughter the satisfaction of knowing what happened to her father."

Seeing Josiah dead will gut Willa.

It will gut the entire pack.

Which is exactly why the sadistic bitch is doing it.

"Leave him here. Let me tell her first. Before we leave, we'll get him."

She pouts. "Oh, sweet, naïve Cole. That's not how any of this works." She reaches out with long fingers and grips my arm, kneeling and pressing a hand to Josiah, before we appear in the woods just outside of the cavern hosting the ley lines.

"What the hell is this?" I demand, feeling the color drain from my face as I take in the dead walkers surrounding us. Lined in perfect rows, they stare straight ahead, unblinking.

Vampires and witches make up another row, though they have varying looks of unease on their faces.

"This is our little army, pet. You didn't think I'd be stupid enough to walk in here unprotected, did you?"

"You promised her we'd all walk away."

She grins. "That's what makes this all the better."

I lunge at her, but she raises a hand. An invisible grip squeezes my throat, and I cough, lungs burning.

"Apparently, you are destined to learn the hard way that there is no beating me." Her magical grip tightens, nearly cutting off all air circulation. "Such a shame the pretty ones are all dumbasses."

"Let him the fuck go."

Delaney's voice is music to my ears. I can barely see her out of the corner of my eye, standing in the entrance to the cavern. Clothed in all black, she's armed to the teeth with daggers. And probably has more where I can't see.

She's beautiful, my hunter. And if I were to draw my last breath right now, at least I got to see her first.

Lucy smiles. "Tell me, witch, where is your fae friend?"

Delaney's mouth twitches as her gaze drops to Josiah's body. Her face contorts, rage overcoming the cool, collected expression I know was a mask. "You killed him," she growls.

"I did. Now, where is Fearghas? Come out, come out, little fae."

Fearghas appears directly beside Delaney, mouth flat, nostrils flaring.

Willa and Jack emerge behind them, and her face falls the moment she sees her father. "Dad!" she screams and rushes forward, but the hunter grabs her around the waist and hauls her back. "You fucking psychotic bitch! I'll kill you! I swear it!" Her voice cracks, and she crumbles to the ground, tears flowing freely down her cheeks.

Z comes up behind her, his face red, eyes hard as he regards Lucy.

It's then that it truly hits me. Everyone I love could die today. "Don't. Trust. Her," I choke out. I still haven't seen Rainey, Elijah, Bronywyn, or Tarnley, so that could mean they have a plan. Why is it that them having one terrifies me even more?

Delaney's gaze shifts to mine, and in them, I see the same understanding. I also know that no matter what I say, she won't leave until it's done. "I'm sorry, Cole." She turns back to Lucy. "Let him go, and I will help you."

Fearghas shifts uncomfortably.

"I know you will." Lucy drops me, and I gasp for air. "But you don't get your boy toy back until I have what I want." Two witches move forward from the back of the crowd and stand beside me. I reach down, trying to urge the wolf to surface, but something in that fucking nightshade venom, or maybe it was something in Lucy's blood, has silenced him.

"Let me talk to him."

Lucy rolls her eyes. "You can have three minutes." She backs away, and the entire army moves back with her. Delaney regards her warily as she moves toward me. I try to stand, but magic holds me in place.

"Are you okay?" Delaney kneels in front of me, cupping my cheeks with her hands.

"I'm fine. You can't do this, Del. You have to walk away."

Her eyes fill as she casts her glance to the side at Josiah. I reach up and cup her cheek, turning her head back to me. "You can't ask me to do that," she whispers.

"You once asked me to walk away, remember? In that alley?" The moment is forever burned into my brain, and I don't miss the irony in the situation we find ourselves in. "You begged me to walk away and let you die."

"And you wouldn't do it," she counters. "You refused."

"I did. But I need you to listen to me this time, please, babe. I can't watch you all die. Take everyone and get the fuck out of here."

"No. If we die, we go down together. You and me. It's always going to be you and me." Fearghas appears beside her.

"What about them?"

"We're here because we choose to be," Fearghas replies. "So stop being a martyr and let us save your ass. Again."

I grin up at him despite the pain, the fear clouding

my eyes and burning my throat. Delaney rests her forehead against mine.

"I love you, Cole. We will be happy."

"We will be happy," I repeat her promise, and hope like hell there's truth in it.

"Time's up."

Delaney glares up at Lucy but gets to her feet and heads toward the cavern. "Watch him," she says as she passes Z. He nods. Jack, Willa, and Fearghas all move to the side in order to let Lucy by.

"You're coming with us, fae. But try anything, and I'll gut the wolf before you can lift a finger against me."

Fearghas doesn't reply, just falls into step beside Delaney. I'm glad she's not alone, that he's with her.

But it should be me, and I hate that it's not.

"You good?" Z questions as soon as they're out of view.

I open my mouth to respond but am cut off by a witch.

"No fucking talking, dog."

Z grins, but there's no humor. It's all savage and promises blood. "I think I'll kill you first."

She snorts and turns her face to cast an amused glance at the witch on my other side. "Doubtful."

Willa straightens and comes to stand beside Z, her cheeks still wet with tears. "I call seconds."

"You've got it, little wolf." Z wraps an arm around

her and tugs her against his side while Jack comes to stand beside her, blade in hand.

They're forming a line in the mouth of the cavern, blocking off the entrance.

I suck in a deep breath and am letting it out as all hell breaks loose.

Someone screams behind me as Z lunges forward and grips the witch by the throat. He shakes, and her neck snaps before she's even able to lift a finger against him. The spell breaks over me, and I lunge to my feet.

Jack reaches me, holding a blade out hilt first. I take it and spin on my heel, diving into the fray of battle.

CHAPTER THIRTY-FIVE

DELANEY

"I have to be honest; I thought you'd put up a bit more of a fight."

"The day is not over yet," Fearghas snaps from beside me.

My magic simmers just beneath the surface of my skin as we move closer and closer to the lines. My hope is that I'll react exactly as I did before. The downfall, though, is that if I feel that way, chances are so will Lucy.

And that could be dangerous. "You shouldn't have killed Josiah." The sight of him...I shake it off knowing that if I focus too intently on it right now, I will be distracted from the coming fight.

And it's more than likely going to be the hardest

"He should have stayed in his own business and not come for me."

"Really? Because we had someone say you came onto pack lands and kidnapped him."

She snorts. "The fool came to me. He wanted to offer me a deal for you and Cole."

I stop in my tracks, and Lucy takes a step past me before turning around.

"Delaney, what are you doing?" Fearghas whispers in my ear.

"He tried to save us?"

"That was his intention."

"And you killed him for it." It's not a question since we all already know what the end result was.

"He refused to take no for an answer."

Power snaps in me, the jolt sending a warm shock through my body.

"Delaney, keep it together." Fearghas's warning is the only thing that keeps me from charging and trying my hand at killing the bitch now.

Based on her smile? She's hoping I will.

It takes all of my strength to take another step and keep moving forward. As I pass, though, I slam my shoulder into hers.

She laughs. "I honestly like you, Delaney Astor. It's too damn bad you've been such a pain in my ass up until this point. I feel like we could have been good friends, you and me."

"Not in this life or any other."

"You and Cole keep saying that same thing."

A handful of yards away is the part of the tunnel where I lost control last time. Fearghas presses a hand against my lower back, out of sight of Lucy, so he can get me out should things get truly complicated once the others reveal themselves.

The tunnel splits just on the other side of the power lines, and while Bronywyn can't risk crossing them, she's hiding just ahead, masking the presence of Rainey, Elijah, and Tarnley.

This is it.

Our final stand.

Fingers crossed it goes a hell of a lot better than last time.

Stopping in my tracks, I turn to Lucy. I'm not quite where I was before, but I can sense the power boost just ahead, which means so can she.

"Why are you stopping?" she demands, her eyes flashing black beneath the tiny lights floating just above.

"We're here."

She turns in a slow circle, dark eyes hardening. "What game are you trying to play, witch? You do realize with the snap of my fingers, I could kill your boy toy." She raises her fingers in demonstration. "One tiny snap, and my dead walkers will eat him alive. I imagine you'll hear his screams even all the way down here."

I glance just ahead. "Can you not feel it?" Why the hell can't she sense it, too? I glance at Fearghas, but he simply shrugs.

"Maybe the lines don't speak psychotic bitch," he offers.

She glares at him. "Watch your tongue, fae. Your sister would be more than happy to know where you are right now."

"I figured she already did and was just too much of a coward to face me."

"Hardly. I simply didn't tell her."

"Not confiding in your new BFF?" Fearghas pouts. "That's hardly the right way to start off a lasting friendship."

"She wouldn't hesitate to kill you. And I promised Delaney here that I would let you walk. Don't make me change my mind." Lucy refocuses on me, and I swallow hard. "Where the fuck are the lines?"

I take a step back and then another. Power builds in my body, and I close my eyes, focusing on trying to channel it and not lose control like last time. My theory about being able to control myself if I knew it was coming?

Thank fuck it was correct.

The magic flows through me. From the bottom of

my feet to each and every strand of my hair, it fills me, making me feel more alive than ever.

My skin begins to glow, the green of my power shimmering around me like glitter floating in the air. And when I meet Lucy's shocked gaze, I can feel nothing but pure joy. "You can't feel that, Lucy? I wonder why."

She rushes toward me and clamps onto my arm with both hands as though she's going to try to siphon the power from my body.

The moment our skin connects, though, she throws her head back and screams as power slams into her. Where she touches me sizzles, the power too much for her.

"Now!" I scream.

Rainey lunges toward her, blade in hand.

Lucy dodges and blasts her with power that sends my sister careening into the side of the cavern.

Elijah rushes toward her, dropping his shoulder and taking her to the ground as Tarnley blurs forward and catches her, wrapping both hands around her arms and pinning them up. Elijah clamps iron around her wrists to keep her from dematerializing.

It's then that Bronywyn steps forward, body blazing gold with the force of the power.

Together, we face off with Lucy. Two beacons of light magic bent on destroying the dark.

She grips my hand, and we both raise our palms.
"Sheelin!" Lucy screams.

Across from me, Fearghas braces for a fight as
Bronywyn and I hit Lucy with all the power we've got.
It slams into her, a steady stream of power that sends
her back a few steps. Tarnley releases her and blurs
away, his body steaming from the transfer of power.

Lucy screams and flings her arms apart, ripping
the iron chain. One by one, she manages to remove the
bracelets. Blood drips from her eyes and nose as she
struggles to stand.

We're giving her everything we've got, but
together we inch forward. Yet, the farther away from
the lines we get, the lesser our magic is.

Tarnley blurs toward Lucy, but in one horrific
move, she spins and grips him.

Bones crack moments before she tosses his lifeless
body to the side.

Bronywyn screams and rushes forward. Lucy
slams a fist into her jaw and knocks her to the side. But
before she comes toward me, she sneers and
disappears.

I lunge forward, rushing for Tarnley, noting his
neck bent at an unnatural angle. I reach for him,
power still flowing through my body. His own jumps
up, arching off the ground as his body knits back
together.

I don't think, don't breathe, because I have absolutely no clue what the hell is happening or why. Just that it's working, and I won't stop until he opens his eyes.

Bronywyn glances up at me, tears in her eyes as she cradles his head in her lap. As soon as the transfer stops, though, I don't wait, I rush forward down the cavern until I see Lucy coming toward me.

"What? You haven't had enough, yet?" I ask as I pummel her with an energy blast that knocks her back a few steps.

"Delaney!" she roars.

"I'm going to kill you, bitch."

When she doesn't blast me with magic, I lunge for her, using my body weight to knock her down. We roll across the dirt until I'm on top, and I slam my fist down into her face.

"That's for Jane!" Again. "That's for Josiah!" Again. "That's for Cole!" Blood splatters my face, but still, I don't stop.

Her arms come up in an attempt to block me, but I know I have her just where I want her. And I will end her this time. Reaching down, I grab my ruby blade, so fucking glad this entire thing is going to be over with.

"Did my magic blast knock the power right from you?" I show her my blade, but she barely sees it, eyes only partially open as she struggles to breathe. "I told you that I'd kill you," I snarl.

"Delaney," she groans.

"Don't bother begging. It won't work." I raise the blade and drive it down into her chest. Bones crunch as the dagger meets its mark and her arms fall to her sides.

She groans and sputters, blood dripping from the corner of her mouth. "Del," she whispers moments before her face shimmers and fades away, leaving me staring down at Cole.

"What? Cole? I don't...I don't understand," I choke out, trying to wrap my brain around what is happening.

Lucy appears just ahead, a satisfied smile on her face. She gasps and covers her mouth with both hands. "What have you done?" When she drops her hands, a smile spreads across her face. "Really is too bad. But I'll be seeing you soon, witch." She disappears, and I turn my gaze back to Cole as Fearghas appears in front of me.

He stares at me, wide-eyed. Then, his gaze moves back to Cole.

"Oh, God, no." Scrambling back, I scream and cover my mouth.

His face turns toward me.

"Cole?"

His hand slides over the dirt, and I rush forward.

"I can save you, just hold on. No, no, no, please."

"Delaney," Fearghas whispers as he drops to his knees beside me.

"Back the fuck off, Fearghas!" I rip the dagger out and press both hands to Cole's bloody chest. I urge the magic forward, not sure what the hell I did to heal Tarnley, but knowing I need it now more than ever. "Please work," I plead. "Please."

Cole coughs, spraying blood into the air. His chest rattles as he struggles to draw breath.

"Please, no, please no. You can't die. I'm so sorry. I'm so sorry. I should have known."

Tears flow down my cheeks as my heart seizes within my chest. Blinding agony, unlike anything I've ever experienced, surges through my body, suffocating me.

"Delaney," Rainey whispers.

"Get the fuck away from me!" I scream.

She backs off.

Tarnley appears in front, Bronywyn at his side. She limps forward and kneels on the other side of Cole. Reaching forward, she covers my hands with her own. Mine warm beneath her touch, letting me know she's trying to use her power.

I watch Cole's face, looking for any changes, but nothing happens.

"I'm so sorry, Delaney," Bronywyn whispers. I meet her gaze, her cheeks stained with tears.

I feel darkness, Delaney. Death and pain are coming for you. Walker's words echo through my brain just as he comes into view in front of me, Z, Willa, and Jack beside him.

"I'm so, so sorry," Bronywyn whispers again.

I shake my head, determined not to hear her words. Because hearing them will make them true. And they can't be true. None of this can be true. "No. Don't you fucking say that."

Her eyes fill again, her bottom lip quivering. "He's gone, Delaney. Cole is dead."

Keep reading with Rise of the Witch!

I killed him.
My life ended as I watched the light fade from Cole's eyes, my hands covered in his blood.
People have always said that something snaps when you lose a piece of your soul. But I couldn't have possibly prepared for the darkness that would take root in the new vacancy.

Heartbroken, I turn toward the only other person willing to do anything to bring Lucy to her knees.

Click here to grab your copy today!

Click here and come join my Facebook group for special sneak previews of what's coming in this series, as well as release day notices!

ALSO BY JESSICA WAYNE

FAE WAR CHRONICLES

EMBER IS DYING.

BUT AS SHE WILL SOON DISCOVER, SOME FATES ARE WORSE THAN DEATH.

ACCIDENTAL FAE

CURSED FAE

FIRE FAE

VAMPIRE HUNTRESS CHRONICLES

SHE'S SPENT HER ENTIRE LIFE ERADICATING THE IMMORTALS. NOW, SHE FINDS HERSELF PROTECTING ONE.

WITCH HUNTER: FREE READ

BLOOD HUNT

BLOOD CAPTIVE

BLOOD CURE

REJECTED WITCH CHRONICLES

SHE'S BACK FROM THE DEAD. THE TROUBLE NOW, IS STAYING THAT WAY.

CURSE OF THE WITCH

BLOOD OF THE WITCH

Rise of the Witch

<u>Dark Witch Chronicles</u>

She sacrificed her soul for her friends...Now they have to save her...or put her down.

Blood Magic

Blood Bond

Blood Union

<u>Sirens Blood Chronicles</u>

He's loved her a millennia, but that love might just be what gets them both killed.

Rescued by the Fae

Healed by the Fae

<u>Mated by Midnight</u>

Barbarian. Beast. Murderer? One thing's for sure, nothing is as it seems in this crazy town.

Midnight Cursed

Midnight Hunted

Midnight Bound

<u>Accidental Alchemy</u>

My job is to keep the things inside these supernatural books from coming out...unfortunately, I suck at it.

Dragon Unleashed

SHADOW CURSED

HE CAN HAVE HER BODY. BUT NEVER HER HEART.

SAVAGE WOLF

FRACTURED MAGIC

STOLEN MATE

BLADE OF ICE

RISE OF A WARRIOR

FALL OF AN EMPIRE

BIRTH OF A QUEEN

CAMBREXIAN REALM

THE REALM'S DEADLIEST ASSASSIN HAS MET HER MATCH.

THE LAST WARD: FREE READ

WARRIOR OF MAGICK

GUARDIAN OF MAGICK

SHADES OF MAGICK

RISE OF THE PHOENIX

ANA HAS SPENT HER ENTIRE LIFE AT THE CLUTCHES OF HER ENEMY.
NOW, IT'S TIME FOR WAR.

BIRTH OF THE PHOENIX

DEATH OF THE PHOENIX

VENGEANCE OF THE PHOENIX

Tears of the Phoenix

Rise of the Phoenix

Tethered

Sometimes, our dreams do come true. The trouble is, our nightmares can as well.

Tethered Souls

Collateral Damage

For more information, visit WWW.JESSICAWAYNE.COM

ABOUT JESSICA WAYNE

USA Today bestselling author Jessica Wayne was only seventeen when she wrote her first full-length novel. Titled *One Lovers Ill Will (A book that never saw the light of day.)*, it was at that moment she realized she wanted to be a full-time author.

Life had other plans, though. After spending seven years in the Army, Jessica finally had the time to push forward with that dream.

Now, a wife and mother of three, Jessica spends her days crafting worlds in which anything is possible.

She runs on coffee, and if you ever catch her wearing matching socks, it's probably because she grabbed them in the dark.

She is a believer of dragons, unicorns, and the power of love, so each of her stories contain one of those elements (and in some cases all three).

You can usually find her in her Facebook group, Jessica's Whiskey Thieves, or keep in touch by subscribing to her newsletter via her website: www.jessicawayne.com.

amazon.com/Jessica-Wayne/e/B01MQ1OH4O

tiktok.com/authorjessicawayne

patreon.com/authorjessicawayne

facebook.com/AuthorJessicaWayne

twitter.com/jessmccauthor

instagram.com/authorjessicawayne

bookbub.com/authors/jessica-wayne

Made in the USA
Columbia, SC
06 August 2024

40072690R00259